Praise for the Mouseheart books:

"For ravenous readers of Erin Hunter, Brian Jacques, and Kathryn Lasky, this is a not-to-be-missed series."
—*School Library Journal*

"Harrowing plot twists, moral dilemmas, and colorful animal characters make this second volume as supercharged and thought-provoking as the first. Atmospheric illustrations add drama. Mouse fantasy fans will cheer brave-hearted Hopper's latest adventure."
—*Kirkus Reviews*

"Sword-wielding rats, feline palace guards, and rebel mice fill this adventure with imagination and heart. . . . For those who love an underdog and some romping good battles, Fiedler thoroughly entertains."
—*Publishers Weekly*

"Captivating and cunning, *Mouseheart* is the next great adventure. *Mouseheart* is the first in the series which promises to deliver grand adventure and great storytelling. Hopper is one little mouse who roars! Readers who loved Jacques' Redwall series and Hunter's Warrior series will love this new series."
—ABookandAHug.com

"The underground world and mix of intrigue, prophecy, and betrayal bring to mind Suzanne Collins' Gregor the Overlander series. . . . Fans of Brian Jacques' Redwall Abbey series may enjoy this modern adaptation of rodent politics and warfare."
—*Booklist*

"A tiny, new hero has arrived! [A] *Braveheart*-style epic adventure . . . The story also emphasizes love and loyalty, and provides clear examples of mercy and restraint."
—*Christian Library Journal*

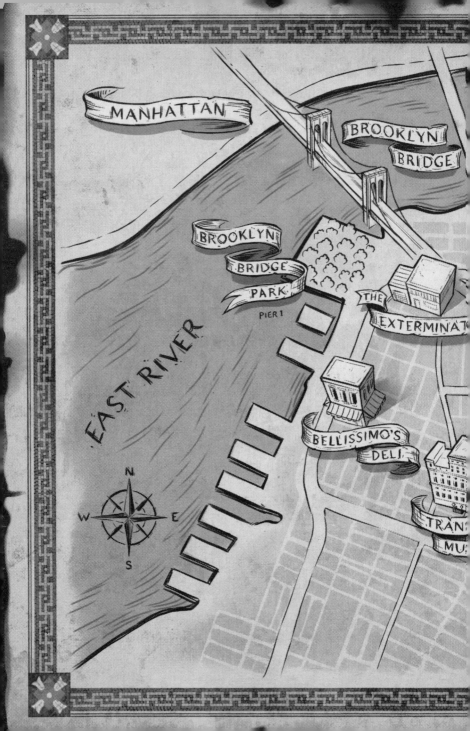

MOUSE

LISA FIEDLER

With illustrations by VIVIENNE TO

MARGARET K. McELDERRY BOOKS

HEART

VOL. 2

HOPPER'S DESTINY

New York London Toronto Sydney New Delhi

Also by Lisa Fiedler

Mouseheart

Mouseheart vol. 3:
Return of the Forgotten

MARGARET K. McELDERRY BOOKS
An imprint of Simon & Schuster Children's Publishing Division
1230 Avenue of the Americas, New York, New York 10020
This book is a work of fiction. Any references to historical events, real people, or real places are used fictitiously. Other names, characters, places, and events are products of the author's imagination, and any resemblance to actual events or places or persons, living or dead, is entirely coincidental.
Text copyright © 2015 by Simon & Schuster, Inc.
Illustrations copyright © 2015 by Vivienne To
Logo illustration copyright © 2014 by Craig Howell
All rights reserved, including the right of reproduction in whole or in part in any form.
MARGARET K. McELDERRY BOOKS is a trademark of Simon & Schuster, Inc.
For information about special discounts for bulk purchases, please contact Simon & Schuster Special Sales at 1-866-506-1949 or business@simonandschuster.com.
The Simon & Schuster Speakers Bureau can bring authors to your live event.
For more information or to book an event, contact the Simon & Schuster Speakers Bureau at 1-866-248-3049 or visit our website at www.simonspeakers.com.
Also available in a Margaret K. McElderry Books hardcover edition
Book design by Lauren Rille
The text for this book is set in Absara.
The illustrations for this book are rendered digitally.
Manufactured in the United States of America
0216 OFF
First Margaret K. McElderry Books paperback edition March 2016
10 9 8 7 6 5 4 3 2 1
The Library of Congress has cataloged the hardcover edition as follows:
Fiedler, Lisa.
Hopper's destiny / Lisa Fiedler ; illustrated by Vivienne To.—First edition.
p. cm.—(Mouseheart ; [2])
Summary: A brave pet shop mouse named Hopper attempts to rebuild a fallen empire in the underground rat civilization of Atlantia, located in the subway tunnels of Brooklyn, while Queen Felina and her band of street cats declare open season on the rodents.
[1. Adventure and adventurers—Fiction. 2. Mice—Fiction. 3. Rats—Fiction. 4. Cats—Fiction. 5. Utopias—Fiction. 6. Fate and fatalism—Fiction.] I. Title.
PZ7.F457Ho 2015
[Fic]—dc23
2014030273
ISBN 978-1-4814-2089-1 (hc)
ISBN 978-1-4814-2090-7 (pbk)
ISBN 978-1-4814-2091-4 (eBook)

To my godson, Cameron Thomas.
Your adventure awaits!

PROLOGUE

IT WAS NOT CRISP, cozy apsen curls he felt beneath him.

It was the cold, hard cement of the pet-shop floor that pressed against the fur of his belly.

Everything hurt—his bones, his teeth, his tail. He was aware of a frenzied scuffle going on around him—sweeping sounds, and Keep's heavy feet, his angry voice.

Pup opened his eyes.

The world from this vantage point was a flat, dusty expanse of floor dotted with the lifeless bodies of his cagemates. His stomach turned with grief and disgust as he blinked away the blur and searched for his siblings.

"Hopper?" he called. "Pinkie?" But his trembling voice was lost in the windy noise of straw against cement and the pattering of rain on the sidewalk outside the open door. Of course Pup did not know the names for straw and rain. He knew nothing of human objects and life outside his cage. But he did know this: he was in trouble.

"Hopper ... Pinkie!" He tried again to holler, but his words were no louder than passing thoughts.

With great effort he lifted his head and scanned the shop. There! His brother and sister, scrambling down the cord that grew out of the money machine like an electrical tail!

They're coming to get me, he thought, relief overtaking him. *Hopper will save me.*

Pup closed his eyes and waited. The vibrations of Keep's tromping feet shook the floor, and damp air swirled in from the stormy world outside the door.

The door ... toward which Pinkie and Hopper were running.

"No!" Pup cried out. "Wait for me."

He tried to lift himself onto his paws, but his fall—a terrifying drop through space, which he was only now beginning to remember—had left him far too sore. He could barely move at all, let alone with enough speed to catch up to his siblings.

Eyes wide with disbelief, he watched as the broom chased Hopper and Pinkie toward the door.

And then, with a bang, it slammed behind them, trapping them, Pup realized, forever out, while he was stuck here, forever in.

However long forever might be he could not begin to guess.

A flicker of motion caught his tear-filled eyes, and he turned toward it. A cagemate, left for dead beside a torn scrap of plaid fabric, had begun to stir. But Keep spotted the movement as well. Pup made to shout a warning, but the stiff bristles of the broom came down hard with a loud slap. Pup could almost feel the impact on his own shivering body as the updraft caused by the swinging broom sent the scrap of fabric fluttering into the air. It hovered briefly, like a checkered kite, then drifted downward to land once again on the dirty floor, this time within paw's reach of Pup.

"Gotcha!" gloated Keep as he shook his broom clean.

Pup gasped, his breath strangling in his throat as he bit back a whimper of terror.

"Nasty little varmints ripped my shirt," Keep muttered, frowning at the piece of fabric. He grabbed a dustpan from the counter and swept the squashed cagemate into it. Then he stamped across the room and bent down, using his boot to kick another unconscious mouse into the rusted dustpan.

Pup felt his blood freeze. Keep was cleaning up. . . . Mouse after mouse was being flattened, then swept or shoveled into the metal receptacle. Unless he could find a way to conceal himself, he would be next.

Muscles aching, he reached his tiny paw toward the fabric scrap. His claws closed around the frayed edge and he tugged it over himself, just as Keep turned to scan the area of the floor where Pup lay.

"That's all of 'em," the human grumbled, heading

for the back exit with his tray full of corpses.

Not all of 'em, thought Pup, quivering beneath the fabric. His brain spun as he tried to formulate a plan. But nothing of his life in the comfy cage had prepared him for a moment like this. He was alone and afraid, with only a torn piece of cheap material to protect him.

His siblings had escaped.

No—they'd gone and left him, without so much as a backward glance.

It was an image Pup would never forget, their two tails disappearing through the sliver of open space between the door and the rain. Part of him understood that they'd been running for their lives and had probably believed him already dead, but another part of him hurt, smarting to the depths of his soul. He'd been abandoned by the only two mice he'd ever trusted. The only two mice who had ever protected him.

As he huddled there beneath the plaid tatter, a small seedling of emotion began to take root. Pup could not identify the feeling, of course; it was as new to him as snakes and brooms and rainstorms. But he knew it did not feel good.

It made his claws clench and his teeth grind and the back of his neck sweat.

Had he been more worldly or educated, he would have known exactly what to call the sensation. But he was neither of those things. He was innocent, and naturally sweet, and until now he'd never had a reason to feel this miserable, gut-searing, heart-chilling *thing* he could not name. He understood only that he did not like the feeling at all.

And so he fought it, let it go, hoping it would never return.

But it would return. It would come for him again, though he could not imagine now how or when or even why. It would visit him in a place and circumstance he was still too inexperienced even to dream of, this biting, clawing feeling that filled him with such darkness. This thing he did not know enough to call anger, which had already given way to fear.

Because it was that moment when the door to the shop slammed open, letting in the noise, the damp, the rain.

And the boy.

The boy with his terrible, vicious, hungry snake.

"You again," snarled Keep, returning with his empty dustpan. "What do you want this time?"

"Same thing I wanted last time," the boy said. "Breakfast for my buddy. I only got two blocks away when I remembered he ain't eaten since yesterday. He can't wait for me to find another pet store, or trap some scrawny subway rat. He needs a meal now."

Keep snorted. "Well, that's too bad, because his breakfast just escaped. Every last hair of it."

Pup peered up at the despicable boy and the repugnant reptile that squirmed on his shoulders. Fangs curved out of its open mouth as its eyes darted around the shop.

Keep walked to the door, but before he could push it closed against the splashing rain, a gust of wet wind blew in, lifting the plaid scrap into the air once again and revealing Pup, curled on the floor.

"There's one," said the boy, pointing a bony finger.

Pup forced himself to lay still, allowing his eyes to open only into the tiniest of slits, through which to watch this sickening transaction.

"It's dead," said Keep.

"So what? Bo don't mind—do ya, boy?"

The snake answered with a hiss. Dead breakfast was better than no breakfast, it would seem.

"Still gotta charge ya," said Keep, ever the savvy businessman, "even if the beast's deceased."

"Half price," said the boy. "It's dead *and* puny." He dug into his pocket and fished out some coins.

"Fair enough," grumbled Keep. "Dead rodents only stink up the joint anyway. Go ahead. Take it."

The boy reached down and scooped up the presumed-dead Pup, who closed his eyes tight and held his breath. He almost wished he *were* dead.

Satisfied with their purchase, the boy and his snake ventured back out into the rain. Listening to the sound of his captor's sneakers slap the wet sidewalk,

Pup kept his body still and his eyes squeezed shut.

If only he had opened them.

If he had, he might have been able to peer through the slender space between the boy's fingers and see his brother and sister in the shadow of a trash barrel, fighting over a discarded piece of hot dog. He might have seen them lunge at each other, then roll toward the rushing water in the gutter.

He might even have seen the raging current sweep them away, to disappear from the Brooklyn outdoors forever.

Or perhaps not forever . . .

But Pup saw nothing except the inside of his own eyelids, pretending for all he was worth to be a lifeless knot of fur in the boy's clammy palm.

He would be dead soon anyway.

He might as well get used to it.

Pup had no idea how long he was clenched inside the boy's fist. They seemed to be traveling a great distance, the boy walking, the snake wriggling. At some point the boy stopped moving and stood still, only to continue to be propelled—not forward, but downward, smoothly. This seemed to trouble the snake, who (Pup could sense from inside the dark cocoon of the boy's curled fingers) grew tense around the boy's neck.

"It's okay, Bo. It's only an escalator. We'll be on the train in no time."

Train, Pup thought. Another word he'd never heard, another concept entirely foreign to him. But the idea of it, whatever it was, managed to soothe the snake.

Then the boy was walking again. Wherever the escalator had deposited them was a place without rain, because the spattering sound had stopped and the occasional drop that dribbled in between the boy's fingers had ceased.

Pup could smell humans—more than he'd ever smelled before, more than there had even been at any one time in Keep's cramped shop—and he could hear their gasps and cries of fear at the sight of Bo, writhing around the boy's neck.

The boy stopped walking, and suddenly Pup's delicate ears were assaulted with a loud growling noise that made his heart thump. The growl was followed by a kind of whistling shriek, as if some enormous beast had just exhaled.

"Best thing about riding the subway with you, Bo," said the boy with a chuckle, "is I get the whole car to myself."

Pup sensed the boy sitting, and then more movement, fast and sleek.

"Okay," said the boy. "Let's get you fed. One dead runt coming up."

The boy uncurled his fist, and Pup felt a chill as he was exposed to the air. Using his other hand, the boy pinched Pup's tail and lifted him up so that he was dangling, presumably, just above those lethal fangs.

"Open wide," the boy told Bo.

Pup was so seized with panic that he forgot to play dead; he opened his eyes and found himself bathed in a sickly greenish light, face-to-face with the diabolical boy.

Startled, the boy let out a shriek, releasing his grip and flinging Pup across the train car.

Bo hissed, furious at having been deprived of his breakfast a second time.

Thwumpff.

Pup landed on the seat opposite the boy's. He quickly scrambled to the edge and dove to the floor, keeping to the cavern beneath the long row of seats, where the boy could not see nor reach.

And he ran.

For a mouse his size, it was a lengthy run indeed. He could hear the wet soles of the boy's sneakers squeaking on the floor as he clambered around the car, searching out his undead prey.

"There he is!" the boy cried. "We got him cornered."

But just as the boy reached out to snatch Pup, the train came to a sudden, screeching halt. Boy and snake were flung forward, stumbling.

To Pup's delight, his pursuer fell hard, face-first onto the dirty floor.

The boy groaned; the snake squirmed.

Pup pressed himself up against the shiny metal door.

A mad hissing filled the car as the snake unlooped his scaly self from the fallen boy's shoulders and began to slither toward Pup.

But the whistling shriek of breath came again, and behind Pup the doors jerked wide, knocking the trembling mouse off balance.

Pup teetered on the edge of the subway car only long enough to see Bo's fanged mouth open.

And then he fell.

Out of the car and into the darkness.

CHAPTER ONE

La Rocha's journal—from the Sacred Book of the Mūs:

I, the mystical and revered La Rocha, look down now upon the remains of the once-prosperous city of Atlantia. It has been a fortnight since the battle—a mere two weeks, yet it feels like two thousand years. Below me the city smolders. The factories no longer produce, and the streets no longer bustle with Atlantia's fortunate citizens, who so recently went about their business, blissfully secure in the guarantee of safety and prosperity.

Safety purchased at an unspeakable cost.

The rats who dwelled here were not directly to blame; they were ignorant to all of it. But then, if they never thought to wonder or investigate, do they not share a fraction of the guilt? The Atlantian citizens only knew that their emperor, Titus, had arranged a peace accord with the feral cats that provided the rodents with comfortable lives and untroubled minds. They never bothered to ask the true cost of that peace.

Now the city is overrun with the refugees

who would have been sacrificed to keep the ferals from preying upon Atlantia. These were mice and rats and squirrels and chipmunks found wandering in the subway tunnels by Titus's soldiers and offered up to the feral queen in exchange for peace. These are the ones who were liberated from Titus's death camps and have now taken up a precarious residence behind Atlantia's once-impenetrable walls.

The rebels acted in good faith when they liberated the camps, but the results are grim. It must be said: they did not think far enough into the future. They were so determined to end the tyranny that they never considered what would happen in the aftermath. Such small crusaders are they! Such high hopes they had! And I count myself among them.

When this rebellion began, long ago, the goal was for all creatures to coexist in peace. A true peace in which we would aid one another, regardless of our species, as we struggled against the daily strife that comes of being tiny and hunted, or far from home and hungry. Of being loved once and then forgotten, turned out, abandoned. For this is the condition of the poor souls who find their way here, to the belly of the earth.

At the heart of this campaign was the belief

we could learn to refrain from preying upon one another. Alas, I see now that this may have been too much to hope for. Because I have come to understand that even in the presence of justice and fairness, nature overrides all. Hunger must be fed, and nature has designed us so that such instinct and need can rarely be entirely quelled. I have learned that there is no evil in the true course of nature, there is only what must be. We form a living chain, from the enormous humans who dominate the upland world to the most humble creatures among us—rodent, insect, reptile.

The so-called peace that Titus brokered was self-serving and entirely against nature—animals were taken randomly from this life before nature deemed it their rightful time. There is no denying that to each of us who walks or hops or crawls or slithers upon this earth or under it, there will ultimately come that moment when we must bid our farewells and breathe our last breath. But what form our exit will take is for nature and destiny, not government, to decide. Nature determines what will come and when it will come, and how. That is the great mystery of being.

Titus upset that fragile balance by attempting to outwit nature, and now all that he twisted and manipulated must be repaired.

Below me the blare of a horn rips through the smoky silence. I recognize it well. In the past the rebel Firren would use this horn to summon her Rangers in a secret call to arms. Now the horn is a warning, and the few rodents who have been scurrying amid the city's shambles—looting, scavenging, begging—scamper off hastily to conceal themselves behind crumbling walls.

"Incoming," a guard's voice bellows. "Ferals approaching. Seek cover!"

I watch in horror as one young mouse, who has been hauling a wagon filled with rotting food scraps, freezes in his tracks in the middle of Atlantia's town square. My heart breaks to see him trembling and unprotected there in plain sight. I wish I could run to him, or at the very least shout out a command for him to run away. But to reveal myself would wreak even more havoc on this forsaken place. I must bide my time and do what I can from the shadows.

Two feral cats stalk into view. They are new to the tunnels, I am sure, for they still have a sense of upland scruff about them. They must be recent additions to Felina's ranks; I can see in their eyes that they remember daylight. And this makes them even more dangerous, because beneath their hunger lurks the need to prove themselves.

The larger of the two felines is reaching out to slam one heavy paw down on the cowering mouse, when from the corner of my eye I spot a flash of silver, a blur of blue and red.

She is here! The rebel warrior. With her she brings a royal heir.

And a Chosen One.

He is the smallest among them, this Chosen One, but he is first to attack. Sword drawn, he barrels toward the startled cats, crying out in a familiar call: "Aye, aye, aye!" He swiftly delivers a warning cut to the larger cat's hind leg. As the cat yowls and sputters, the petite rebel in her silver cape catches hold of the other villain's tail and sinks her sharp rat teeth into it. The bitten one hisses and roars.

Now the royal heir steps forward, brandishing a dagger.

"I'd really rather not kill you two," he says. "There's been far too much bloodshed already. But I will if I must."

The larger cat licks a trickle of red from his leg and speaks with an upland accent. "We gotta eat," he says in his own defense.

"Well, do it elsewhere," says the Chosen One. "These citizens of Atlantia are under our protection."

"Citizens?" The cat snorts. He shifts a yellowy

glance toward the refugees, who peek out from their hiding places. "They ain't citizens, they're squatters. Rodent rejects. They're feline food."

At that the Chosen One raises his sword. "Not while there's breath in my body, they aren't!"

Then the rebel plants her hind legs and rests one ready paw on the handle of her sword. She makes no other move, just waits with coiled fury. The ferals sense immediately how very much she'd enjoy plunging that blade right between their eyes. The royal heir simply crooks a grin and spins his dagger between his claws in a showy gesture. The message is clear: he, too, is prepared to fight.

Then the little warrior draws himself up; the words he speaks are ground out between his tiny mouse teeth. "Be gone," he orders. "Or die."

The ferals hesitate only a moment before turning to run back the way they came.

From my perch above Atlantia, a feeling swells up within me, a warm sensation that prickles along my fur. It is pride. And hope.

Now the Chosen One rushes toward the quivering victim, who is still huddled in the middle of the dusty square; he sweeps him into his arms.

"It's okay," he says in a gentle voice. "They can't hurt you now."

The mouse wriggles free and regards the hero with a sneer. "Of course they can! Don't you see? We're doomed. You've solved nothing. You've failed!"

With that, the mouse runs off, leaving his cart behind.

The Chosen One turns to his friends, his eyes moist and his whiskers twitching. They know that the mouse's words ring with the prevailing sentiment of all who still dwell here. The suffering rodents feel no gratitude. They give no credit to the Chosen One and the rebels for trying; instead they place blame for falling short.

With the weight of this knowledge pressing heavily on my heart, I bow my head and slink away.

As Hopper watched the last of the crickets spring away from the palace, he was reminded of the one that had played a delightfully impromptu concert for him on that first dark day when he'd awoken and found himself in the tunnels. A lifetime ago, it seemed.

At the height of the rebel invasion this writhing swarm of insects had, at Firren's command, attached itself to the sprawling palace and transformed it into a prison, where the emperor Titus had been contained these past two weeks. Hopper had not seen Titus since the bugs had sealed him within the beautiful palace, but he could imagine the craggy old rat at turns pacing in fury over his imprisonment, then dissolving into weeping fits, grieving the loss of his city and mourning the end of his regime.

And maybe—just maybe—lamenting the wickedness of his death deal with Felina.

Today the crickets had been relieved of their duties; they had been ordered to take their leave by Firren, who now stood before the palace with Hopper and Prince Zucker.

Hopper was still smarting from the insult delivered by the mouse in the town square. The resentment in those little black eyes stung more than any battle wound Hopper had endured. Did he really deserve such contempt?

As he looked around at the waste and the chaos, it was hard to be sure that he didn't. Most of the grand buildings of Atlantia had been stormed by rodents desperate for shelter. Some had been set ablaze and were still smoldering. The stalls and carts of the market were toppled and broken, and the streets were filled with litter of all sorts. Nearly everything of value had been stolen, swept out of the city in the exodus, and the rodents who remained cowered in their hiding places or crept through the city with frightened expressions on their gaunt faces.

Zucker, who always seemed to know what Hopper

was thinking, laid a gentle paw on the Chosen One's shoulder. "These are confusing times, kid," he said softly. "You did what you had to do. We all did."

Hopper sighed. "But we never expected this."

"I'm not sure what we expected," Zucker admitted. "All we knew was that those refugee camps had to be eradicated and Titus had to be stopped."

"In that regard we've succeeded," said Firren.

Zucker grinned. "And now, like after any good party, somebody's gotta clean up."

Hopper shook his head. "It wasn't a party."

"I know, kid. I'm just trying to inject a little levity."

Hopper supposed he was grateful for the prince's attempt at lightening the mood. He was not looking forward to what was about to happen.

With a deep breath he focused his gaze on the tall, wide doors of the palace. A moment later the soldiers Bartel and Pritchard appeared from inside, pausing at the threshold. They were young, sturdy rats, impressively decked out in the uniform of Zucker's private guard—purple tunics embroidered with a silver *Z* over the heart. In a way it was Hopper who had first recruited them to duty when he'd enlisted their assistance in retrieving a wounded Zucker from the tunnels.

"Come along," Bartel called over his shoulder. "The prince, the Chosen One, and the rebel leader await."

There was a slow shuffling sound as Titus emerged

from the palace. When the disgraced emperor stepped into view, Hopper's breath caught in his throat. Even Zucker, who had more reason than anyone to harbor a deep, unrelenting anger toward the old rat, had to look away.

This once-formidable rat sovereign, who mere weeks ago had sat upon a gilded throne and ruled a prosperous underground kingdom, was little more than a shriveled shadow of his former self. His broad shoulders were hunched, and the heft he'd once carried was gone. He seemed deflated, a sack of wrinkled skin and bones.

"Didn't they feed him in there?" Hopper whispered to Zucker.

"They tried." The prince gave a grim shake of his head. "He wouldn't eat."

Even at this distance Hopper could see that Titus's eyes no longer burned with keen intellect; now they were sunken, vacant, and afraid. His paws trembled, his whiskers drooped. In places his fur had gone from iron gray to dull white. Worst was the pinkish welt of a scar that snaked across his face. If it had been unappealing before, it was downright ghoulish now, standing out from the sagging flesh of his snout more than it ever had before.

"Step lively," Pritchard said. "And mind the stairs."

Titus's paws were tightly bound with rope, as were his hind legs. He took tiny, mincing steps as

he followed his military escorts down the sweeping front steps of the royal residence.

Was he always a self-serving and diabolical tyrant? Hopper wondered. *Is it possible that at the start of it all his heart was pure?*

"Where do you want him?" Pritchard inquired.

"Take him to the town square," Zucker directed. "We'll be along straightaway."

An old rickshaw with wobbly wheels stood at the base of the staircase, towed by a burly squirrel with a wounded tail. Injured in the battle, no doubt, Hopper thought.

The twin soldiers guided Titus toward the shabby conveyance.

"Why are you taking me to the square?" he asked, addressing his question to no one directly but looking pointedly at his son. "Am I to be hanged? Tortured?" The confident boom of his voice had been replaced by a trembling rasp.

When Zucker did not answer, Titus hung his head. Bartel hoisted the old rat into the cart and climbed in beside him. Pritchard hopped onto the running board, nodding to the squirrel, and they rumbled off.

"I'm sending the Rangers in to guard the palace," said Firren. "If we don't, the looters will have a field day."

"Good thinking," said Hopper.

Firren blew her horn to summon her Rangers. They

were at her side almost instantly. Hopper recognized them because they had joined him and Firren on the long trek to the Mūs village. One of these Rangers was called Leetch, Firren's second-in-command. He was the biggest, and the deadliest with a sword, after Firren.

Over the past weeks Hopper had come to like and respect Leetch as they worked together in their attempts to maintain order or scare off the occasional feral. But even as Hopper had devoted himself to that task, he'd been deeply preoccupied with thinking about his family. Images of Pinkie and Pup on their way back to the Mūs village besieged by enraged cats haunted his nightmares. Many nights he'd woken up shivering and shouting in terror. He tried to convince himself that since he had heard nothing to the contrary, they must have made it safely back to the Mūs encampment, even though it broke his heart to know that Pup was so far away. Hopper's only comfort had come from knowing that if Pinkie had indeed reached the Mūs village nestled so deeply in the earth, and protected by a great gray wall constructed of human-fashioned bricks, Pup would be safe there for the rest of his life.

But without Hopper.

That thought had him choking back tears; he put his pain aside and tried to focus on what Zucker was saying to Firren.

"While the Rangers are in the palace, you might wanna . . . ya know . . . have them execute a thorough search." Zucker shifted his weight from foot to foot, avoiding eye contact with the rebel leader. "Titus has probably been stashing away . . . whaddya call 'em . . . *valuables* for years. Weapons, too."

"Got that, Leetch?" said Firren.

The Ranger nodded. "What shall we do with the booty when we find it?"

Firren turned a questioning look to Zucker.

"Bring it to my chamber and store it there."

Leetch gave the prince a curt nod, then led the other Rangers up the stairs and into the palace.

Zucker scratched his head and continued his strange little weight-shifting dance. Hopper would have laughed if the change weren't so distressing: lately he'd noticed a peculiar tension simmering between the prince and Firren. They seemed to have trouble meeting each other's eyes, and whenever she was around, the typically quick-witted Zucker became instantly tongue-tied.

"We should be on our way," said Firren, tilting her head in a gesture that was surprisingly shy. "It's almost time."

"Right," Zucker agreed. "Although I'm not exactly looking forward to this."

"You sent your soldiers ahead, didn't you?" asked Hopper, the dread squirming in his guts like an enormous earthworm. "In case there's trouble."

"It'll be fine, kid." Zucker patted Hopper on the back. "We've got to assure the rodents this miserable state of affairs will only be temporary. We need to let them know we intend to rebuild and revitalize, and make Atlantia safe and prosperous again. We'll be able to get them on our side, I'm sure of it. After all, becoming a guiding force in the future of Atlantia is pretty much your destiny, right? All you've got to do is be positive and tell them your grand plan."

"That would be a wonderful thing to do," muttered Hopper, "if only I had one."

CHAPTER TWO

WHEN THEY ARRIVED IN the town square, a crowd had already gathered. Hopper felt a plummeting in his chest at the sight of the small mouse who'd sneered at him earlier. Many of those present were refugees who'd been freed from the camps during the raid. He recognized Driggs, the hefty young squirrel who'd fought beside him in the hunting ground. He also spotted the brave old lady mouse, whose name Hopper had since learned was Beverley. During their trek from the refugee camp she had faked an injury in order to steal the guard's dagger. She still wore the apron she'd used to hide that cleverly appropriated blade, but now it was filthy and tattered. When Hopper caught her eye, she smiled at him; the kindness in her expression did wonders for his morale. But he noticed that she was much thinner than she'd been two weeks ago. Her eyes seemed tired, and she moved gingerly, as though every action was taxing to her. . . . Living in the aftermath had clearly taken its toll on her. On all of them.

Only a few who had gathered were Atlantian citizens—most of that population had quit the city the minute they learned of the end of Titus's secret peace treaty. Still, a handful remained, among them the merchant who'd once tried to sell Hopper his cherished Dodgers pennant. Hopper guessed that prize was long gone now, carried off or destroyed in the exodus. Marcy, the darling palace chambermaid, and a small number of the palace serving staff were also in attendance. Every mouse, rat, chipmunk, and squirrel looked exhausted. Haunted. Angry and in desperate need of answers—answers that it would be up to Hopper to provide.

Answers he did not presently have.

News of the assembly had gone out the night before. Zucker had issued a royal decree inviting any and all who still resided within the walls of Atlantia—legally or otherwise—to attend a meeting in the town square. The big draw was that the dethroned emperor Titus would be formally and publicly charged with his crimes. Rumor had it an official apology might be forthcoming. Not that anyone would have accepted it. They most likely turned out because they were curious as to what such an act of contrition might sound like; how would the beast Titus possibly explain himself? How could anyone express sufficient regret for offenses as great as his?

Bartel and Pritchard had handed Titus off to Zucker's most trusted soldier and close friend, Ketchum. Now the former emperor stood on a platform in the center of the square. The crowd milled around him. Some shouted taunts and insults, others just fired hateful looks. Titus flinched each time someone hurled a name like "evil dictator" or "wicked despot" at him. The worst was "feline-feeding fiend." Hopper supposed there would be no point in reminding the small Atlantian contingent within this angry mob that just fourteen days ago they had all but worshipped Titus for the safety and comfort they'd enjoyed under his reign. Certainly, Hopper had no sympathy for Titus; the rat deserved not an ounce of compassion. But it was troubling to see how quickly the tide of public opinion could turn, how even the most civilized rats defined right and wrong chiefly in terms of how it applied to them.

"You're a monster!" one bedraggled chipmunk hollered, shaking her fist at Titus. "When my babies were taken off to a colony months ago, I rejoiced! I thought it was a blessing."

Hopper, who stood between Zucker and Firren at the front of the crowd, felt Firren's muscles tense. He wondered if she was remembering the day she and her family had been taken away as eager "colonists" and delivered to the hunting ground instead.

"Now I know the truth," the chipmunk continued. "Now I know what really became of my children, you horrible, vile rat!" Her voice trailed off as she broke down in wracking sobs. Titus covered his face with his bound paws as the crowd booed and hissed. It occurred to Hopper they would probably be throwing rotten food at the emperor, except there was almost no food left in the city to throw. Those who had fled had wisely smuggled out as much of the city's store as they could carry.

When Zucker climbed onto the platform beside his father, the shouting ceased. A hush fell over the assemblage. Hopper's heartbeat quickened.

"Good rodents," Zucker began. "We gather today to discuss the future of our city and life in these tunnels."

"What future?" the merchant heckled. "What life? Our only destiny now is to wait for Felina's ferals to come for us."

"That's not true!" said Zucker. "Atlantia is now under the rule of a new leader—"

"A *new* leader who just happens to be the only son of the *old* leader?" scoffed a chubby rat. "Namely, *you*! How do we know you don't take after your old man?"

"And who will join you in your leadership?" cried the grieving chipmunk mother. "That puny mouse who claims to be the Promised One?"

Hopper had almost forgotten about that title. Titus had bestowed it upon him when he first realized that Hopper was the Chosen One of the Mūs prophecy. The emperor had thought to keep the Mūs' Chosen One in Atlantia as a well-treated hostage, in the hopes that a Mūs attack could be thwarted by using Hopper as a bargaining chip. Zucker, acting as a double agent, had encouraged the plan. It had enabled the prince to protect Hopper and finally reveal the truth to him about Titus's dirty dealings. Hopper's real identity had never been disclosed to the rat citizens of Atlantia, who considered the Mūs their enemy.

Hopper saw Zucker's jaw tighten; the prince's paws balled into fists. "Listen, folks, whether you like it or not, I'm still the heir apparent to the royal throne. So how about a little respect, huh?"

"Ha!" A skinny squirrel sneered. "Maybe you're just a spoiled royal brat who'll strike another dastardly deal the first chance you get!"

At that Zucker's paw flew to his sword. Hopper immediately leaped onto the platform to position himself in front of Zucker. Again the mob settled into a charged silence.

"We're getting ahead of ourselves," said Hopper. "Rest assured the prince here is a good rat who deeply regrets the terrible crimes his father has perpetrated. Through all of it Zucker has been on the side of the camp refugees. He fought against the emperor on your behalf!" Hopper shot a cool look at the merchant. "And for the record, I don't remember anyone complaining about Titus's politics when you were enjoying the freedom his peace accord brought you. He wasn't just sacrificing innocents for his own purposes, he was doing it for *your* safety as well."

"We didn't know!"

"You didn't *ask!*" Hopper shot back. "As far as I'm

concerned, that makes each and every Atlantian citizen an accomplice."

The rat merchant scowled, then gulped as some of the former camp dwellers turned angry glares in his direction.

"Easy, kid," Zucker whispered. "We don't want to cause a riot. These rodents fighting one another isn't going to help anything. Your destiny isn't to get trampled by an angry mob, ya know."

Hopper knew Zucker was right. At the moment the crowd had a common enemy in Titus, and a common threat in the ferals. Hopper would do well to shift their focus back to that.

"Titus has been brought here today to be sentenced and to extend an apology to you all," said Hopper. "I suggest we all be quiet and listen."

Once more the crowd settled down, and all eyes bored into Titus. Zucker and Hopper stepped aside, but Hopper noticed the prince's paw remained firmly on his sword.

The defeated emperor took a long, shaky breath. When he spoke, his voice sounded as if it were being scraped out of his throat.

"I loved this city," Titus began. "It was my dream, my great creation." He paused to blink a mournful tear from his eye. Or perhaps he was just bothered by the sting of smoke that still lingered in the air. "I came below as all of you did. I was without a home in the daylight world above. Humans had laid bare my outdoor nest with their digging machines and steel beams and black tar. I was chased indoors, and for a short period, a shining moment, I was safe and warm and happy. Soon the humans came for me there, too. Came with a vengeance. But I dodged their stomping boots and refused to eat their poison, and I dove into the darkness of these tunnels, hoping for respite."

Hopper found himself riveted. In spite of everything else Titus was still quite the orator. His voice may have been raspy and weak, but his words were entrancing. Hopper was beginning to understand how this rat had gone from being a lost soul to the leader of a great kingdom. It didn't make him like Titus any better, but he couldn't deny that the disgraced emperor knew how to work a crowd. No one moved as he spoke; they were utterly captivated.

"I know you will not believe me, but I did not embark on my road to royalty with evil in my heart. I never meant to hurt anyone. The abomination of the peace accord came about because I was forced to think quickly, to act in desperate haste in order to spare what I loved most in the world."

At this Titus's eyes darted to Zucker. Again the prince's jaw flexed, but with what emotion Hopper could not tell.

"I confess to all of you now that back then I was not thinking clearly. I could see only as far as the split second before me . . . a split second that would mean the difference between life and death. And so I chose. I struck a dark bargain, the ramifications of which I was far too desperate and naive to even consider at the time." His voice broke, and when he spoke again, it was in a beseeching tone. "Haven't any among you ever been forced to make an urgent choice? Haven't you ever been compelled to act without the luxury of taking the time to consider what might follow?"

Hopper felt his blood go cold. *Yes I have. And this war-ravaged city is the proof.*

Now Titus shook his head, a gesture of sadness and shame. "I am sorry. I am sorry to the depths of my soul. My early intentions were good, but it wasn't long before I realized what a mistake I had made. And although there were tens of thousands of opportunities between then and now when I could have made it right, I elected to leave things as they were—an evil status quo. And *that* is my true crime: striking the accord was an act of ignorance and desperation, but allowing it to continue even after I understood what a truly sinful thing it was . . . *that* is my most profound trespass. I cannot say what the result of defaulting on my agreement with Felina might have been—I suspect if I had refused to honor her conditions, Atlantia would have fallen long ago. Which is precisely why I did not try to undo what I had done."

Titus closed his eyes and sighed heavily. "It was so much easier to simply put the truth out of my mind and let myself live the lie. As those who will rise to power in my wake will soon discover, the right path is often the steepest and most difficult to climb. For some, wickedness is effortless. Goodness is a far greater challenge—but a true leader welcomes that challenge and rises to meet it. Justice is worth whatever work it requires. But sooner or later even the purest of hearts will face temptation. I regret that I was not strong enough to resist it. And so, what I wish for all of you now is a leader who will be more steadfast than I. And even as you judge me, which is surely your right to do, I would ask that *you* ask yourselves this question: In my place . . . what would you have done?"

With that, the former ruler of Atlantia bowed his head and let the silence surround him.

No one moved. No one blinked, no one spoke, perhaps no one even breathed. Hopper wondered if they were all suddenly remembering how, in recent days, they had been forced to steal from their neighbors in order to feed their children. Were they recalling some dark moment back on that battleground when they'd callously shoved a smaller, weaker rodent in front of them to shield themselves from a slashing cat claw or a ferocious feline fang? They had looted abandoned buildings and destroyed property, all in an attempt to survive. Hopper guessed that if he'd asked the merchant or the chipmunk or the squirrel a mere two weeks ago if they could ever imagine themselves doing any of these things, they would have said, "Never! Of course not! I am good and just and noble."

But it's so much easier to be those things when your loved ones are not crying out from hunger. Perhaps the true test of righteousness is being good and just and noble when your children are starving.

Now Beverley broke the silence. "I would like to hear what he has to say." She pointed at Hopper, her eyes twinkling warmly. "You will help us find peace again, won't you?"

Hopper looked at her trusting face and wanted more than anything to say that he would. But right now the task seemed insurmountable. He glanced down at Firren, who smiled her lovely smile, then at Zucker, who gave him an encouraging nod.

Hopper answered the only way he knew how—with the truth. "I can only say that I will try," he said. Jamming his paws into the pocket of his tunic, he closed his eyes and wished for words of wisdom to form on his lips. Surprisingly, his wish was granted . . . in the form of a crumpled scrap of paper, stuffed deep into his pocket.

The note from La Rocha. It had been mysteriously delivered to Hopper following the bloody liberation of the camps.

He'd forgotten he'd kept it. But it was all the inspiration he needed. He didn't even have to look at it, as he knew by heart the words the great mystic had written:

> CHOSEN ONE,
> THERE IS STILL SO MUCH TO BE DONE.
> HAVE FAITH AND BE STRONG, FOR I
> SHALL COME FOR YOU.

It was that simple. Faith. And from it, strength.

What these rodents needed was something to believe in. Maybe if they had that, everything else would follow.

Hopper looked out over the waiting crowd. He must make them believe in *him*. And for that to happen, he needed to believe in himself.

"There is much to be done," he boomed, the words of La Rocha's note echoing over the crowd. "We must have faith and be strong. We have liberated the camps, but clearly, this has left us with an even greater battle to be won. We need to have faith . . . in ourselves, and in one another. If we work together to rebuild, a whole new Atlantia awaits, where all rodents will be safe and welcome. But if we fail to unite in this worthy cause, we are all doomed to live in fear." *Or die in it*, he added silently.

The rodents murmured among themselves, mulling this over.

"Okay, so let's say we do unite," snorted a scruffy factory rat. "That still won't keep the ferals out. Sure, maybe by banding together we can fight off a few of the beasts, one at a time. But how long can that go on? We're hungry and weak and we're smaller than they are. And with the city in ruins there are no safe places to hide."

"It'll be the hunting ground all over again," wailed a refugee. "Except this time it's open season on all of us! Refugee and Atlantian alike."

This was true, of course. Faith and unity were only part of the equation. They were lacking strong, towering walls and a well-trained army to guard them. In its present condition the city was anything but secure. What these rodents needed was an impenetrable fortress . . . and they needed it fast! They needed a place where no feral could trespass. Hopper believed fully that Atlantia could be reconstructed into that safe haven over time, but these rodents needed a more immediate solution; Felina's hungry ferals would soon be back, and in greater numbers, to hunt the unprotected streets of the ruined city.

"I know a place where we will be safe!" he cried. "There is a village that lies behind a sturdy wall built of human-made bricks and mortar. In other words, it's catproof!"

This glimmer of hope caused a few of the mice to cheer.

"Take us there!"

"Yes! Lead us, mouse!"

"Where is this wondrous place?"

Hopper beamed. "It's far away from here, but we will make the journey together! We will seek sanctuary there, and I know they will allow us entry."

"*How* do you know?" someone in the crowd demanded.

"Well, because . . . ," said Hopper, preparing to reveal to this gathering the shocking truth. "Because although I came from above, like most of you, I have since learned that I was actually born of tunnel dwellers. And not only was I born of them, but as it turns out . . ." He paused to allow a modest shrug. "I also happen to be their foretold leader. I am the Chosen One of the Mūs tribe. And it is to their fortified dwelling place that I am going to take you."

The cheering stopped abruptly and was overtaken by an angry gasp, followed by a grumble of disbelief.

"He's a *Mūs?*" someone shrieked.

"He wants to take us to live among monsters!" another cried out.

"The Mūs are barbarians," a hostile voice shouted. "And that would make their Chosen One the most barbaric of all."

"I'd rather take my chances with those mangy cats!"

"The Mūs are Atlantia's greatest enemy!"

"They most certainly are *not!*"

It was Titus who had spoken this last. The emperor's face was filled with shame as he continued: "The savagery of the Mūs is merely another falsehood I invented to keep my unworthy backside securely upon the throne. I vilified them because I feared them. In truth, they are peace-loving creatures, wise and fair and strong . . . all the things I set out to be but ultimately abandoned."

"Wait a minute. So you're saying the Mūs *aren't* dangerous?" someone shouted.

"Only to me," Titus confessed. "Their noble leader knew the real purpose of the camps, and he would have fought valiantly to bring me down so that he might put an end to them." His gravelly voice caught when his gaze fell on Firren. "He deserved much better than he got for his efforts."

Hopper felt a tear trickle through the white fur that encircled his right eye.

"Thank you, Titus," came a voice from the back of the gathering, "for finally speaking the truth about the Mūs."

Every head turned in the direction of this proud new voice. Even Hopper went up on the tips of his hind paws, searching out this new speaker. A murmur of interest rippled through the crowd as it parted to make way for the stranger who was now moving in brisk, purposeful strides toward the platform.

The Chosen One gasped.

There was something undeniably familiar about this stranger.

Small of stature, but with a proud bearing.

And dressed in a robe of shimmering gold.

CHAPTER THREE

"PINKIE?"

The name escaped Hopper's lips in a whisper. For the briefest of seconds he thought his sister was approaching through the crowd. But as the stranger drew nearer, Hopper could see that this golden-caped creature was not his acid-tongued, bite-first-ask-questions-later sibling.

"Sage!" he cried, jumping down from the platform to meet the leader of the revered Mūs Tribunal. Hopper hadn't seen the council members at the camp raid or the hunting ground, and with good reason. The three elders were philosophers, not warriors. Hopper assumed they'd remained behind in the safety of the Mūs village, strategizing and planning for whatever would arise in the aftermath of the battle.

He grinned now, fairly certain that the one thing they most definitely had *not* imagined would arise was that Hopper would be bringing a whole gathering of displaced Atlantians and nomad refugees to live among them while the great city was being rebuilt.

"How are you?" Hopper gushed, throwing his arms around Elder Sage. "How's Pinkie? How's Pup?"

When Sage replied with a grim shake of his head, Hopper felt the panic seize him.

"Are they hurt?" Hopper asked anxiously. "Didn't

they make it back to the village after the battle? What's happened to them?"

From beneath the golden hood Sage frowned. "Nothing's happened to *them*," he said archly. "*They've* happened to *us!*"

Zucker quickly called the anxious crowd to order, commanding them to waste no time in finding whatever shelter they could. He explained that he and Hopper would return to the palace to confer with their unexpected visitor, and promised that when plans to transition them all to the safety of the Mūs village were finalized, he would send his soldiers to notify them.

"At which time," the prince declared confidently, "a calm and orderly departure from our compromised location will commence." Then he turned to Hopper and added in a grim whisper, "Let's hope so, anyway."

Hopper rolled his eyes. "Don't be such a pessimist, Zuck-meister. It's a great idea!" He flashed an eager grin at Sage. "Isn't it a great idea? If we can just get all these rodents through the tunnels unharmed, they'll be able to live behind your wall until Atlantia is up and running again. We can pool our resources, build an army. . . ." He broke off when he saw the doubtful look in Sage's eyes. "What? We *can't* build an army?"

"There is much to discuss," the elder said in a solemn tone. "But not here."

Zucker immediately dispatched Polhemus and Garfield to escort Elder Sage to the palace in the ramshackle rickshaw.

Marcy also hurried ahead to see what meager refreshment she could find to serve their honored guest. Hopper reminded her to take care. There was no telling what dangers the streets of Atlantia held these days.

"And what of me?" Titus asked quietly. "Will you leave me here to rot? Or perhaps to fall prey to some hunger-crazed feral skulking within the city limits?"

Zucker glared at his father. "Either works for me."

The iciness in his friend's eyes made Hopper shiver.

"We've set up a makeshift cell for him," the soldier Ketchum reported, "in the basement of one of the abandoned factories. I'll deliver him there and post a guard."

"Excellent," said Zucker. After a moment's hesitation he sighed. "You might as well unbind his paws. He poses no threat now. And make sure he gets something to eat."

"Thank you, Your Highness," said Titus, his voice wavering. "It is a powerful leader who can show mercy where none is warranted."

Zucker did not reply. When Ketch had taken Titus away, the prince clapped Hopper on the back.

"Great speech, kid. You really can think on your

feet when you have to." He grinned, but there was concern in his eyes. "Let's get back to the palace and see what old Sage has to say about this plan of yours."

They had gotten only a few steps out of the square when Hopper remembered Firren. She was in the same spot where she'd been standing during Titus's mea culpa address, only now her eyes were focused on the ground and she was fiddling with the handle of her sword. This was odd. Firren wasn't ordinarily a fiddler.

"Aren't you coming, Firren?" Hopper asked.

"Hmm?" She lifted her face, and her gaze went right to Zucker. "Oh. Well . . . I don't know. Should I?"

Hopper was about to say, "Of course you should," but Zucker spoke first.

"Sure. I mean, if you want to, that is." He gave an awkward shrug. "But only if you want to. It's entirely up to you."

"Right." Firren cocked her head. "Do you think you'll be needing my help?"

"Obviously we need all the help we can get. And your help is always very . . . you know . . . helpful." Zucker kicked a pebble on the ground and scratched the back of his head. "Which helps. A lot."

"Okay, so then maybe I will come along." Firren shifted her weight from one hind paw to the other. "Then again, I was just thinking, maybe I should go make a quick sweep of the tunnels. Some of the Rangers are still unaccounted for since the raid. That is, if you don't *really* need me."

Zucker gave a slow nod. "Tunnel sweep. Lost Rangers. Also good ideas."

"Okay. So . . . I *won't* come with you, then? Or . . . ?"

"Nope. No need. Unless . . . you *want* to."

"Do *you* want me to?"

Hopper listened to this exchange in utter bewilderment. It was by far the stupidest conversation he'd ever witnessed. What in the world had gotten into these two? Since when did the mighty Firren have difficulty making a simple decision? And Zucker—what was with all the shrugging and stammering and head scratching? He was acting like a total nincompoop—a nervous young rat, fresh out of the schoolroom.

"Well, I don't *not* want you to come with us," said Zucker. "But then again, like I said, it's your call."

"All right, then." Firren drew her sword and forced a smile. "The tunnels it is."

"The tunnels. Okay." Zucker snapped her a clumsy salute. "Have at it."

Firren frowned, returned the salute, then turned to leave.

Just as she reached the edge of the square, Zucker suddenly cupped a paw to his mouth and called, "You be careful out there!"

Firren turned back and smiled over her shoulder. "I will."

"Good." Zucker nodded and smiled back. "Good."

When Firren took off toward the gates, Zucker let out a long sigh and rolled his eyes.

"What was *that* all about?" Hopper asked.

"Forget it, kid," Zucker grumbled. "You wouldn't believe me if I told you."

They entered the palace to find the once-gleaming floors and furnishings thickly coated with dust and grime. The opulent halls, which had bustled with such energy and excitement, were now silent.

And of course, there was the cricket poop.

Scads of it.

Everywhere.

"Ewwww," said Hopper, wrinkling his nose in disgust. "Yucchhkk."

"Couldn't be helped," said Zucker with a shrug. "In war we call it collateral damage."

"I call it poop," said Hopper.

Sage, who had been waiting in the grand foyer, simply lifted the hem of his golden robe and followed Zucker to the Conflict Room.

Holding his nose, Hopper tiptoed gingerly behind them and tried to ignore the unpleasant squishing sensation beneath his feet.

When they reached the Conflict Room, where

the sinister General Cassius had once presided with such arrogance, they each took a seat in a plush chair around the broad, dusty table.

"Tell us what's going on," Hopper said. "If I know my sister, I'll bet it's not good."

"Not good," said Sage, shaking his head. "Not good at all. She's dismissed us, Temperance, Christoph, and me."

"She dismissed the Tribunal?" said Zucker. "Why?"

"Because she wants complete authority over the Mūs. She's parlaying her success in battle into a campaign to turn our peaceful village into a military state. Her first official act was to institute a conscription policy."

Hopper's courage may have increased tenfold in recent days, but he was still a relative novice when it came to issues of war. "What's conscription?"

"It's compulsory enlistment in the armed forces."

Hopper frowned, still not understanding.

"It's bullying, plain and simple," Zucker clarified. "She's forcing every capable and able-bodied Mūs to join her army."

"Right," said Sage. "Every last one of us. Whether we're willing or not."

"I take it you weren't willing?" said Hopper.

The elder considered the question a moment before responding. "Although I value peace above all," he said at last, "I would never object to fighting for what

I believe in. But Pinkie has gone too far. She's turning the village into a police state. We're practically living under martial law."

Two more terms with which Hopper was not familiar. He guessed what it all boiled down to was just Pinkie being Pinkie. Now that she'd put herself in charge, she was ruling with nothing less than an iron paw, and there would be only one law: hers.

"Pinkie's always been the bossy sort," Hopper observed.

"Oh, this is much, *much* worse than bossy," moaned the beleaguered elder. "She has taken an if-you're-not-with-Pinkie, you're-against-Pinkie stance. Many Mūs citizens have been forced to go against their beliefs and principles just to keep from being turned out into the tunnels to fend for themselves." He paused for a long moment, then placed his tiny paw on Hopper's arm. "We were hoping you might be able to talk to her and convince her to just . . . to just—"

"To just get over herself?" Zucker finished.

"Precisely!" said Sage. "We followed her into battle, and she proved herself a strong leader. But now that the fight is over, we feel she needs to let us govern as we always have."

"With all due respect," said the prince, "the fight is not over. Not yet. As heinous as Titus's agreement with Felina was, it did at least guarantee safety in the tunnels. Now it's a free-for-all out there. Those cats are hunting day and night, even when they aren't in need of nourishment. No rodent is safe to roam. My soldiers are doing all they can, but it's a big job." He leaned forward with a thoughtful expression, his paws splayed upon the tabletop. "Maybe, if we can get Pinkie to make military duty a matter of choice rather than obligation, having a powerful Mūs army standing at the ready wouldn't be the worst thing in the world. We could all benefit from the presence of a highly visible peacekeeping force."

Sage nodded. "On that point I agree with you, Your Highness. If Pinkie the Chosen, as she's taken to calling herself, would allow our forces to patrol the tunnels in defense of *all* creatures, I would be wholeheartedly for it, as long as no one was pressed into service. But she's got quite a different agenda."

Hopper was almost afraid to ask. "What do you mean?"

"She's created this new and improved army of hers for the benefit of Mūs citizens only. Her orders are such that Mūs soldiers may not, under any circumstances, defend, protect, or come to the aid of any creature who is not one of us."

"That's horrible," said Hopper. "What about Pup? Surely he's tried to talk her out of this."

Sage gave a mirthless chuckle. "Pup is a whole other story entirely. At first your little brother seemed to be brainwashed by Pinkie. She made him her right-hand rodent, and he reveled in it. He was so innocent he really didn't know any better. I think his experience in the hunting ground frightened him so deeply that he was willing to do whatever it took to feel safe. So for the first few days he jumped to do her bidding and never questioned her politics."

There was an ominous note to Zucker's voice when he asked, "And now?"

"Now the little scamp is showing some real spunk. He's talking back to Pinkie and speaking his mind, challenging her—but not on our behalf, on his own. He seems to have a rather large chip on his tiny shoulder."

Sweet little Pup . . . first a sycophant, now a malcontent? It made Hopper's heart hurt just to picture it.

"I'll talk to them," he said, popping up from his chair. "But if I know Pinkie, she won't agree to anything unless there's something in it for her." He turned to Zucker. "Any ideas?"

"A solid alliance should be enough," the prince grumbled. "If she helps us now, we can promise to do the same for her should she ever need us—that is, once the Atlantian army is up and running again. You know . . . kind of a quid pro quo."

Hopper pondered this a moment. "And if the squid fro-yo doesn't do it for her?"

Zucker laughed. "How about this? If the Rangers

find any treasure hidden in the palace, it's hers."

Hopper nodded. "Good. I think Pinkie will like the idea of being rich. If that doesn't work, maybe I can at least snap Pup out of this spell he's under and bring him back here."

Zucker gave him a dark look. "Back here to what? Certain death? Our plan was to ask Pinkie to let us all take refuge in the Mūs village, remember?"

Hopper deflated. "Oh, right."

"But you will try to make Pinkie see that her ways are wicked?" Sage pleaded. "You will come and meet with her in an attempt to find a solution that will benefit the Mūs and the Atlantians alike?"

"I'll give it my best shot," said Hopper. But deep down he had his doubts.

What was it Titus had said in the square? *For some, wickedness is effortless.* That was certainly true for Pinkie. But for the first time Hopper found himself wondering *why*. What had caused this deep anger in his sister's soul that made her so quick to turn against others? What had happened to her to fill her with such malice? Until the day they escaped from their cage in the pet shop, they'd led the exact same life. Well, except, of course, for the fact that Hopper had endured the agonizing experience of watching their mother being stolen away in the night. So shouldn't *he* be the one with the ax to grind?

"All we ask is that you try to make Pinkie see

that our only hope of survival is for us all to work together," said Sage.

"Getting Pinkie to work on any creature's behalf but her own?" Hopper sighed. "Good luck with that. Still, I don't think I could live with myself if I didn't at least try."

"Let's go, then," said Zucker. "The sooner we have a face-to-face with that maniacal little mouse master the better. With any luck, we'll be making her see things our way by lunchtime."

"Lunchtime?" Sage repeated. "It's a three-day trek under ordinary circumstances, but now, with the ferals terrorizing the tunnels, it takes twice that, what with all the hiding and backtracking."

"Oh, don't worry about that." Hopper grinned, striding toward the Conflict Room door. "We'll be there in no time."

"But how?"

"Easy. We'll take the subway."

CHAPTER FOUR

IT TOOK SOME DOING to get the Mūs elder to even consider leaping onto the speeding metal monster, but at last Hopper and Zucker talked him into it.

"What if it takes us to the wrong place?" Sage asked, his whiskers twitching with trepidation. "Such a swift and evil thing! How do you know it won't carry us to the dwelling place of some great demon?"

"Doesn't going to see Pinkie fall under that category?" Hopper muttered.

"The Chosen One's figured out the migration patterns," Zucker informed Sage proudly.

"Actually, one of the pages of your Sacred Book was a subway map," Hopper explained. "So it was only a matter of matching the numbers to the tracks and the platforms. According to my calculations, the next train should be along any moment."

"You speak in a foreign tongue," said Sage, shaking his head. "But as you are the Chosen One, I suppose I shall have to trust you. And if your miraculous understanding of these speeding things was indeed gleaned from the book of La Rocha's prophecies, well, then surely I have nothing to fear. The mystic provides the answers to all life's mysteries."

"Yeah," Zucker snorted. "That La Rocha really knows his stuff."

The sarcastic tone in the prince's voice caused Sage to blink with surprise. "You are not a believer, I take it?"

The prince turned up his palms. "I mean, c'mon. A cockroach? No one's ever actually gotten an up-close-and-personal look at this magic bug, have they? He only communicates with you Mūs through written documents, right?"

"That is correct."

"So . . . doesn't that seem just a little bit weird to you? I mean, wouldn't it be easier to just have a conversation? Even for a cockroach."

Sage stiffened. "One so great as La Rocha would never deign to allow mere mortals to hear the melodic majesty of his voice!"

"Okay." Zucker shook his head "Whatever."

Hopper frowned. He hadn't realized how skeptical Zucker was when it came to La Rocha's prophecies. "I don't understand," he said. "You believed the prophecy about me. You believed I was the Chosen One."

"I believed you were my old friend's kid," Zucker corrected. "And that was all I needed to know in order to put my faith in *you*."

This made Hopper smile. Then something else occurred to him. "Did Dodger believe in La Rocha?"

Zucker thought for a moment. "Well, he believed there was someone or something down here bringing hope to the masses, and that was okay with him. La

Rocha was helpful in spreading the rebel message to the believers."

"That is exactly why La Rocha imparts his wisdom through cryptic messages," Sage went on, indignant. "So that those who are not worthy of his wisdom do not receive it. Puzzles, poetry, ciphers, codes. In this way he confuses the skeptics and reserves the gift of his knowledge for the true believers." The golden-caped elder turned to Hopper. "You've seen the book. Tell him how wondrous and complex it is."

"Well, um . . ." Hopper didn't want to insult Sage, but now that he thought about it, to him the Sacred Book *had* looked more like a collection of discarded human wastepaper than an old mystical tome. "It was definitely complex."

"What are you saying?" gasped Sage.

"I'm saying I don't know what to think," Hopper admitted. "The pages I saw were all different shapes and sizes, and of varying degrees of quality. Some of the messages did appear to be written in La Rocha's own script, but I noticed that others—like the subway map, for example—featured very different presentation styles. Intricate, flowing script; clear, bold print; and so many colors! I don't see how such a wide range of effects could possibly have been produced by one tiny creature."

Sage huffed. "You doubt his existence based on variations in his font choices? He is a mystic, not a scribe!"

"I'm sorry," said Hopper. "I didn't mean to upset you. I do believe in La Rocha. Honest! After all, he said I'd be here. . . ." He flashed his most glowing smile at the elder. "And here I am! See?"

Sage gave a curt nod, signifying the end of the discussion. That was fine with Hopper. Still, he wondered about the true origins of the Sacred Book. He remembered some of the pages he'd spied when the Tribunal had been poring over it in search of an answer to the question of two Chosen Ones. He'd spied a few "messages" that had been too baffling to even try to interpret:

One had the words "Jamba Juice Smoothie—Buy One, Get One Free" scrawled whimsically across a bright red rectangle.

Another read, "*The New York Times*—August 9, 1974—Nixon Resigns," all smudged in a banner of boldface black on a brittle yellowed page.

And then there was the one that announced "Madison Square Garden—Bruce Springsteen and the E Street Band—July 1, 2000, 7:30" in squared-off print on a small cardboard stub.

What in the world could any of that possibly mean? And how could it ever be useful to a mouse? But Hopper had no intention of pondering these particular mysteries at the moment. He had much bigger things on his mind. His confrontation with Pinkie was just a short train ride away, and for that

he was going to need more than wondrous, mystical wisdom.

For that, he was going to need guts.

Sage had loved every minute of his subway ride, racing through the darkness, clinging to the metal knob on the back of the train. He'd delighted in the sound, the speed, the motion, turning his pert brown face into the wind and letting it pummel him until his fur was slicked back flat against his head and his little black eyes watered.

Once, he'd lost his grip and nearly fell off, but Zucker had reached out just in the nick of time and caught him by the hem of his golden cape.

"One of these days we're gonna have to figure out a way to get *inside* that thing," Zucker had muttered when they finally hopped off. "I think a couple of my whiskers blew off that time."

"Whiskers don't blow off," Hopper had said, and laughed.

As they traveled the rest of the way to the Mūs village on foot, they kept to the shadows. Twice they saw ferals hunting and had to hide behind stones or deep inside the slender cracks of the tunnel wall. The exodus from the city had left the tunnels teeming with rodents, and the felines were taking full advantage. The distant sounds of scampering paws and hissing cats made Hopper sick to his stomach.

He was relieved when they arrived at the door in the enormous gray wall that shielded the Mūs village from the open tunnels. It was the same door he'd gone through with Firren, to meet the Tribunal and beg for their help in the battle to liberate Titus's refugee camps. He'd had to keep his face averted that time because Firren knew the villagers would instantly recognize him as the Chosen One. That was a revelation she'd wanted to save until he was standing directly before the three most powerful figures in the entire Mūs tribe.

What a very different life he'd been living then, he reflected. He hadn't known he was the son of the great Dodger, the brave and valiant Mūs leader who'd gone to his death fighting against the devilish Atlantian general Cassius.

My father died a hero, Hopper reminded himself now. *And here I am, shaking in my boots, dreading a conversation with my own sister.*

Summoning his courage, he knocked. The door opened and a sentry mouse poked his face out. Hopper's eyes were instantly drawn to the uniform the sentry wore.

The guard's military-style jacket was obviously brand new. It was clean and crisp, trimmed with heavy silver braid and accented with decorative buttons. And it was *pink*!

Pink. For Pinkie.

Hopper turned to Sage with an incredulous look. "Seriously?"

Sage replied with a grim sigh. "She works quickly."

"Welcome," said the guard, although his voice was anything but welcoming. "Do you have business behind this wall?"

"Uh, *yeah*," said Hopper, jerking a paw toward Sage. "He lives here, and I'm Pinkie's brother."

"I thought Pup was her brother."

"I'm her *other* brother," Hopper snapped. "Now please let me in so I can have a word with my sister!"

The guard scowled. "Gonna need some identification."

At this, Zucker shot forward, bending down so he was nose to nose with the diminutive soldier. "Look, buddy, I know you're probably feeling terribly official in that brand-spankin'-new uniform of yours, but I gotta tell ya, your attitude is getting on my last nerve. So I suggest you take a good look at my friends." He pointed first to the white fur around Hopper's eye, then to Sage's shimmering gold cloak. "Check the circle, check the cape. And look close, because that's all the identification you're gonna get!"

The sentry took in Zucker's imposing size and the sword at his hip. He swept his eyes quickly over Hopper and Sage, then wisely stepped aside.

"That's what I'm talkin' about," grumbled Zucker, giving Hopper a nudge through the door.

"I'll summon a foot soldier to escort—"

"No need," said Sage. "I will see us to Pinkie the Chosen myself."

The guard looked as if he might argue, but one glare from Zucker took care of that.

"You may proceed," he squeaked.

"Thanks." Zucker grinned. "And by the way, pink is definitely *not* your color."

As they made their way toward the locomotive, Hopper took note of the troubling changes to the village. Last time he was here, the neat little yards and tidy huts had looked cozy and inviting. Now most of them had been commandeered by Pinkie's army to be used as barracks, training stations, or storehouses for military equipment. Through an open door in one of these houses Hopper saw a Mūs blacksmith laboring frantically, forging all manner of weaponry. The sparks from his fire had singed the pretty checked curtains that hung at the window, and instead of bread and fruit, the dining table was piled high with swords, cutlasses, and rapiers. It took Hopper a moment to realize this was the very same house where the sweet elderly couple had provided a meal for him and Firren and the Rangers. A cold feeling settled in his belly as he wondered where that kindly old couple was now.

Hopper pulled his gaze and his dark thoughts from the house and focused on the locomotive ahead of him.

In days past the locomotive had housed the Tribunal. It was also the occasional lodging place of the elusive La Rocha, who from time to time would visit here to avail himself only to the elders—but never allow them to see his face. He would hand down voiceless proverbs and prophecies, adages and advice (written, always written). La Rocha would reside in the privacy of the cylindrical smokestack that rose up from the imposing lump of mechanical cranks and metal wires inside the engine. From there he would shower his followers with mystic revelations that became part of the stylistically eclectic Sacred Book (as Hopper had pointed out). Then, without warning, he would vanish . . . to where, no one could say for certain. Maybe he disappeared into the tunnels, or perhaps (depending on one's willingness to suspend one's disbelief) he evaporated into the very air itself, in a magical puff of smoke.

Now the black steel behemoth that loomed at the center of the village was Pinkie's command center, and Hopper thought the once-gleaming locomotive seemed to have lost some of its luster.

At the base of the engine, in the shadow of its towering metal wheels, stood a line of soldiers in pink uniforms, shoulder to shoulder, ears thrust back, and each holding a newly forged blade. The expressions on their furry brown faces were blank, and they formed an imposing, albeit pastel-tinted, blockade.

One Mūs soldier at the end of the line had slightly darker fur. The tilt of his ears was different, and there was a shimmer of anticipation in his eyes. Hopper could tell he had big military aspirations. What was the word Sage had used? Conscription. Hopper guessed that this soldier had not been drafted, but had signed on to Pinkie's army eagerly and with great purpose. The others did not look quite so enthusiastic about this new path.

Oh, Hopper could certainly relate to that! He'd never planned to fall into a subway tunnel and join a revolution; he'd never aspired to topple an empire and fight a depraved cat queen and her band of ferals. But here he was. And although things looked glum at the moment, Hopper was grateful for every minute of it. He was right where he belonged, and he knew it, believed it, felt it deep in the marrow of his bones.

Because being the Chosen One may not have been his idea. But it *was* his destiny.

The blockade stepped aside to allow the former elder and the Atlantian delegates access to the metal ladder. Hopper, Zucker, and Sage climbed into the cavernous engine, where more pink-clad soldiers awaited. Pinkie was seated at the rough-hewn table in the middle of the space, rifling through the Sacred Book.

Hopper scanned the room for Pup. He found him seated on a stool in a corner, bent over a page Hopper immediately recognized as the one containing the paw-written prophecy that had foretold the Chosen One's arrival.

. . . He alone brings purity of vision
Exalt and hail Him!

More than anything Hopper wanted to run to his brother, but he feared he might wind up impaled on the tip of some overeager soldier's blade. Pup was so intent on his task, he didn't even notice Hopper and the others were there.

But Pinkie did; she looked up from the table and eyed her brother with disdain. "What are you doing here? I don't remember sending an invitation to the creep who tore this hole in my ear."

"*After* you tore one in *my* ear!" Hopper shot back. He glowered at the sister who was practically his twin. With the distinctive white circle of fur around her left eye and the jagged wound to her right ear, they were truly mirror images of each other. Opposites, inside and out.

"What do you want?" she growled.

"I've come for two reasons," Hopper began. *Three, if you count wanting to take Pup home with me.* "First, I've come to request asylum for all the Atlantians and refugees who are currently struggling to survive in the tunnels."

"Asylum?" Pinkie looked as though she'd never heard the word.

"It means a safe haven," Sage explained, shaking his head sadly. "You see, Pinkie? You still have so much to learn before you can lead this tribe. You do not yet possess the proper skills to be a ruler. You don't even possess the proper vocabulary."

Pinkie folded her arms across her chest and glowered. "Didn't I throw you out of here a week ago?" She turned back to Hopper. "The answer to that request, as I'm sure you expected, is a big ol' no. Next question."

Hopper ground his teeth and clenched his fists. "Why?"

"Because effective immediately there will be no non-Mūs allowed behind the gray wall, that's why. No squirrels, no chipmunks, no chirpy-jumpy-buggy critters." She gave Zucker an icy smile. "And no rats. You're lucky I haven't already tossed *you* out on your tail."

"I'd like to see you try," Zucker retorted, seething, his paw resting on his blade.

"And I'd like to see you go up against my personal guard. You're outnumbered here, so don't get cocky."

"Please, Pinkie," said Hopper, trying to keep his voice steady. "The animals are in grave danger. Why won't you help them?"

"Why can't they help themselves? Why should I be responsible for them? Rats and squirrels are bigger than we are. They'll need more food, more water, more everything. I don't want those overgrown rodents using up precious resources that rightfully belong to the Mūs." She paused to smooth her golden cape, which was now emblazoned with a bold pink *P*. "Remember how it was in Keep's shop? Remember how the swimmy things lived among the swimmy things, and the feathery flyish creatures shared their cages with other feathery flyish creatures? Those of us who were furry lived among others who were furry, and the slimy things slithered with the—"

"What's your point?" Hopper demanded.

"It was a good system! Do you ever remember any epic battles being fought in the pet shop?"

Hopper cocked an eyebrow. "You mean other than between you and me? And since when is Keep your role model? Pinkie, how low have you sunk?"

"*I'm* not the one begging for help," Pinkie replied. "So I guess not as low as you. Your raggedy rodent rejects will not be welcome *here*."

"There is a name for what you're describing," murmured Sage. "An ugly name: segregation. And as a practice, it is shortsighted and ill advised."

"Call it whatever you want," Pinkie said, and waved a dismissive paw. "It's the law."

Now Pup jumped up from his stool and skittered over to bring Pinkie the page he'd been working on. When he spotted Hopper, a sudden smile spread over his face.

"Hopper!"

"Pup . . ."

But when Pinkie threw Pup a look, his smile faded as quickly as it had appeared; in the next instant he was regarding his brother with cool eyes. "Hello."

"How are you, Pup?"

"Wonderful," Pup boasted. "I'm Pinkie's second-in-command. I help her run things around here." He puffed out his little chest, but the look in his eyes was not the glow of pride, rather it was the glint of entitlement.

Hopper's heart sank.

"Let's not get carried away, Pup," Pinkie scoffed. "You don't exactly run things. You just help me out so it's easier for me."

Pup's jaw flexed and his eyes flared. It was the first time Hopper had ever seen his darling little brother express anger.

"Here, Pinkie," said Pup, handing the page to his sister. "I've made some alterations to this document. I think you should read it. All of you."

Pinkie took the page and laid it on the table where Hopper and the others could see it. As she deciphered Pup's changes, her fur began to bristle and her fangs seemed to bare themselves of their own accord. Hopper's mouth dropped open; Sage actually gasped in horror.

"I can't read, so I had one of the guards point out all the 'he' and 'him' words for me," he explained in a voice filled with self-satisfaction. This appeared to be true, because Pup had taken a dark, powdery stone to the page and scribbled over every "he" and crossed out every "him." Then, because he couldn't write, either, he had replaced those words by drawing in primitive little hieroglyphs—one depicted a mouse with a white circle around her left eye, which was obviously intended to be Pinkie.

And sketched in beside Pinkie's image was that of a much smaller mouse who wore a ferocious expression

on his face and had a dark, soot-colored circle drawn around his left eye.

With a chill creeping along his flesh, Hopper looked up from the page to his brother's face and shuddered at what he saw. While they'd all been looking at the prophecy page with its foreboding alterations, Pup had engaged in an additional bit of artwork.

With the same black stone he'd used to edit the prophecy, he'd chalked a dark, severely perfect circle into the fur around his own left eye.

CHAPTER FIVE

"**You defiled the prophecy!**" Sage cried.

Pup crossed his arms. "You say defiled . . . I say updated."

"Are you out of your little runt mind?" snarled Pinkie, whipping around to glower at Pup. "This looks like you expect to lead with me and be considered my equal."

Pup nodded.

"Change it back!" Pinkie demanded. "Immediately!"

Zucker frowned at Pinkie, then at Pup. "The thing about mystical prophecies," he said, his voice echoing off the metal walls, "is that if you're going to believe in them, then you kind of have to take them as they are. You can't just rewrite them to suit your own tastes."

"I can do whatever I want," Pinkie snapped. "I'm Pinkie the Chosen, and the Mūs answer to me." She grabbed the stone from Pup's paw and scribbled out his little doodles. "*Not* the Tribunal, not Hopper, and definitely not Pup!"

Hopper snuck a glance at Pup and caught a glint of a small fang as his brother's upper lip curled in fury. Hopper expected him to reply, but the small mouse simply stood there.

"Now," said Pinkie, tossing the stone over her

shoulder, "I've already denied your request for asylum, so what was your second order of business?"

Hopper let out a long breath. "If you won't let the homeless rodents temporarily live here in safety, then will you consider commanding this fashionably dressed army of yours to defend them in the tunnels? They need protection from the ferals. Without it, they can't scavenge for food. They'll either starve to death or be eaten themselves."

Pinkie stared at him silently; her expression seemed to ask, *And how is this is my problem?*

"Don't you remember, Pinkie?" Hopper urged. "You were lost down here once yourself. You wandered the tunnels and hid from the predators, and listened to your stomach growling with hunger. But then you knocked on that door in the big gray wall, and they took you in and cared for you."

"They had to!" Pinkie snapped. "I was their Chosen One."

"Well, then do something good with it!" Hopper challenged. "Choose to protect the innocent, whether they're mice or rats or squirrels or . . . or . . . or crickets who poop all over the place."

At that Pup let out a snort.

"Please, Pinkie," Hopper continued. "Right now you command the only army in the tunnels. Atlantia will raise a new militia, and then, I promise, we will gladly take over the job. But that's going to require time. So for now please say you'll let your soldiers look out for all of us."

Pinkie remained silent. Hopper held his breath. He could feel Zucker tense behind him. Sage tapped one hind paw nervously against the metal floor. But no one spoke. All they could do was wait for Pinkie to give her answer.

Finally she did.

"No."

"No?"

"No. My army fights for me and me alone. The safety of the Mūs is guaranteed. Everyone else is on his own."

"I don't understand," Zucker bellowed. "You fought to free these rodents in the camp attack. You battled right along with them in the hunting ground. Why don't you want to finish what you've started?"

"The prince is right," said Hopper. "Just a fortnight past you led the Mūs soldiers into battle on a quest to free the refugees. The only reason we emerged victorious was because we fought *together*! Squirrel fighting beside chipmunk fighting beside mouse fighting beside rat! Even the crickets helped. They were your comrades-in-arms, Pinkie! How can you turn your back on them now?"

"Because I realized what a waste of time it was!" Pinkie's whiskers were trembling with anger; she planted her paws on her hips and fired her words at Hopper. "Our father fought against those camps, didn't he? And where did it get him? It got him *dead*, that's where. No squirrels or chipmunks or rats protected him, did they? So here's where I stand: the Mūs army protects the Mūs. That's Pinkie's law. And while we're on the subject, I've decided to pass another new law." She turned to Sage. "There will be no more La Rocha."

"Blasphemy!" hollered Sage.

"I've checked out that dwelling place of his," said Pinkie, flicking her head in the direction of the metal mountain that separated the main interior of the locomotive from La Rocha's private chamber in the smokestack. "Tore it apart, actually, looking for some sign that he was all you Mūs believers said he was. But guess what. He wasn't there. In fact, all I found was some blank paper, some torn blue fabric, and a writing utensil or two. Nothing that proved any marvelous mystical being had ever dropped by for a visit. So as far as I'm concerned, the myth of La Rocha has been officially debunked. Any Mūs who invokes his name or his teachings will be punished!"

Hopper opened his mouth to remind Pinkie that the only reason the Mūs had hailed her as the Chosen One in the first place was because La Rocha's prophecy had predicted her arrival. But his words were cut off by paws gripping the collar of his tunic.

The next thing Hopper knew, five pink-clad soldiers

of Pinkie's private guard had succeeded in shoving him and his two companions out the engine door.

The two remaining elders, Temperance and Christoph, were brought to the bottom of the engine ladder and told they would be taking their leave.

In total eight soldiers escorted Hopper, Zucker, and the three demoted Tribunal members back to the gray wall.

"I guess we shouldn't be surprised she turned us down," said Zucker.

"True," said Hopper. "But I am surprised by Pup. Did you see how cold he was? He seemed so bitter. He was never like that before."

"He's seen battle," Zucker reminded him. "That changes a rodent. And I'm sure Pinkie's influence isn't helping. She'd make anybody go a little wacky."

Just as they were about to depart through the hidden door, Hopper heard a familiar voice calling out to him.

"Wait! Hopper! Don't go yet."

He whirled, his heart soaring to hear Pup crying out for him. His brother was scrambling to catch up. He was carrying a parcel wrapped in faded blue fabric. When he skidded to a stop before them, Hopper opened his arms. "Pup! You've decided to come with us?"

"What? No!" Pup lowered his eyebrows. "I've come

to give you this." He shoved the blue bundle at Hopper.

Hopper opened it to peer beneath the folds of blue felt: he saw chunks of bread, a bit of fruit, some water in a small apothecary jar. The gesture of kindness caused a lump to form in his throat. Perhaps there was hope for his tiny sibling after all. "Thank you," he whispered. "This is very generous of you, Pup."

"It wasn't me. It was Pinkie's idea. She gathered up the food and dispatched me to bring it to you." Now Pup stomped one hind paw in the dirt. "But you mark my words, Hopper, I'm not going to be her little delivery boy much longer. I can do great things too. I can be a hero."

"Of course you can," said Hopper. "If you come with us—"

Pup shook his head. "I don't need help from any puffed-up Chosen brother or sister."

As Pup headed back toward the engine, Hopper turned to Zucker, looking troubled and perplexed.

"I think somebody needs a nap," said Zucker.

"I heard that!" Pup shot back. He paused only long enough to cast a withering glare at the rat prince, then took off at a scamper, kicking up dust as he ran.

Hopper was simply too overwrought to ponder Pup's strange behavior. He sighed and looked down at the tidily packed meal his sister had wrapped in felt. "I guess despite all her bitterness, Pinkie knows that family still counts for something."

"Yeah," Zucker muttered. "Either that or the food's poisoned."

Hopper's gut told him it wasn't. As he tucked the edges of the fabric back into place, his eye was drawn to a splash of white inside. Sewn onto the royal blue felt was a large white letter *D*.

This was a scrap torn off the Dodgers pennant he'd once seen in the marketplace. In the exodus someone must have taken it from the city, and it had somehow made its way to Pinkie's village. Seeing the piece of pennant made Hopper's mind flash back to his first walk through the city, and a feeling of loss welled up within him.

He decided that after they had dined on Pinkie's food offering, he would save the soft blue scrap of material, this relic from the recent past. He would keep it to remind himself of how great the city once was and how great it could be again. Only this time it would not be built on dark lies and savage bargains. This time it would stand for community and decency.

He hadn't been able to sway Pinkie; and Pup, it seemed, was on his way to becoming just as hard-hearted and dangerous as their sister. But that didn't mean Hopper wasn't going to keep trying to make things right. With one last glance over his shoulder, he followed his companions through the door and out into the tunnel.

They ate quickly, sharing the meal Pinkie had provided. When they were through, Hopper tucked the parcel's blue wrapping into his pocket alongside the note from La Rocha. Then they began their march to the place where Hopper knew they would meet up with the train. He had some niggling concerns about how all five of them would manage to leap onto the speeding vehicle at once, but he kept these to himself. Christoph and Temperance were already terrified enough at the thought of riding one of the monsters they'd never seen but had heard growling and rumbling menacingly above their heads for their entire lives.

It was Sage who ultimately convinced them. He pointed out that as scary as it would be, it was a lot safer than taking their chances against the ferals. He also reminded them that he had ridden a train from Atlantia and had arrived in one piece.

By a stroke of sheer luck the 2 train did not rocket past them as it usually did; instead, for some reason unknown to Hopper, the serpent came to a full stop in the same dark stretch of tunnel where he had leaped aboard the first time. The travelers took full advantage of this lull in motion, clambering safely aboard the metal hitch that jutted out from the back of the last car.

"This is a gift from La Rocha," said Temperance.

"He's used the benevolent power of his spirit to bring the beast to a halt, in order that we might board with ease."

"I thought La Rocha was a philosopher and a prophet," said Zucker. "Now he's a magician, too?"

"He is a little bit of everything," Christoph clarified, positioning himself on the hitch and grasping the metal knob.

"Yes," said Temperance. "He guides and watches over us at all times."

"And was he watching when Pinkie booted us all out on our backsides?" Zucker muttered under his breath.

"What was that?"

"I said, uh . . . that La Rocha must be a real busy guy."

When the train started up, Temperance screamed and Christoph covered his eyes, but their panic didn't last long. The rodent riders were soon enjoying the sensation of speeding through the shadows with the wind in their whiskers. Hopper reveled in it too. The vibration of the metal perch made the bottoms of his paws tickle.

By the time the train pulled up to the Atlantic Avenue platform, the Tribunal was cheering for joy.

"This is us," said Hopper, jumping nimbly from the hitch. "Everybody off."

"Can't we ride a bit longer?" Christoph asked.

"Yes, can't we?" echoed Temperance. "Where does

this miracle of motion go from here?"

"Good question," said Hopper. "I could tell you if I had the map, but I assume it just goes on to another platform like this one. And then another. And another."

"Eternally!" cried Sage, liking the concept. "An infinite journey. I say we ride on and see where it takes us."

Zucker frowned. "You sure you want to do that?"

"We have nothing to lose," Temperance reasoned. "And if we do not find that which we seek up ahead, we can always locate this same sleek silver beast with the number two marking on its forehead and command it to return us here."

Hopper and Zucker exchanged glances. The thought of the Mūs elders all alone and unchaperoned in the tunnel world was disconcerting. Then again, Atlantia was in such a state of upheaval that they would not be able to offer the exalted Tribunal members adequate safety, or even comfort. Perhaps it *would* be wise to let them go off in search of better things.

"All right, then," said Zucker. "Bon voyage. And you know where we are if you need us."

"And we can always look to La Rocha for guidance," Sage reminded them.

Hopper quickly explained how they could find Atlantia, if indeed they did decide to return. He told them the exact location of the crack in the floor that would drop them into the abandoned tunnel where the city of Atlantia had once thrived. *And will thrive again*, he added silently, reaching into his pocket to feel the soft scrap of blue felt. He added a caveat about bracing themselves for the long fall into the lower tunnel, then gave each of them a hug.

"Good luck," he cried as the train's wheels began to screech against the metal track. "I hope you find what you're looking for."

"We wish the same for you, dear Chosen One."

"Good-bye, Hopper! May La Rocha bless and keep you!"

"Farewell!"

Hopper and Zucker watched as the train departed with the tiny adventurers aboard. Then the prince and the Chosen One ducked their heads and made their way through the gauntlet of human shoes, boots, and belongings. With a singular purpose they ran—full speed toward the gap between the wall and floor, the portal that would drop them back into the long-forgotten tunnel where the future of Atlantia waited.

CHAPTER SIX

THEY ARRIVED AT THE city to find the gate flung wide. Rodents streamed out, shouting, crying . . . running for their lives. The soldiers Ketchum, Garfield, and Polhemus were doing their best to exert some degree of control, but the panicked mob was having none of it.

"What's going on?" the prince demanded. "Why are they fleeing? Is it Felina?"

"Worse," replied Ketchum. "Exterminators!"

Hopper looked beyond the gates, and sure enough two enormous humans in coveralls were tromping through the city. Rats and chipmunks squealed in terror as they dodged the heavy boots and scampered desperately to escape. Every so often one of the exterminators would shout out, "There's one!" and swing his heavy shovel; the shovel would come down with an earsplitting clank . . . and there would be one less screaming rat.

Zucker grabbed Hopper and pulled him to crouch in the shadow of the city wall. "Stay low, kid," he said. "These guys are trained to kill on sight." Then the prince beckoned his soldiers over.

"It's madness, Your Majesty!" breathed the exhausted Garfield. "Atlantia is being destroyed!"

"What are they doing here?" Zucker asked. "Humans

never come down this deep. The tunnel's abandoned. There hasn't been a train through here in ages. What could they possibly want with Atlantia?"

"I heard them talking," Polhemus offered. "They said the Transit Authority sent them."

"What's the Transit Authority?" asked Hopper.

"We aren't entirely sure," Ketchum admitted. "Best we can figure, it's some powerful supernatural force that lords over lesser humans and gives them subterranean quests and trials to perform, such as this one. These exterminators said that the Commuters— whatever they are—have been complaining to the Authority about a lot more rats on the platforms lately."

This made perfect sense to Hopper. The freed refugees and former Atlantians who feared the tunnels must have run for higher ground in their efforts to escape the ferals.

"There is more to report," Ketchum said to Zucker. "It seems, in the chaos, your father has escaped. The factory where he was being held was one of the first the exterminators destroyed. His guard was badly injured, and Titus fled."

"We thought to give chase," Garfield added, "but decided our efforts would be better spent here, helping with the evacuation."

Zucker nodded. "Good call. Titus is no threat without Felina supporting him, and even if he goes to her for help, I doubt he'll be able to con her into reinstating their agreement. She'd rip his head off before he even made the proposal."

"So . . . you do not wish us to hunt him down."

"No." Zucker frowned. "He'll just have to try and survive in the tunnels . . . like the rest of us."

The sound of human voices interrupted them, thundering off the high arched walls of the tunnel.

"Look at this place, Erik," boomed one of the exterminators. "It sure isn't your ordinary rat's nest, is it?"

"Sure isn't, Buddy," Erik agreed.

"Ya know," said Buddy, "if I didn't know better, I'd say these tunnel vermin had designed this nest to function like an actual city."

Erik snorted out a chuckle. "Right. Only in Brooklyn would you find a bunch of rats that also happen to be civil engineers." He swung his shovel again. "I think you've been breathing in too many subway fumes."

"I'm not kidding," Buddy insisted. "I saw one section of this nest that actually looked like a market. And I swear there was a coffee shop. And there's a pile of stuff over there that looks like . . . a castle."

"A rat castle?" Erik's guffaw echoed over the city walls. "Well, we'd better leave that alone, then, just in case the rat king comes back. You know how I hate to tick off the royalty."

"Zucker," Hopper whispered. "What if Firren's in

there? What if she finished her tunnel sweep and went back to the palace to await our return?"

A storm of emotions passed over the prince's face, then he turned and grabbed Polhemus by the front of his tunic. "Did you see her?" he croaked. "Did you see Firren in there?"

Polhemus shook his head. "No, Your Highness. I didn't, but—"

"How about you, Ketch?" Zucker released Polhemus and turned his fiery eyes to Ketchum. "Did you see Firren?"

Ketchum swallowed hard and shrugged, then winced as another shovel hit its mark.

Zucker sprang to his feet. "I'm going in!"

At the same instant Hopper leaped up and cried, "Let's find her!"

For a moment the rat and the mouse just stared at each other.

"No way, kid," said Zucker. "You're staying here."

"Firren is my friend too," Hopper countered. "We have a better chance of saving her if we both go."

"I can't be looking for Firren and worrying about you at the same time!"

"I can take care of myself."

Hopper was surprised when Zucker grinned. "Yes, you can. You've proved that many times over. But this is different, kid. These guys are *big*. Have you not been listening to those shovels banging around in there?"

Hopper opened his mouth to argue just as Zucker nodded to Garfield and Polhemus. Before he knew what was happening, the two muscular rodents had him by the arms and were holding him against the wall.

"Zucker! Tell them to let go."

"I will, kid. Soon as I get back." The prince took a deep breath. "I mean, as soon as *we* get back. Firren and me."

"Zucker, no!" shouted Hopper. "Highness! Your Majesty . . . *Zuck-meister!!*"

But it was too late. The prince's tail had already disappeared through the open gate.

It seemed an eon had passed before the metallic rattling of cages being placed and the hollow thumps of slamming shovels finally fell silent.

In all that time the soldiers' grip on the Chosen One's arms had not faltered. Now, as the giants strode toward them through the decimated city, Hopper's captors pressed him farther into the shadows of the wall.

"We'll come back for those cages tomorrow," Buddy was saying. "Should be a good haul."

"Yeah," Erik agreed. "Now how about we go for a pepperoni slice at Spumoni Gardens? My treat. And you can tell me all about this rat kingdom with its coffeehouses and rodent palaces."

"Very funny."

"I'm serious, Bud. Maybe you should quit the exterminating business and take up writing kids' books."

"Ah, shut up."

The rodents stayed perfectly still as the humans approached, their leviathan boots kicking up a thick cloud of dust when they stepped over the wall. The scuffed toe of one boot missed flattening Ketchum by half an inch.

Hopper glared up at them, seething with anger. Even through the veil of dust he could see the diabolical words printed on the backs of their coveralls:

PIER ONE EXTERMINATORS, BROOKLYN, NY
WHEN IT COMES TO
E-RAT-ICATING
YOUR PEST PROBLEMS, WE'RE "PIER-LESS."

As the human footsteps echoed away into the darkness, all eyes turned to the gate. Hopper knew they were all hoping the same hope: that Firren and Zucker would appear any second now, safe and unharmed.

But any second turned to many minutes. And still no sign of them.

"Where are they?" Garfield whispered. "Why aren't they coming out?"

Polhemus shrugged. "Maybe they can't come out," he whispered back.

"Shhhh!" said Ketchum. "Patience . . ."

Hopper's heart beat a wild rhythm as he trained his eyes on the opening in the wall; he squinted through the brownish haze. But still no one emerged.

And then . . . finally . . . motion! Two figures, obscured by the swirling dust, came stumbling through the open gate.

"Zucker?" Hopper cried. "Firren!"

"Help us . . . ," came a dry voice from deep within the dirty cloud.

The soldiers released Hopper and ran in the direction of the plea. Hopper could see now that it was not the prince and the rebel. It was Driggs the squirrel and old Beverley. She was limping and seemed to have trouble breathing. Driggs looked dazed; there was a trickle of blood spilling from his forehead. Overall, though, they seemed hardy enough. A shiver of relief went through Hopper to know that these two good rodents had been spared.

Ketchum helped the old lady to the wall and sat her down, while the others assisted Driggs.

"Did you see Zucker in there?" Hopper blurted out. "What about Firren? Are they alive?"

Driggs gave him a forlorn look. "Hard to say, Chosen One."

"What's hard about it?" Hopper asked, frantic. "Dead or alive? Which one?"

"Trapped," Beverley squeaked in a tremulous voice. "Those human beasts laid traps all over the city. Some were metal cages, others were just sticky pads, like movable tar pits or quicksand. I was trying to avoid one of those when I twisted my leg and fell down. Firren came running to aid me, but one of the beasts spotted her and used his shovel to swat her into a metal cage."

"It was awful," Driggs confirmed, shaking his head as if he still couldn't believe what he'd seen. "Firren just wouldn't give up. . . . She kept throwing herself against the cage door, trying to get out."

"Oh, how she fought!" cried the old lady.

"She struggled so powerfully," said Driggs, tilting his face back so Garfield could inspect his wound, "that for a minute there I thought she might actually get out. But on her last attempt to break down the door, she hit her head against the bars." He lowered his eyes and added softly, "No more struggling after that."

"Then the prince came galloping in, screaming her name!" Beverley continued. "He went right for her cage, but Firren wasn't moving. He tried to pry the door open, but the sleeve of his tunic got caught in the clasp! He pulled and he pulled. The door didn't open, though he managed to disengage the sleeve; a whole piece of it tore away."

"Then he flung himself at the human giant," said Driggs, "and sank his teeth into its ankle. The giant growled and spit, then it swung its shovel. Poor Prince Zucker went flying. He crashed into the side of the cage. And then . . ."

Hopper felt tears well up in his eyes. "No!"

Driggs sighed. "He wasn't moving. He was just sprawled there right next to Firren's cage, perfectly still. I couldn't tell if he was . . ."

"Couldn't tell if he was *what*?" Hopper prompted.

"Breathing."

Hopper didn't need to hear another word. He ran for the gate.

Inside the walls the dust was settling and a deadly silence had fallen over the city. The only building still standing was the palace, but it had sustained a fair amount of damage—an entire wing of the sprawling manse had been crushed.

But the demolished buildings were nothing compared with the sight of so many trapped and wounded rodents. Hopper averted his eyes from the ones who had fallen prey to the glue pads. He knew there would be no hope for them. But those who had been forced into cages were a bit luckier; at least they were still alive.

"Chosen One!" cried a chipmunk. "You've come to save us!"

"Yes, but—"

"Let me out first," begged a field mouse. "I need to find my family."

"No, let *me* out!" pleaded a lanky rat. "And I can help you free the others."

Hopper looked from one desperate prisoner to another. He didn't know what to do. The weight of his responsibility pressed down on him like a brick. He could take the time to open these cages, but every second would be one more that Zucker lay unconscious. What if the difference between the prince's life and death pivoted on how soon Hopper could reach him to attend to his wounds?

"Don't just stand there," snarled the chipmunk. "Are you the Chosen One or aren't you?"

"Are you a hero?" taunted the field mouse. "Or a useless phony?"

Hopper's head spun. It was his duty to help these rodents, even as they insulted him. But Zucker and Firren . . . they could be dying.

Or dead.

And these animals were still alive.

Hopper dashed to the cage of the lanky rat who had offered his help. If two of them were working to free the others, Hopper could get to Zucker that much faster. His claws shook as he worked the clasp. It took three tries, but finally the lock came free and the door swung open.

The rat leaped out.

"Over there," Hopper instructed, pointing toward the field mouse. "Set him free and then—"

The rat laughed. "Are you kidding? I'm not sticking around here one minute longer. Those humans might come back! Sorry, Chosen One, but I am out of here."

Hopper felt the words like a kick in the gut. "What about the others?"

"Not my problem."

"But you said you'd help me!"

"And it worked. I'm free, they're not." Then, in a final insult, the rat reached for Hopper's sword and yanked it from its sheath. "Might need this out there," he sneered. "See ya."

With that, the rat sped off toward the gates, taking Hopper's weapon with him. Hopper could only stare after him, sputtering in shock and sorrow.

And anger.

"Did he say those humans might be back?" cried the chipmunk. "Hurry! Let us out!"

Hopper was sick with fear for Zucker, but he knew that the prince would have wanted the safety of his subjects seen to before his own. Fueled by the heat of his fury, Hopper ran from cage to cage, struggling with locks, pulling open doors. Of all the rodents he freed, only one—a half-blind old rat who walked with a cane—stayed to help him.

When all the caught rodents had been freed, Hopper guided the blind rat to the gate and deposited him into Ketchum's care.

"He's a hero," Hopper declared. "Treat him as such."

"Yes, Chosen One."

When Hopper turned to reenter the city, Garfield was right on his heels.

"I'm coming with you this time!" Garfield insisted.

"So am I," cried Polhemus.

"No," said Hopper. "It's a minefield of traps in there. You could get hurt. I'll need you to be safe and ready when I bring Zucker and Firren back."

If I bring them back.

With that thought and no other in mind, Hopper bolted back through the gate.

Hopper sped through the crumbling city and finally found the prince in what had once been the children's playground. His heart lurched as he knelt beside his friend.

"Zucker! Answer me! Can you hear me?"

No word came from the prince's lips. Hopper saw no flicker of his eyelids, no movement from his body.

"Zucker, please! You have to be all right! You have to!"

The prince did not respond. Hopper didn't realize he was crying until he saw the teardrops falling on

Zucker's purple tunic. It was filthy and torn from his struggle with the cage door.

The cage . . .

Firren!

Only now did Hopper become aware of the cage. It was quite a ways off from where Zucker lay, which was strange, since Driggs had said Zucker had fallen right beside it. Could the prince have awoken briefly and crawled the distance to where he was now sprawled? And had that effort been his last?

Hopper pushed the dread aside and ran to the cage.

The door was open. But Firren wasn't inside.

What could that possibly mean? Had she come to and broken out? Had the exterminators done something even more horrific with her after she collapsed?

Hopper did know that if Firren had been able to free herself, there was no doubt as to where she would be—right here beside Zucker, with whatever strength she had left, doing whatever needed to be done to help him.

But she wasn't here. And that could only mean something terrible had happened to her.

The pain filled him, rising and swirling like the tornado of dust the humans had brought forth. Without thinking, Hopper reached for the shred of purple fabric that still dangled from the cage's metal lock and gently slipped it into his pocket.

Then he let out a wail, a bellow from deep in his soul.

They were gone. He had lost them both. His two brave friends . . . *gone.*

And around him so many others lay dead, or nearly thus. The city was in ruins. The tunnels were a death trap. The future held no promise, and the past was tainted with disappointment and shame. Hopper's heart felt as if it were splintering into pieces inside his chest.

He really *had* failed. Again. And again. And again.

With a writhing sickness in his belly and a pounding in his skull, he began the long, slow walk back to the gate.

And then he heard the meows.

Hopper's nose twitched of its own accord; he could smell the felines approaching. He imagined their stomachs rumbling eagerly in anticipation of such an abundant and easy meal.

It must have been the scent of widespread rodent fear—now mingling with the sickening aroma of death—that had alerted the ferals.

And now they were coming to feast!

Hopper knew he should hide, but the city offered no shelter; it was all but flattened. His eyes scanned the area until he spotted a giant heap of shiny dark-green fabric. He didn't recall ever seeing such a large pile of material left about in Atlantia before the attack. Perhaps then it had been hidden by the buildings, which had since collapsed. To Hopper it appeared to be some sort of lightweight tent that had caved in on itself.

The cats were closer now, so close that he could hear them purring. And rising above this terrifying noise was another sound . . . voices. Human voices!

The exterminators were returning.

CHAPTER SEVEN

THE ONE CALLED ERIK was still teasing his partner, Buddy, about his fantastic story of a rat-run city, and Buddy was grumbling his displeasure.

Cats! Humans! It was all Hopper could do to keep from freezing in his tracks.

But as the footsteps of the exterminators drew nearer, Hopper sprang into action. He needed to conceal himself, or else he'd be risking the wrath of not only the ferals but that infernal shovel as well. Having no other option, he ran for cover under the fallen green tent, jerking his tail beneath it just as the exterminators pounded back toward the city.

It was dark beneath the fabric, but Hopper was able to make out a narrow, slashlike opening cut into it. It led to a blousy pouch sewn into the folds. The opening was trimmed on both sides with strips of jagged metal teeth.

Hopper dove for it, scrambling through the slash and grimacing as the metal points pinched at the delicate skin of his ears and tail. He bit back his gasps of pain and slipped inside, forcing himself to go still just as the exterminators arrived—and right along with them, the slinking ferals.

"Get a load of all these mangy cats," the one called Erik snickered.

"They look awful mean," Buddy noted nervously.

That's because they are, thought Hopper.

"Hey, Erik, did you know that a group of cats is called a glaring?"

"No, Bud. I didn't know that."

"Well, that's what it's called. And now I can see why. That white cat over there with the two different-colored eyes . . . I think she's actually staring me down!"

"Now the cats are givin' you dirty looks?" Erik hooted. "Oh brother!"

"I ain't kidding!"

"Oh, I know, Bud. I know. Hey, you think maybe they've got their own little cat kingdom over on the other side of the tracks, with catnip farms and hot and cold running litter boxes?" Erik erupted in laughter.

"Look, now she's takin' one of the dead rats and runnin' off with it. Just one! That's strange, ain't it? Why would she do that when there's such easy pickin's?"

"Maybe she's watchin' her waistline. Or maybe she thought *you* were givin' *her* dirty looks."

"Aw, knock it off already," Buddy shot back. "Let's just find my darn jacket and get out of here."

"That's an official company Windbreaker, ya know. If you'd have lost it, the boss would've made you pay."

"Believe me, Erik, every day I get stuck being your partner . . . *I pay!* Boy, do I pay."

"What's *that* supposed to mean?"

Buddy didn't bother to answer. The next thing Hopper knew, the green tent was being lifted off the ground. It only took him a second to understand that the heap of cloth he thought was a tent was actually Buddy's misplaced jacket. Hopper had hidden himself under the Windbreaker. And he'd made it even worse by trapping himself inside the enemy's *pocket*!

"So, Erik...," Buddy began. (He was brushing off the jacket now, shaking it, so that Hopper nearly bounced right out of the pocket. A few coins that were in there with him jangled around and almost clonked him on the head.) "Whaddya figure we should do about the cats?"

"Just leave 'em be. The boss don't pay us enough to start killin' house pets. That's the animal shelter's job." Erik let out another cackle. "Besides, these cats are about to have themselves a nice dinner. Rat carcass à la carte."

"That's disgusting." The Windbreaker swung sideways, jostling Hopper, as Buddy stuck one arm, then the other, into the sleeves and began to walk away.

"The best part is, after these cats eat their fill, there'll be a lot fewer rodent corpses for us to cart out of here tonight."

Deep in Buddy's pocket, Hopper bit his tongue to keep from crying out in horror.

"Come 'n' get it," sang Erik. "The rat buffet is now open."

"Yuucchhkk," said Buddy, walking faster. "You're makin' me sick!"

Hopper heard the meows grow louder as Felina's glaring descended upon the wreckage. The arrival of more hungry cats caused Buddy to double his pace; the Windbreaker made a swishing sound as the frightened exterminator hurried to exit Atlantia.

Hopper clung to the slippery material, and his thoughts whirled. He had to get out. Maybe he could escape through the same opening he'd come in by. He could claw his way to the toothy gap and jump! It would be a long way down, but he'd fallen from greater heights than this.

But surviving that dive meant he'd literally be throwing himself at the feet of the exterminators; he would be trampled beneath their enormous boots. Worse yet, his escape might somehow alert Erik and Buddy to the presence of the soldiers and refugees who (Hopper sincerely hoped) were still waiting safely outside the gate. The soldiers might have a chance to escape if they scattered, but Driggs was probably too woozy from his head injury to run fast enough, and Beverley could barely hobble, let alone sprint.

"Better zip up your pockets, Bud," Erik was advising. "You don't wanna drop any of that loose change. You're gonna need it to pay for your pizza."

"What? I thought you said *you* were buying."

Buddy reached for his pocket; his fingers gripped

the zipper and tugged. Hopper burrowed into the lowest corner of the pocket, but the noise of the metal teeth locking together was deafening to his tiny ears. Swallowed in darkness, he could feel the steady beat of the exterminator's step as he traveled farther and farther from the city.

Suddenly the trajectory of the motion changed; Buddy was still walking, but instead of propelling himself forward, he seemed to be going up. Rising somehow—ascending . . . slowly, steadily, higher and higher.

Stairs!

Hopper's blood went cold. Buddy the exterminator, in his zip-pocket Windbreaker, was climbing a set of stairs. And stairs could lead to only one place . . . a place above and beyond the subway.

Buddy was heading out of the tunnel.

And Hopper was going with him.

Hopper chewed.

He nipped and he bit and he scratched at the silky green material of the Windbreaker pocket, tearing it, shredding it, piercing it with his incisors. Snatches of fabric snagged on his teeth, and once he nearly choked on a knotted clump of string. Fraying threads wrapped around his tongue; he spit them out and kept chewing.

And as he gnawed and gnashed and nibbled, Hopper

had only one goal: to create a hole big enough to slip himself through.

He knew, because he sensed light filtering through the Windbreaker, that Buddy had already transported him out of the tunnel. He was above, upland, in the daylight world.

Sunshine . . . he remembered seeing it through the window of Keep's shop, wondering what it would feel like on his fur, how warm it would be. He had longed for it his whole caged life. But now it terrified him. He would be separated from Ketchum and the others, and he would be alone in the human world.

He chewed.

Then Buddy stopped moving and bent himself into a sitting position. Hopper heard a grinding sound, a mechanical growl, and felt movement again. But this time it wasn't Buddy's body that was creating the motion. He'd placed himself inside something, and that something was moving. That something was carrying Buddy, just as Buddy was carrying Hopper.

A train perhaps? As far as Hopper knew, trains only lived and moved and carried humans down below in the tunnels.

He thought back to the rainy night he'd escaped the pet shop. There had been rolling machines with lighted eyes and round feet. They had sped past him with humans inside. Buddy had to be sitting in one of these upland vehicles. Hopper realized that, as with the trains, the whole purpose of these round-footed creatures was to allow humans to travel great distances in short periods. That meant that the longer he and Buddy stayed inside this rolling monstrosity, the farther away from Atlantia they would get.

Hopper chewed harder and faster, fighting the green fabric of Buddy's pocket as though it had attacked him first. Finally the fibers gave way and split open into a hole just large enough for Hopper to wriggle through.

He tumbled out of the pocket and onto Buddy's lap beneath the billowing tent of the Windbreaker; Buddy twitched.

It was considerably brighter outside the pocket. Hopper could see through the green curtain of the jacket that Erik was seated to Buddy's left, gripping a large circle, which he rotated from side to side. The vehicle swerved in keeping with the motion of Erik's hands.

Quivering with fear, Hopper inched his way to where the edge of the jacket met the coarse white material that made up the leg of Buddy's coveralls.

Buddy flinched.

"Whatsa matter with you?" snapped Erik. "I can't concentrate on the road with you doing the passenger-seat mambo over there! Now sit still! We're almost to the bridge."

"But there's something crawling on me!" Buddy protested, and he began to wiggle.

"Crawlin' on you? What could be crawlin' on you?"

It was at this moment that Hopper poked his nose out from under the hem of the Windbreaker.

Buddy squealed as if he were a giant rodent himself.

"MOUSE!" he screamed, bouncing up and down hysterically in his seat. "Erik, there's a *mouse* on my *lap*!"

"So maybe he wants to tell you what he wants for Christmas."

"Erik! Help!"

"Oh, for Pete's sake!"

Hopper made a mad dash toward Buddy's knee, but Erik was quick. He let go of the circular thing and reached out, pinching Hopper's tail and plucking him off Buddy's leg and dangling him in midair. Now it was Hopper who squirmed and wiggled.

"Cute little guy," Erik observed. "Don't usually see markings like that."

"J-just get r-rid of him, will ya?"

Erik let out one of his rollicking chuckles. "Ya know, Bud, for a professional exterminator, you sure ain't too good around rodents. Now open your window."

Hopper watched with wide eyes as the square of glass to Buddy's right magically slid downward. A gust of cold air blew in; its icy bite stood his fur on end.

"Lean back so's I can fling him out."

Fling him out? Hopper did *not* like the sound of that.

Buddy pressed himself backward against the seat, and Erik gave a good flick of his wrist, releasing

Hopper's tail and sending him sailing past Buddy's terrified face.

The sensation was almost like riding the train—but with no sturdy hitch beneath his paws to anchor him. Hopper flew sideways toward the cold, spinning over himself, soaring out of the vehicle and plunging through the atmosphere.

Wooommppffff.

It was a punishing landing, but it didn't end there. Hopper's momentum bowled him onward, somersaulting his bruised little body across a rough black surface and directly into a speeding parade of roaring, round-footed monsters. How he avoided being squashed by one of them, he would never know; he could feel their powerful, whirring whoosh as they zoomed over his head, but somehow he managed to evade their heavy rubber feet and roll out the other side . . . tumbling still, but to where . . . toward what?

The world was a revolving blur. Overhead Hopper caught glimpses of blue—a bright, endless expanse. Rising into this he saw two stony towers. Radiating out from these was an intricate, crisscrossed web of steel.

Then the solid surface ceased to be, and Hopper felt nothing but a cold rush of . . . *nothing.* All around him—air and more air, above, beneath. Cool emptiness, everywhere. His stomach sprang into his mouth; he was falling again.

Chapter Eight

La Rocha's journal—from the Sacred Book of the Mūs:

I have been hiding forever, it seems. And of late I do so with the aid of a hooded cloak I fashioned from a piece of blue cloth I found during the mad exodus from the city. I believe it may have held significance once. In any case, it makes a warm garment. And a good disguise.

La Rocha must always be unseen. That is the first rule.

And unseen I was when I slipped into the palace to listen to the elder Sage give his report to Zucker and the Chosen One. Pinkie of the Mūs, it seems, is causing an entirely new brand of trouble. She is single-minded, that one, and not inclined to compromise. There is steel in her soul, and I can't help but admire that. She is proud and smart—two characteristics I very much respect, although she is far too stubborn and selfish to rule; one must have compassion to lead. But Pinkie has no talent for the softer emotions, and for that I cannot blame her. Deep hurt often results in this sort of temperament, and I alone shoulder the responsibility for that.

Pinkie is Pinkie and I am to blame. This is another of my secrets. And so I remain hidden.

Hours have passed since the Chosen One, the prince, and the elder boarded their train to the Mūs village. I wait on the outskirts of Atlantia for their return. I want to learn whatever I can of their meeting with Pinkie.

But a commotion begins, and I see the humans making their approach.

It has been so long since I've seen any of their kind—I last encountered the hulking beasts on my one and only upland journey. Such height, such power, and so clearly bent on destruction.

On the backs of their uniforms is an insignia, which brands itself on my memory.

As expected, they rain doom, thrashing and crushing what is left of the city, taking as many prisoners as they can. And all I can do is sit and watch, which shames me to the depths of my soul. I was a warrior once! I knew how to fight! But on this day I must keep still, stay back, and watch the chaos erupt.

Now I see Firren entering the fray. She brings courage and might enough for the both of us, storming in with her sword swinging. But she is small and they are large, and she is soon taken captive. Secrecy be damned! I prepare to risk all by running in to aid her. But now

Zucker arrives . . . and I have to smile. How could I have doubted that he would come? He would do anything to aid the girl rebel.

Oh, but these humans are cold blooded. They take their shovel to the prince and he falls. I am overcome with rage and helplessness, waiting, watching. . . .

It is not long before Hopper is here. The sight of him fills me with relief but also guilt. I told him I would come for him, and I had every intention of doing so. Alas, much has transpired to make that impossible, even at this very moment, when I am close enough to call out his name. But this is not the time to reveal myself.

His presence is the distraction I need. While he frees what rodents he can, I creep into the ruins of Atlantia and drag the unconscious Firren from her cage. I bring her to my latest hideout in the darkness of the tunnels, not far from Atlantia, but still a long way to carry someone. Lucky she is small, for a rat.

Many days ago I found this artifact where I now live. A human castoff—a suitcase, I believe it is called. I cannot go back to the locomotive in the Mūs village, so I have made this my dwelling place. Who knows how long it has been lost and moldering here in the darkness. It bears a medal that tells me it is named for an ancient who was

known for his great strength—Samson. This is a good sign, for what I need is a fortress. A roomy one that will prove difficult to breach. Thus far the cats have paid this item no notice, so I am safe. And so shall Firren be.

When she is securely ensconced, I hurry back to the city, eager to see if I can be of similar assistance to the prince. I arrive just in time to see Hopper taking cover beneath a heap of green fabric. Zucker is not where he was when I went in for Firren. In fact, he is nowhere.

I can only hope that his soldiers have come to his rescue. A chill shoots through me when I hear the ferals lurking, because it is equally possible that the cats have stolen Zucker away in my brief absence. For all I know, he is already disemboweled and scattered in bloody pieces throughout the tunnels. Or perhaps the humans have scooped him into an airless sack to be carried away and incinerated like so much garbage. Truth be told, I do not know which scenario sickens me more.

And now Hopper's hiding spot is being plucked up from the ground by a human hand. I watch with wide eyes, horrified. Wherever that fabric is going, the Chosen One is going with it.

Only once in my life before this have I felt such a sense of loss.

I turn and rush with all my strength back to the place where I have hidden Firren.

When I arrive at my fortress, someone is waiting for me. A female rat who, after mere moments in my company, seems to ascertain exactly who I am and what I'm about . . . what I have always been about.

"La Rocha?" she asks.

"If you choose to believe it," I reply.

She smiles and explains that she, like Firren, who still lies motionless but alive inside my fortress, has just escaped the violence in the city. This is how she has come to be here in my hiding place. I tell her she is welcome to stay, for I see a brightness and a sensitivity about her that one does not often encounter. She could easily be the one to succeed, the one who comes next . . . if she is willing.

I tell her so. It is a great risk to share such a secret so quickly, but I can tell she is trustworthy. She is flattered by my offer. More than flattered . . . interested. But she tells me she must go back to the city to seek her family. She has brothers, she tells me.

But we can meet again?

Yes.

For there is much to be taught, and much to be learned.

The rat, whose future is now entwined with my own, takes her leave with a blessing from me, and I return my attention to Firren. With Zucker gone and the Chosen One taken, she is the only one left. It is up to me to care for her and see to her comfort.

With any luck she will live.

And if she does not, I will give her a hero's farewell. She deserves at least that much from me.

After all, we are old friends.

CHAPTER NINE

REACH!

The word exploded in Hopper's head; it was half thought, half instinct, and he did not question it. As the air took him, he shot both arms upward.

Grab!

He grabbed. His paws connected with something— an edge, an unyielding permanent thing that seemed to hover there alongside the sky—mouse claws on metal, grasping, clutching, clinging. Again words pushed through his terror, instructing him:

"Hold on! Hold on tight!"

But these words were not inside his head. Someone was shouting to him.

"I'm coming. Just hang on!"

Hopper gripped as tightly as he could, his muscles burning with the strain; he hazarded a downward glance and saw that he was dangling high above something blue gray and flowing. Water. A river, like the mad rushing one that had swept him into the tunnels in the first place. But compared with this river, that first one had been little more than a trickle. This river was massive, sprawling, and unfathomably deep. The drop from where he dangled was immeasurable.

"Now listen . . . ," said the voice. "I'm going to swing my tail toward you, and I want you to catch it. Got me?"

Hopper grunted an affirmative reply.

A rope of silky black fur unfurled and flicked toward him. "Grab my tail!"

Hopper told himself to reach for it, but his paws would not let go of the edge.

"Don't be afraid," cried the voice. "You have to let go of the bridge and grab my tail."

Bridge. So that's where he was. Suspended in midair from the edge of a bridge over what appeared to be a frigid, bottomless body of water. *Wonderful.*

His paws were beginning to go numb, and his muscles were cramping.

"Here comes the tail again! Now just reach out and grab on."

The sleek black lifeline swished into view once more. This time Hopper reached out. He felt himself beginning to plummet, but only for a heartbeat—in the next second his paws were gripping fur.

"You did it!" The tail swung once, then jerked upward, and Hopper found himself back on the bridge. He fell to his knees, pulse thumping as he sucked in mouthfuls of cold air. The graceful stone towers and metal netting still loomed above him.

Infinite water and certain death loomed below.

But thanks to that tail—and whoever belonged to it—Hopper was alive.

He took a moment to allow the blood to return to his paws. The air was chilly, and after his time in the tunnels he found the sensation of so much space and atmosphere intoxicating. He was dizzy and sore, but also extremely grateful.

"Thank you," he said, turning to smile at his rescuer.

His blood turned to ice.

A black-and-white cat smiled back at him.

"Ahhh!" Hopper let out a squeak and leaped to his feet, springing backward and once again tottering over the edge of the abyss.

The cat shot out a paw, caught hold of Hopper's tunic, and yanked him back to safety.

Hopper reached for his sword. But it wasn't there. He held up his front paws in a gesture of surrender, but as he stared into the clear green eyes of the stranger, he began to relax. These eyes did not have the fiendish look he recalled seeing in Felina's mismatched eyes or in Clops's single good one. These eyes looked friendly. *And besides,* Hopper reasoned, *if this cat wanted to eat me, I'd be dead already.*

"I'm sorry," he said, lowering his paws. "It's just that where I come from, cats don't usually rescue mice. In fact, cats are the ones the mice need rescuing from."

"I can see why you'd be worried," the cat said, nodding. "But I promise, you're safe with me. Welcome to Brooklyn. The name's Eugene. But everyone calls me Ace."

"Hopper."

"*Hop*per, huh?" Ace lowered one whiskery eyebrow. "You sure it's not *Jump*er?" He glanced meaningfully toward the metal ledge from which Hopper had so recently been dangling.

"Huh? Oh . . ." Hopper shook his head hard. "No, no, no . . . I wasn't trying to . . . ya know . . . jump off, if that's what you mean."

"Didn't really think so," Ace said with a nod. "You don't exactly strike me as the Good-bye-cruel-world type."

Hopper took a moment to study the cat. He was mostly black, with a brilliantly white chest and paws.

He had a lithe and limber way about him, and Hopper guessed it was only recently that Ace had grown out of his kittenhood. He was strong and agile, with a ready grin and a youthful confidence.

"Just so I'm clear . . . you're not going to eat me, right?"

Ace laughed. "Not to worry, friend. I don't eat mice. I prefer to stick to table scraps and store-bought bagged food."

That was some of the best news Hopper had ever heard. He was fuzzy on the actual meanings of "bagged food" and "table scraps," but he did understand that Ace presented no immediate gastronomic danger. He relaxed, but only a bit. After all, he was still standing on a gigantic bridge in the daylight world, where he had no home, no friends, and very little hope for the future.

"So how did you get here?" Ace asked. "Did a bird drop you?"

The only birds Hopper knew of were the candy-colored ones who had sung so cheerfully back in Keep's shop.

"No, a human did." Hopper pointed to the rolling monsters, still zooming past mere inches from where he and Ace stood. "Flung me out of one of those."

"Wow." Ace looked impressed. "You must be one tough little mouse to survive that."

"Must be," said Hopper, although he wasn't feeling very tough. He was feeling shaky and scared and very,

very lost. His two best friends in the whole world were gone and he'd left behind scores of others who were depending on him to help rebuild a safe and prospering city. He was suddenly overcome with misery. "Maybe you should have just let me fall."

"Aw, c'mon, Hopper. Things can't be that bad."

"Trust me." Hopper sighed. "They are."

"Maybe all you need is a good meal and a little rest," Ace suggested. "I always find that things have a way of getting better if you just wait 'em out. You have to put the bad stuff behind you and get on with your life."

"Easy for you to say," Hopper muttered. "You have nine of them. The odds of at least one of them turning out right are definitely in your favor."

Ace laughed. "Tough *and* witty. I like that in a rodent. Now let's get off Mr. Roebling's masterpiece, all right? Being this close to traffic gives me the willies, and we need to put a little food in you."

Hopper didn't know what willies were, but he followed Ace to the end of the bridge. A meal sounded good.

"Where are we going to find this food?" Hopper asked warily.

"My place," Ace answered, then gave Hopper a big grin. "Hope you like Italian."

On the walk to Ace's "place" they kept to the sidewalks to avoid the round-footed beasts that seemed to be everywhere. Ace explained that these were called cars and were, in this cat's opinion, an animal's worst nightmare. Hopper thought Ace might feel differently if he ever found himself in the path of an oncoming subway train.

The humans who hustled about the sidewalks of Brooklyn ignored the odd duo of cat and mouse for the most part, although a few stopped to pet Ace or give him a scratch between his ears. On these occasions Hopper pressed himself against the nearest wall and tried to be invisible.

"You're awfully popular around here," Hopper observed. "I didn't know humans could be so pleasant."

"It's the same as it is with cats and rodents, I guess," said Ace. "Some are okay, some . . . not so much. You've just got to know who to trust."

They turned into an alleyway and approached the back entrance of a building.

"This is it," Ace announced. "My pad."

"Your *what*?"

"Where I live." Ace leaned his shoulder against a tall glass door; when it swung inward, he motioned for Hopper to go in ahead of him.

Hopper was immediately hit with an onslaught of smells. Good ones. His nose went into a twitching frenzy as he tried to breathe in so many aromas, none of which he'd ever experienced before. All of them exotic, delicious, and savory.

"What is this place?" he asked.

"Guido and Vito, the guys who run it, they call it Bellissimo's Deli. Me, I call it home." Ace sniffed the air and smiled. "Smells like today's special is eggplant parmigiana."

Hopper's mouth watered. "That sounds incredible."

"Oh, it is!" said Ace, licking a paw and giving his face a quick wash. "I'll go out front and see what I can rustle up. You stay here."

"Why do I have to stay here?"

"Because mice and food-service establishments definitely do not mix." Ace pressed his head against a creaky swinging door and disappeared through it.

Hopper looked around the room. It was snug and cozy, lined with tall shelves well-stocked with cans, jars, and tins. The labels on them read: ROASTED PEPPERS, IMPORTED OLIVE OIL, SEMOLINA FLOUR.

A skinny, treelike object stood by the door with white aprons and heavy coats hanging from its branches. Pinned to the wall was a rectangular piece of paper with the word JANUARY printed across the top. Hopper would have to ask Ace what "January" meant.

Over in one corner on the scuffed wooden floor were arranged four metal bowls—two large, two small—and beside them was a gigantic, pillowlike bed. The scent emanating from it was new to Hopper—not human, not feline, not rodent, but absolutely animal.

On closer inspection he realized the indentation in the pillow's middle was much too large and deep to have been made by the lissome Ace. Judging by the size of the impression, it was clear the creature that slept in this bed was no lightweight.

"*Buon giorno.*"

Hopper gulped. Deep voice. Hot breath. Right behind him.

"*Come si chiamo?*"

Slowly Hopper turned, and found himself staring into what was perhaps the oddest and ugliest face he'd ever seen—broad and flat, with wrinkled skin and droopy eyelids. The bottom teeth jutted out farther than the uppers, and a long pink tongue lolled out from one side of the mouth, producing a ridiculous amount of drool. Even Titus's scarred snout was a thing of beauty compared with this face. And the body was not much better: stubby, built low to the ground, with coarse hair and a stump of a tail.

But the stump was wagging. And the folds of the homely face suddenly widened into a lopsided grin.

"*Ciao, piccolo.*"

The words were unfamiliar, but the tone was friendly and Hopper could tell that the smile was genuine. Despite this creature's unseemly appearance, he exuded warmth and kindness.

The creature tilted his big head. "Another of Ace's foundlings, I take it?"

"Yes," said Hopper with an ache in his heart. Zucker had called him a foundling once. "Yes, I suppose I am."

"I'm Capone," said the creature, then, to clarify, he added, "Dog."

"Mouse," said Hopper.

"Yeah," Capone said with a laugh. "I got that." The folds of skin around the dog's saggy chin jiggled. "That cat saved my life. Found me half starved on Navy Street, a fugitive from justice."

"Justice?"

"Well, maybe not justice. More like the pound. Point is, Ace brought me here and the Bellissimo brothers took me in. I'm not by nature inclined to feel friendly toward creatures of the feline persuasion, but Ace is different. There's nothing I wouldn't do for that cat."

"So you live here?" Hopper asked.

"Only during the day. The Bellissimo brothers take me home with them at night. Ace is a little more independent; he's here round the clock."

The swinging door banged open and Ace returned, looking anxious. "I see you've met my roommate. Great. But Hopper, would you do me a real quick favor?"

"Sure. What?"

"Hide!"

Hopper dove under Capone's bed just as the swinging door creaked open again. He peered out from beneath the pillow and saw a pair of human shoes—they looked more pliable than the boots the exterminators wore, less bulky, with springy soles, and there was a brightly colored swoosh marking on the side.

"Here you go, fellas," said the human. He filled the metal bowls with the delectable-smelling meal, then reached down to scratch Ace underneath his chin. "Yo, Acey boy. Got a job for you. Mrs. Fiorenza saw a couple-a mice in her basement. Thinks they've got designs on her biscotti! I told her you'd swing by the bakery tomorrow to take care of things."

The cat purred contentedly. It sounded like he was accepting the job.

So Ace had lied! He *did* eat mice . . . and he was probably going to eat Hopper! Today's special: eggplant parmigiana *with a side of mouse*! Hopper stung with anger as he watched the deceitful cat rub up against the human's leg.

The human bent down to give Capone's belly a quick scratch, then pushed his way back through the swinging door.

Hopper crawled out from beneath the bed and scowled at Ace. "I thought you said you didn't eat mice."

"I *don't* eat them," said Ace, dipping his head into the bowl for a bite of eggplant. "I *relocate* them. Of course, the shop owners don't know that."

"I don't understand," said Hopper, but he was

finding it hard to keep his mind on the conversation. The smell of the human food was too wonderful to be ignored.

"Ace is the neighborhood's premier mouser," Capone explained. "When the storekeepers find rodents on their premises—mice, rats, what have you—it's real bad for business. Since exterminators are expensive and not exactly discreet, the store owners just borrow Ace for an afternoon and he gets rid of the problem."

"That's the part that worries me," muttered Hopper, stepping closer to the food. "The getting-rid-of part."

"I told you," said Ace. "Mouse meat doesn't appeal to me. No offense."

"None taken." Hopper took a nibble of the cheesy, saucy entrée in the bowl and nearly cried out in delight. "Wow. That's delicious."

"Exactly," said Ace. "I don't *have* to eat mice because I've got an endless supply of this! Which is why I follow a strict catch-and-release policy. I catch the rodents, I offer them a quick lesson in how to survive in the great outdoors, and then I bring them to the grasslands and let them go. Live and let live. That's what it's all about, Jumper."

"Hopper."

"Right."

"So what are the grasslands?"

Ace took a big bite of eggplant. "The humans call it

a park. Lots of open space, plenty of places to burrow, and always food to scavenge."

Hopper considered this. "That's very noble of you, Ace," he said. "I wish all cats felt the way you do."

Ace swallowed his eggplant and motioned for Hopper to help himself to more. "Sounds like you speak from experience."

Hopper opened his mouth to reply, which he intended to do with a simple yes. But what came out instead was his whole horrible, exciting, triumphant, and tragic story.

CHAPTER TEN

THROUGH A STREAM OF hot tears Hopper told Ace and Capone everything, from the skinny boy and his snake, to the escape from the cardboard box, to the waterfall that deposited him into the tunnels. He told them about Zucker, and Firren, Pinkie and Pup. He explained the emperor rat's unthinkable peace accord with the feral queen and told them about all the poor innocent rodents who'd been jailed in the refugee camps and sacrificed in cold blood.

With unrestrained pride he described the rebel victory in the hunting ground, and with profound distress he confessed that the aftermath had turned out to be an unqualified disaster. He spoke of his missive from La Rocha, who'd promised to come for Hopper but never had, and he relayed the grisly tale of the giant exterminators tromping through the city. Finally, he admitted to Ace and Capone that until the moment he'd seen Zucker sprawled beside Firren's empty cage, he'd still foolishly believed that somehow, some way, he could make it all right.

"Wow," said Ace. "No wonder you were afraid of me. Sounds like the cats you've met have been pretty nasty. That feral queen in particular had a serious mean streak."

Felina, Hopper thought, picturing her fluffy coat

and strange two-toned eyes. "Felina is a monster."

"What?" Ace's black ears perked up. "What did you call her?"

"Felina. That's the name of the feral queen. The one with whom Titus had the peace accord."

Ace stiffened. "Did she, by any chance, have pure-white fur?"

"Yes," said Hopper. "She did."

"And her eyes. Were they two different colors? One blue, one green?"

Hopper nodded. "How did you know?"

"We've met," Ace answered tightly. "Long time ago. I spent some time in the shelter when I was a kitten, and . . . well, this Queen Felina of yours was there too."

"She's no queen of mine," Hopper assured him. "She's the stuff of nightmares."

Capone took in Ace's snarling expression. "No wonder you remember her."

"I'll never forget her." Ace's eyes grew distant, as though he were looking into his past and not liking what he saw. "Felina was vicious. Heartless. She was never happier than when she was watching others suffer." He jolted out of his daydream and asked, "Does she still have that red collar with the jewels on it?"

"Last I saw, she was still wearing it," Hopper confirmed. "Why?"

Ace did not answer. He curled his tail around his body and looked away, saying nothing for several minutes. When he finally spoke again, Hopper was shocked to hear what he offered.

"I'll help you get back there, Hopper. I'll personally see to it that you return safely to those tunnels to finish your fight."

Hopper blinked in amazement. "There's nothing to go back to. I've failed. My friends are dead, my family despises me. I have nothing. Why would I ever want to go back?"

It was Ace's turn to look surprised. "Because you still have work to do. You've got to defeat Felina and rebuild your city. You can't just abandon your destiny."

"Who says I can't?" Hopper sighed and licked a spicy smudge of marinara sauce off the back of his paw. "Why should I go back? Zucker and Firren are dead. The underdwellers who remain don't care about anything but themselves. And they all hate me for failing them."

"You said the prince's soldiers were still willing to fight."

Hopper felt a stab of guilt, thinking of Bartel and Pritchard and the others. "Yes, but they're overwhelmingly outnumbered. It's a fight we can't win."

"You can't win if you don't *try*."

"But I *did* try. And I failed." Hopper dropped his face into his paws. It was clear to him that the others would be better without him. Chosen or not, he'd ruined everything. "Can't I please just stay here with you, Ace? I won't let the Bellissimo brothers see me, I promise."

Ace considered this request with troubled eyes. It was so long before he answered that Hopper was afraid he was going to say no.

"All right, you can stay," said Ace at last. Then he gave Hopper a crooked smile. "I just hope you can handle the snow."

"Oh, I can!" Hopper assured him. "I definitely can." He didn't actually know what snow was, but if it came for him, he would fight it off with his bare paws if he had to. "Thank you, Ace."

"My pleasure. Now, first thing tomorrow morning, let's you and I go see if we can help Mrs. Fiorenza with her pest problem. For now, you should get some rest."

"Yes, let's," Hopper said as he snuggled into the enormous pillow. Moments later he was sound asleep.

The next morning Hopper followed Ace down the block to the bakery. Mrs. Fiorenza's pest problem turned out to be a very sweet family of mice seeking shelter in the warmth of the building's old stone basement. They'd been forced to move in after the abandoned tenement building where they'd been residing was purchased by a conglomerate of humans who were planning to redevelop the neighborhood.

"Gentrification," Ace explained, "is almost as bad as traffic. Rodents rarely survive either one."

Ace sent Hopper into the bakery first, to warn the mice that a cat was about to pay them a visit, pointing out that this was always the trickiest part of the relocation process: rodents weren't used to being helped by felines, and Ace usually had to calm them down quite a bit before explaining that he was there to help. Hopper could now act as the vanguard, and he was glad he could be helpful.

He wouldn't have thought it possible, but the bakery smelled more marvelous than Bellissimo's did. Hopper found the mice in their nest by the furnace and told them all about Mrs. Fiorenza's request to have them removed. He told them there was a cat right behind him, but they shouldn't be afraid. When Ace came slinking in, the mice were wary, but they didn't become hysterical.

Ace told them about the grasslands and gave them detailed directions to the park. He also told them to look for a chipmunk named Valky—another of Ace's rescues—who would be happy to help them settle in.

The mice were grateful and insisted on giving Ace and Hopper a token of their thanks. It was in this way that Hopper discovered the indescribable joy of cannoli.

"For a little guy, you've sure got a good appetite," teased Ace on their way back to Bellissimo's.

"I think I like Brooklyn," said Hopper, wiping cannoli crumbs from his whiskers.

"What's not to love? It's the best . . ." Ace stopped speaking midsentence.

Hopper followed Ace's gaze to where a trio of rough cats were stalking a wounded pigeon. The poor bird hobbled about, trying to escape, and with good reason. Hopper could see the ferocity in those three pairs of sulfur-colored eyes.

Ace hissed at the cats; the biggest of the three hissed back.

"Well, look who it is! Ace, the Good Samaritan, all dressed up in his tuxedo."

"Leave the bird alone," Ace growled through his teeth.

"Why? We ain't gonna eat him. We're just havin' some fun with him."

"*That's* why I want you to leave him alone." Ace hissed again. "Now scram!"

The other two cats arched their backs; their fur bristled menacingly. Hopper could see their glistening teeth, but neither of the felines made a move to attack.

"How about I trade you the bird for that mouse you got there," said the big cat. "I could use a little snack."

Shivering, Hopper stepped closer to Ace. He

thought of Cyclops with his many battle scars and his nasty disposition. Compared with these wild cats, Clops had been a gentleman.

"No chance," said Ace.

The big cat let out a shrill meow, and the other two laughed. Then, without warning, the big cat's paw darted in Hopper's direction. Ace's reaction was like lightning; he swiped his claws at the big cat, and narrowly missed taking a chunk of flesh out of its neck. It was clear to the big cat, as well as to Hopper, that the miss had been intentional.

It was also clear that the next swipe would have a vastly different outcome.

The three cats bolted.

"Yeah, that's what I thought!" Ace called after them. Then he turned to the wounded pigeon. "Hey, Pilot."

"Ace." The pigeon bobbed his gray head. "Thanks for that. I owe you one."

The bird's voice came as a surprise to Hopper; Pilot spoke in a deeply pitched coo that was accompanied by a musical burbling—a warble. The sound had a soothing quality that reminded Hopper of the bubbling aquariums back in Keep's shop.

He'd often watched pigeons swooping through the air outside the pet-shop window and heard Keep complaining about those "rats with wings." Of course, now that he was personally acquainted with so many rats, this no longer seemed to be the insult Keep had intended it to be.

Hopper had never seen a pigeon up close before, and he'd certainly never expected that one could be handsome. For the most part the bird was a speckled mix of gray and white, with two darker, scribblelike stripes across his lower back and wings. He had a full, proud chest and craggy orange talons on which he strutted and bounced with a kind of jaunty grace. But it was the bird's long, slender throat that was truly a thing of beauty. The feathers there were shiny and colorful, catching the winter sunlight in a shimmery wash of iridescent pinks, greens, and purples.

"Happy to help," Ace told Pilot. "And if those bullies bother you again, you know the signal, right? Three short, three long, three short."

Pilot bobbed his head and let out a series of whistles exactly as Ace had described: three short, three long, three short.

"Perfect," said Ace, grinning. "That's the S.O.S. signal. If I ever hear that, I'll come running. Now, how's that wing coming along?"

"Getting better," the bird replied. "Still a little sore, but I think I'll be airborne again in a day or so."

Ace nudged Hopper forward. "Hopper, say hello to Pilot. Pilot, this is Hopper."

The pigeon bobbed his head in greeting, and Hopper offered a wave. Then, with his lame wing drooping, the bird trotted away.

"You stood up to those cats, even though there were three of them," said Hopper.

"Somebody has to," said Ace, padding toward Bellissimo's. "Those cats spend their whole miserable lives tormenting weaker creatures just because they can. They hunt for fun, not for survival. Seems they get some kind of nasty kick out of it. I keep hoping they'll grow out of it."

This surprised Hopper. "Do you really think animals can change their ways?"

"Sure," said Ace. "With the right motivation. Take Capone, for example. He was the scariest stray on the block when I met him. Even the humans at the animal shelter were afraid of him. I think that's why they sort of looked the other way when he broke out."

"He broke out of the animal shelter?" Hopper was amazed. Capone sounded pretty daring.

"He was in a bad way when I found him. But now ... well, Capone is as loyal as they come. All he needed was someone to care about him. There was goodness in him; it just had to be coaxed to the surface."

Hopper pondered this. He thought of Titus giving his apology in the town square. Could he have been sincere when he said he regretted what he'd done? And Pup ... he'd been turned into a cold mouse by Pinkie, but maybe with enough patience and attention he could become sweet again. Though he doubted there was any hope for his sister. Pinkie was a lost cause.

He said as much to Ace, who laughed.

"Anyone can change, Hopper," Ace assured him. "Like I said, it just takes the proper motivation. For Capone, part of that motivation was imported salami and provolone cheese. Which I suppose explains his breath."

Hopper chuckled. Then a thought struck him. The exterminators had said there was a problem with rodents on the subway platforms. Was it only a matter of time before the tunnel cats headed north as well? He frowned, trying to picture it.

"What are you contemplating so intently?" asked Ace, giving Hopper a gentle swat with the soft tip of his tail. "What's on your mind?"

"I was just thinking . . . now that the ferals don't have Titus's sacrifice to look forward to, they might be desperate enough to venture upland for food."

"They can try," said Ace, "but the local cats won't stand for it. The natural resources here at ground level are limited. I don't care how tough Felina's guerrilla warriors think they are, they're no match for a Brooklyn stray."

Hopper tried to picture Felina tangling with the three tough cats he'd just seen. "You think the neighborhood cats would fight the ferals?"

"They'd fight and they'd win," Ace predicted. "And that's only fair. I may not consider any of the feline rabble who roam these streets to be personal friends of mine, but this *is* their neighborhood, and if anyone's going to hunt here, it should be them."

Hopper was stunned by Ace's nonchalance. The same cat who refused to eat mice and had just gone out of his way to defend an injured bird was discussing feline hunting practices without so much as a shudder of revulsion.

"How can you say that?" Hopper gasped. "You're talking about cats eating mice. And rats. Don't tell me you're actually in favor of that kind of atrocity."

They had reached the back door of Bellissimo's; Ace pushed it open. Inside, Capone was lying on his back on the comfy bed, snoring peacefully.

"There's nothing atrocious about it, Hopper," said Ace. "It's the way of the world. The natural order of things. It's . . . life."

"But . . ." Hopper's eyes were wide. "When I told you about Titus's agreement with Felina, you were appalled."

"Because *that* was not natural. *That* was evil. But when a cat in the wild hunts for his food, it's part of a larger chain of events. It's survival."

"No!" Hopper shook his head. "You can't mean that. Innocent mice being devoured by evil cats . . . ?"

"Innocence has nothing to do with it, Hopper. And there's a big difference between evil and hungry." Ace flopped down in a triangular shaft of sunlight, swishing his tail lazily across the floor. "Have you ever been hungry? I mean really, *really* hungry?"

Hopper was about to answer with an emphatic yes—there had been precious little to eat in Atlantia these last two weeks—but then it occurred to him that even in the face of a virtual famine, Zucker had somehow seen to it that Hopper and the soldiers were fed. Maybe his time living as a guest in the palace had spoiled him; before the battle there had been sumptuous meals every night, prepared by the royal kitchen staff and delivered to Hopper by liveried servants. Even back in the pet shop Keep had seen to his nourishment. Pellets were placed in his bowl every day; they weren't fancy, but they were filling. And guaranteed.

"I stopped those hooligan cats from hurting that bird because I knew they weren't hungry," Ace explained. "They were just looking for an easy fight. And that would have been wrong." The cat paused to yawn and stretch. "What do you like to eat, Hopper?"

"Eggplant parmigiana," Hopper blurted out. Then he thought harder and said, "Fruit. Seeds. Stuff like that, I guess."

Ace nodded. "Did you know that there are some species of mice who eat meat?"

"Really?"

"Yep. They eat critters. Worms, centipedes, insects."

Hopper's insides knotted up as he remembered the musical cricket who'd serenaded him in the tunnel.

He couldn't even begin to imagine.

Or could he? If he were hungry enough ... if he were starving ... if Pup were starving ... could he do it?

"I would never!" he answered, stomping his foot. "I would find something else to eat. Dirt, if that's all there was."

Ace smiled. "I do believe you would," he said gently. "And that's your choice. But that choice isn't what makes you a good mouse. And choosing differently, in the name of survival, wouldn't make another animal bad. Those of us who can fight, fight. We run when we can, we hide when we're able. Sometimes the hunter wins, and sometimes the hunted goes free. It's not really up to us. We're part of a larger chain of events. Nature decides."

"Nature is unfair," Hopper protested.

"I don't know about that," Ace said, and sighed. "Maybe it's more fair than we think. We all win and we all lose. Give and take, up and down. In the end maybe it all comes out even."

"That's incredibly confusing," said Hopper.

"It sure is."

Ace put his head down on his white paws and closed his eyes. Hopper curled up in the sunshine beside him. He knew Ace was telling the truth. It was a tough lesson, but Hopper was beginning to understand that it was one he must accept.

Felina's bargain had been an ugly one. It had

nothing to do with nature, only power. Hopper knew he had been fighting on the side of right. For now he wouldn't think too much about the bigger mysteries, the ones he couldn't solve. The wins, the losses, the surprises, the challenges, eating or going hungry, building a mighty city or watching it get obliterated beneath an exterminator's boots—in the face of all these things one could only be brave and do his best. Hopper was starting to see that there would be times when he would grieve and times when he would rejoice. And there would be times, like now, when he would simply sit and wonder. *That* was nature; that was *life*. It was not wholly good or wholly bad. It just *was*. And what it was, more than anything else, was an adventure.

Strangely, Hopper found this to be the first truly comforting thought he'd had in weeks.

Moments later, snuggled safely beside Ace in the sunlight, he nodded off to sleep.

CHAPTER ELEVEN

LA ROCHA'S JOURNAL—FROM the Sacred Book of the Mūs:

I have just visited the Runes, where I used a chalky stone to write a very important message, perhaps the most important yet. It is a cryptic notation intended to relay information. I can only hope it will be read by one who might know what to do with it.

To my great relief, I find Firren stirring. It has been three days since I rescued her from Atlantia. She opens her eyes, no doubt surprised to find herself recovering in a suitcase. There are a thousand words I would like to say to her. But most of them will have to wait. I keep my hood close around my face and tell her of what has occurred in Atlantia while she slept. She is by turns amazed, angered, saddened, and bewildered.

"Hopper was taken by the humans?"

"Yes."

"And Zucker . . . do you know if Zucker is dead or alive?"

"I do not. For now I choose to call him absent."

"But you are La Rocha."

I nod.

"Tell me honestly, then: Do you really see more than the rest of us? Do you know things we cannot?"

"If I see more, it is because I look more deeply and with greater care. And what I know is knowable by anyone who takes genuine interest. If I have any power at all, it is the ability to contemplate. As to Zucker's present whereabouts, I, like you, can do nothing but wait and hope."

Firren takes a moment to think on this, then laughs her shimmering laugh. "You really are a puzzle. A riddle."

"Yes. But aren't we all?"

She stands up, works a kink from her neck, then reaches for her blade. "I'm going to the Mūs homeland," she announces. "I have to find out what went on when Hopper appealed to his sister for help."

"I would think, since he did not come back with her army marching behind him, that she was disinclined to assist him."

"Well, maybe I can change her mind." Firren raises her sword and spins it in a tiny circle above her head. "Maybe what that little uplander needs is some good old-fashioned girl talk."

At this, I laugh. "Does girl talk typically require heavy weaponry?"

"Depends on the girls who are doing the talking."

"Firren, there is much you don't know about Pinkie," I tell her. "Perhaps engaging with her is not in your best interests just now."

"Is that a mystical prophecy or a lucky guess?"

"Most mystical prophecies are born of lucky guesses."

"Then maybe you can reason with her," Firren suggests. "The Mūs revere you, and being that she's their leader now, I bet she'll be willing to at least hear you out. We need the Mūs army to bring safety to the tunnels."

There is a look of nostalgia in the warrior's eyes.

"What is it?" I ask.

"What I just said . . ." Firren sighs. "Dodger wanted to assemble a Mūs army to bring down Atlantia. Now we need them once again to march against Felina. We're right back where we started."

"That is more true than you know, Firren."

She blinks at me, not understanding.

In response I begin to push back my hood to unveil myself.

But before I can do this, there is a noise outside the Samsonite fortress. At first I think it might be the pretty rat coming back. I remove my paws from my hood just as the suitcase lid is banged opened. In the space of a second there is a dagger pressed to my throat. And it is Pinkie who holds it there.

"La Rocha," she scoffs. "I believe you're losing your gift for mystery. That little trip you took to the Runes just now was a big mistake. You see, when I didn't find you in the smokestack, I knew you'd show up there at graffiti central eventually, to scrawl more of your silly predictions and platitudes upon those walls." She laughs; the sound is cold and brittle in my ears. "You led me right back here."

Now her eyes go to Firren, who stands poised to strike, her sword lifted, her body radiating fierceness.

"And isn't this fortunate? I've managed to capture the mighty rebel Firren as well. I'm turning out to be quite the excellent leader, aren't I?"

"Dumb luck does not make a leader, Pinkie," Firren snarls.

"Maybe not, but it's about to make you my captives."

"Why?" I ask. "What need have you of

captives? Your village is once again a neutral entity, secluded behind a wall, separating itself from the strife of the tunnel dwellers and those who would fight to protect them."

"You are correct about that," says Pinkie. "But this has nothing to do with tunnel politics or rodents' rights. This has to do with me. My power. My plans."

"Explain yourself," says Firren.

Pinkie snorts. "There are Mūs who are, shall we say, reluctant to recognize me as their Chosen leader. This white circle around my eye helps, of course. They really loved that Dodger character, and I suppose the marking reminds them that I am his daughter."

Her dagger wobbles in her grasp.

"You may be his daughter," Firren growls, "but you are nothing like him. He was righteous and kind."

"He was a deserter!" Pinkie shouts.

This brings Firren up short. "What are you saying? He didn't desert the cause. He was believed dead and used that misconception to escape, to buy time, to go upland and recruit—"

"I didn't say he deserted the cause. He deserted his family! Me, Hopper, Pup . . . our mother. He left us alone in a cage. He chose you and the refugees and those sniveling little mice

145

who live behind that wall. He chose all of you over us. He never deserted you . . . he deserted ME." She draws in a long, shuddering breath. "And I watched him do it."

I feel her paw clench around the dagger, then she gives a firm tug on the back of my robe. Her eyes stay fixed on Firren, whose eyes stay locked on Pinkie.

"Don't try to fight me," she warns, backing toward the rim of the suitcase and pulling me with her. "I've got plenty of soldiers just outside. If you're smart, and I think you are, you and the hallowed La Rocha will just come along and keep quiet."

"But why?" Firren presses. "What is it you think we can do to help you secure your authority?"

"Most of the Mūs are willing to follow me, no questions asked, but as I said, some are still not on board with me taking control. They say they would feel a whole lot better about submitting to my reign if their beloved La Rocha would endorse me." She spins me around, so that she is now pushing me instead of pulling. "And that's exactly what he's going to do."

"You will make me your puppet?" I whisper.

"I will make you my prisoner. And you will support me, preaching only on my behalf and saying only what I command you to say."

With that, she shoves me out of my hiding place and into the hands of her personal guard. Firren is taken roughly by the arms and dragged along behind me.

Pinkie walks ahead of us, chin up, ears back, shoulders squared.

She looks every bit the leader.

But as I had hoped to prove to Firren, had I had the chance to remove my hood, what one looks to be is not always what one is.

CHAPTER TWELVE

OVER THE NEXT SEVERAL days, Ace showed Hopper around the neighborhood. They feasted on scraps of food from places called "restaurants," and Hopper decided that after eggplant, chimichangas were his favorite food. Not only did they taste good, but saying the word made him giggle.

Zucker would love chimichangas, he thought. Suddenly he didn't feel like giggling anymore.

One morning Hopper awoke late after a night of horrible dreams filled with images of the grim aftermath wrought by the exterminators. He saw bloody fur and broken necks and wide, sightless eyes.

Even in his nightmare he searched for Zucker and Firren, but always the dust rose up in choking clouds and made them impossible to find.

He awoke trembling, damp with sweat from the top of his bitten ear to the tip of his pointy tail. And yet, even in the most frightening moments of the dream, he'd still felt a deep longing for the tunnels. He missed the way the shadows fell and how the whole place shook when the trains rocketed past. What had terrified him at first had become a kind of comfort. He missed the gleaming wood of Zucker's desk, where the prince had taught him to read and write, and he yearned for the way the tunnels made him feel like part of the earth, living deep inside it, close to the heart of the planet itself. The tunnels were not perfect, but they were home, and even in his darkest dreams that feeling of home called out to him.

"Rough night?" Ace asked, offering Hopper some scraps of Italian bread for breakfast.

"Nightmares," said Hopper.

"Well, then," said the cat, "I think what you need is a little distraction. Something to keep your mind off your troubles."

Hopper smiled. "I'd like that. I'd like that a lot."

Ace reached into a box labeled LOST AND FOUND and removed a red mitten. After making some artful changes, he gave it to Hopper, who wriggled into it.

"That should keep you warm," said Ace.

"Thanks," said Hopper.

Outside the sky was a blustery gray. Hopper shivered, but the cold air was exhilarating. He thought of the stale, dusky air of the subway tunnels and decided this was one aspect of upland life he could get used to.

"How about a ride?" said Ace, going down on his haunches so Hopper could climb on.

"Okay, but I don't mind walking."

"It's a bit of a distance for those little legs of yours," said Ace, not unkindly. "And we're running late." He gave Hopper a mysterious grin. "We don't want to miss the game."

Hopper didn't know what that meant, but he obediently scrambled up onto Ace's back.

"Won't the humans think it's strange when they see a cat giving a ride to a mouse?" Hopper asked.

Ace laughed. "This is New York, Hopper. They've seen a lot stranger. Besides, I doubt anyone will even notice. And if they do, we just might become the next YouTube sensation."

Hopper positioned himself between Ace's shoulder blades, and the tuxedo cat glided along the sidewalk with the mouse on his back.

"One of these days we'll have to do some real sight-seeing," said Ace. "You would love the Botanical Garden, and Coney Island—"

"Stop!" cried Hopper. "Stop right here!"

Ace came to such an abrupt halt that Hopper almost slid off the silky fur of his back.

"What is it? What's wrong?"

"This is where I used to live," Hopper whispered, pointing to the big glass window of Keep's shop. "This is where I was born."

Ace lowered his head so his passenger could slip safely to the sidewalk.

For a moment Hopper just stood there, staring at the tall door—the door he and Pinkie had run for and escaped through, leaving Pup behind for dead. Hopper remembered the guilt and the grief he'd experienced, believing he'd lost his little brother forever. He remembered his fight with Pinkie just before, on the counter of the pet shop, in which she'd bitten his ear so hard she'd maimed him . . . and in a thoroughly uncharacteristic move, he'd bitten and maimed her right back.

Now he crept closer to the door and pressed his face to it for a better look. He expected to see Keep waddling around from cage to cage, feeding the small animals and grumbling to himself like always.

But the shop was deserted. Completely *deserted*. No Keep, no cages. Just a few empty boxes and forgotten leashes strewn about. And the broom—the broom Keep had used to swat at Hopper as he'd dashed for the door—propped in a corner. Hopper squinted harder and saw the jangly bell that used to hang on the door handle; it was still lying on the floor, right where it had landed the morning Hopper had made his escape. If he closed his eyes and imagined, he could almost hear the rusty jingling sound it used to make. But today it was silent, dented, forgotten.

"Where is everybody?" Hopper whispered. "They're gone. All gone." He was shocked to realize that all this time he'd been harboring a sliver of hope that at least one or two of the cagemates had survived. Pup had, after all.

But then, even if they had lived through the commotion of that morning, how long would they have lasted after that? They were feeders. Any who'd survived would have been dumped back into the crisp blanket of aspen curls to await the next skinny kid who wandered into the shop with a snake around his neck.

Nature. Not good, not bad . . .

Hopper sighed and stepped back to study the shop's facade. He wanted to get a picture of it in his mind so he could tell Pup about it someday . . . if Pup ever spoke to him again. Hopper had never thought about how the pet shop might look from this vantage point. The night he ran away was the one time he'd been outside, and he'd certainly had no interest in looking at it then! But now his curiosity got the better of him, and he tilted his head upward, starting at the top. There he saw a rusted light fixture over the entrance and some faded numbers nailed beneath it. Only now did he notice the hand-lettered sign taped to the glass—OUT OF BUSINESS.

Just below the sign a narrow slot was cut into the glass of the door. This slot was protected by a swinging brass flap. Hopper recalled that this opening was some kind of communications portal through which a uniformed human would drop messages hidden in paper envelopes. The mail slot, Keep had called it. Hopper's paw went to his pocket, where the note from La Rocha and the piece of Zucker's tunic were still safely tucked. What would he give for a message now? About Zucker or Firren. Better yet, *from* Zucker or Firren. He shook off the thought and continued his examination.

As ever, the words BROOKLYN SMALL PET SUPPLY were painted across the big glass window. It occurred to Hopper this was the first time he wasn't seeing them backward. Of course, back then he hadn't known the difference. But since Zucker had taught him to read . . .

No. Don't think about Zucker. Too sad, much too sad.

Hopper's gaze moved down from the window to the brick half wall below it. At the bottom, where the wall met the sidewalk, was a small gap where a chunk of mortar had crumbled away. No wonder Keep's business had gone bust; the place was falling apart.

"Well, this is depressing." Hopper sighed. "I can't say I miss the place, but I do have one or two fond memories from my life here."

He remembered how it had felt to curl up beside his mother, even if she hadn't been with them very long. And the laughter of his cagemates as they played, tumbling over one another, kicking up aspen curls.

"Sorry you had to see this," Ace said gently. "But I think there's an old human saying: 'You can't go home again.'"

"Who says that?"

"Old humans, I guess." Ace dipped his shoulder in invitation, and Hopper scooted back up to his seat between the cat's shoulders.

"Where are we going, anyway?" he asked.

"To the Barclays Center!" Ace announced. "Are you a fan of the Nets, by any chance?"

"I don't think so," said Hopper. "What are they?"

"Well, they're a team of extremely agile and powerful fellas who fight together like a well-oiled machine in pursuit of victory and honor."

"Oh!" said Hopper, remembering Firren's highly trained rebels. "Like the Rangers!"

Ace shrugged. "I'm more of an Islanders fan myself, but yeah, just like the Rangers."

With that, the cat quickened his pace to a canter, and Hopper held on tight.

Hopper stared up, up, up at the imposing structure, mouth open, eyes wide.

The Barclays Center. It was the color of a rusty subway rail, and also like the subway, it had a serpentine quality; the whole thing seemed to slither and writhe, circling in and out of itself without actually going anywhere. At the same time, it appeared to hover in the air . . . but it never left the ground. Glowing blue letters across its forehead seemed to scream out its name. And from deep within came a muffled rumble, a deafening purr that was occasionally broken by a single roar made up of ten thousand individual voices.

"What *is* it?" Hopper gasped. "Does it move? Can it talk? Do we ride it?"

"It's a sports arena," Ace explained. "We go inside and watch the Nets do their thing."

Hopper imagined that the "fellas" who made up this band of rebel athletes called the Nets must be beyond enormous to need such a gigantic arena to showcase their talents.

"Will it just be us watching?" Hopper asked.

Ace laughed.

Hopper followed the cat toward a door propped open by a human; the human carried a broom (bigger than Keep's) and leaned against the door from the inside. Hopper wondered if the Barclays Center had swallowed this human whole and hadn't finished digesting him yet.

The closer they got to the open door, the louder the roar became. Hopper could see that the human's uniform had the name MAINTENANCE embroidered over his heart. When the human spotted Ace, his face broke into a grin. "There he is! The only basketball fan I know with a tail. C'mon in, Slam Dunk!"

"Slam Dunk?" Hopper whispered.

"That's what he calls me," Ace whispered back.

Ace scampered inside, curling once between Maintenance's burly legs in a friendly greeting. Then Hopper found himself in a very different kind of tunnel, filled with a thundering echo. The noise made by the Barclays Center was no longer a purr *or* a roar . . . it was tumult, louder than anything

Hopper had ever heard before, louder even than the subway trains and the round-footed traffic monsters put together. He covered his ears, but only for a moment, because he soon realized that this noise was not dangerous or threatening; this noise was filled with happiness and excitement.

It was coming from the thousands of humans who filled the arena; all of them were adding to the chorus of shouts, hoots, and hollers.

"Why are they so excited?" Hopper asked.

"My guess? Because the Nets are winning!"

Ace guided Hopper farther into the mass of human spectators until he could finally see what all the fuss was about. Far below them, in the belly of the Barclays Center, ten colossal-size human men in short pants and baggy sleeveless tunics were jogging madly back and forth on a gleaming wooden floor. Every one of them seemed intent on capturing the same prey—a bouncing orange sphere.

"That's the basketball," Ace explained. "The goal is to shoot it through those hoops on either end of the court."

As Ace said this, one of the men achieved exactly that; from the midway point on the court he hurled the ball—it was an elegant, catapulting motion in which the human's wrists and knees appeared to be doing most of the work. And what aim! The ball sailed in a perfect arc, hitting its mark—the hoop—and swishing through the roped web that hung from it. Hopper would *not* like to meet the spider who'd woven that.

When the ball hit the floor, the human crowd erupted, leaping to their feet, clapping their hands. . . .

And spilling things everywhere.

"Is that what I think it is?" Hopper breathed.

"Yes it is," said Ace, grinning broadly. "Food! *Stadium* food. The best kind there is."

"Better than eggplant and cannoli?"

"Okay, well, maybe the second-best kind." Ace gave Hopper a little push with his nose. "Go get some. But watch out for stamping feet."

Hopper squirmed his way under a row of seats and began to feast. He lapped up puddles of sugary soda and munched on more different kinds of crunchy candies than he could count. He tried popcorn but didn't like the way it stuck in his teeth, so he went back to the sweets. Some were sour, some were tangy, some melted in his mouth, others took forever to chew. But the flavors were scrumptious—cherry, lime, butterscotch, chocolate. Hopper washed the candy down with even more soda—cola, orange, and something called 7UP. Hopper definitely understood where the "up" came from; he was beginning to feel like he could fly!

"Maybe you'd better slow down," Ace advised. "You've had an awful lot of sugar, and your system's not used to it."

Hopper wiped a sticky smear of something

strawberry-flavored from his lips. When he replied, his words came in one long, breathless ramble: "My-system-is-fine-honest-I'm-perfectly-okay-this-candy-stuff-is-delicious-I-would-love-some-more-can-we-bring-some-home-with-us-Ace-and-can-we-only-get-it-here-in-the-belly-of-the-Barclays-beast-or-will-we-be-able-to-find-it-somewhere-else-because-I-really-think-I'd-like-to-eat-it-every-single-day-oh-my-goodness-how-do-they-make-it-taste-so-wonderful?!?!"

Ace rolled his eyes. "That's it. You're done with candy for today."

Hopper's blood seemed to be moving at double time through his veins, and his whole body was tingling. "Where are we going now?" he asked, forcing his words to come out one at a time.

"There's another game I want to see."

Hopper followed Ace across the shiny-floored concourses, then through a maze of hallways and more tunnels until they reached a door with a sign that read STORAGE. Ace knocked on a loose vent cover toward the bottom part of the door. After a moment the grate swung open. Standing on the other side was a rat.

And he was wearing a Nets jersey.

Inside the storage room were eight more rats, all outfitted in some manner of sports attire. Hopper could see that their jerseys had been extensively cut down to size, fashioned from old versions of the human uniforms that had been relegated to this seemingly forgotten closet. Some of the jerseys were black and white, like the real Nets', but others were blue, gold, green, white . . . or some combination of all these colors.

Ace quickly introduced Hopper to his athletic friends—first Julius (who'd opened the door), then Dawkins, Kidd, and the rest, whose names Hopper was too revved up on sugar to remember.

"How do you know these rats?" Hopper asked Ace.

"I rescued most of them. Julius, Kidd, and Dawkins were living in the attic of a sporting goods store before I relocated them to Barclays. The others were scattered throughout the arena, mostly setting up house near the food concessions."

"I bet that didn't go over well," said Hopper.

"No, it didn't," said Ace. "Which is why my pal Maintenance brought me in. I realized this place was so enormous the rats could actually stay on-site as long as they kept a low profile and stuck to the nondining areas. When I discovered this forgotten storage room, I knew they had a new home."

The rats had cleared a wide section of the floor to use as their court; it did not have the wood sheen of the court in the actual arena, but it did have two soda cups with the bottoms torn out of them tied to mop

handles and positioned at either end to act as baskets.

Hopper and Ace watched as the rats got busy choosing up sides. "They're down a rat today," Ace explained. "One of their best players injured himself running away from an angry hot dog vendor."

"Where did they get the ball?" Hopper asked, noticing the extremely bouncy rubber orb the rats were tossing back and forth. Truth be told, he was still feeling extremely bouncy himself.

"That's my contribution," Ace explained. "It's from the gum-ball machine at Bellissimo's."

Just then Dawkins sent a powerful pass to one of his fellow players; the player missed his catch and the ball went rolling out of bounds. Unable to stand still a second longer, Hopper took off after it, zipping across the rat-size court and skidding to a halt just before crashing into an enormous old sneaker. Kidd jogged over to retrieve the ball.

"Whoooh!" cried Julius, eyeing Hopper with interest. "You're one fast little mouse."

"Not usually," Hopper admitted. "I've just had a lot of candy."

"Maybe so," said Julius, smiling. "But let's see what you've got in the way of skills." He turned to the rat called Kidd. "Give this tiny rodent that ball."

Kidd bounced the springy rubber ball to Hopper. Hopper leaped up into the air, caught it, landed on his hind paws, then spun around and aimed for the soda cup on the opposite end of the court.

Swish!

The rats gaped.

"Three-pointer!" cried Dawkins. "The kid hit a three-point shot his first time out."

"Do that again," said Julius, throwing the ball back to Hopper.

Hopper didn't have to be asked twice. His muscles buzzed with energy and his limbs just wanted to move. He caught the ball, bounced it once, and copied the form he'd seen the human Net execute—ankles and knees, graceful arc—to send the ball soaring through the air and into the farthest soda cup. Another flawless three-pointer.

"I choose *him*!" said Kidd. "He's on my team!"

Ace clapped Hopper on the back. "How do you like that, Hopper? You've been chosen."

Hopper grinned. "I get that a lot."

For the next forty-eight minutes the Chosen One dribbled, passed, and fired off three-point shots like a pro. By the time the game was over, Hopper had earned the respect of the athletes and made nine new friends.

"Did you have fun?" Ace asked as they sat down to rest.

Hopper nodded. "It was great!"

In fact, there was only one thing that could have made the great afternoon even better . . . and that was if Pup and Zucker had been there to see it.

So much for taking his mind off his troubles. The thought of his brother and friend had Hopper feeling sad and guilty all over again.

If only he could have been as good at being the Chosen One as he was at basketball, he thought.

If only—

He was startled out of his thoughts by the sound of the door grate rattling. And then . . .

Thwump!

The enormous door slammed open.

There, holding a pile of old towels and fraying sweat socks, stood Maintenance.

CHAPTER THIRTEEN

WHEN THE JOLLY HUMAN saw the gathering of rodents, he squawked.

"I thought I got rid of you rats!" he cried, tossing his laundry aside and grabbing one of the mops which held the soda cup baskets. When he saw Ace, his face registered shock.

"Slam Dunk? I thought you were on my side. And here you are . . . f-*rat*-ernizing with the enemy!"

Maintenance's boot sideswiped Ace, scooting him out the open door. The basketball rats scattered, taking cover behind old gym bags and broken stadium seats. Hopper was too terrified to move; he stood alone in the middle of the rodent-size basketball court. Apparently, this unwitting tactic translated into hiding in plain sight, because Maintenance ignored the mouse completely and began shoving the dusty mop top into all four corners of the storage room.

"Get outta my nice clean arena, you dirty little buggers!" he commanded.

The rats cowered and ducked, but the raglike tentacles of the mop head reached for them, sweeping them out of their hiding places.

"Help!" cried Kidd as the mop encroached upon him. "Hopper!"

Hopper gaped at the mop. The cottony ropes of its

head seemed alive as they slithered closer to Kidd. His mind flashed on a memory of another slithering foe—the skinny kid's hungry snake!

Fueled by fury and fear, Hopper dove for the mop, sinking into the dried grime of its ropes. With dust stinging his eyes, he clawed his way to the long wooden handle, dug his claws into it, and began to climb.

Again Maintenance poked the mop toward Kidd, which jolted Hopper as he climbed, but he clung to the handle and made his way to the summit, balancing precariously on the rounded top. He was looking right into the human's eyes.

"W-what the heck . . . ?" Maintenance blinked at him.

Hopper blinked back. Then he jumped . . . launching himself right at Maintenance's face.

He landed belly-first on the human's nose, his claws digging into the skin around it, his hind paws scratching at Maintenance's upper lip.

"Aaaahhhhhgggg!" Maintenance dropped the mop handle; it landed with a loud smack. Hopper held on tight as the human slapped at his face, trying to dislodge the mouse from his nose.

"Get offa me, you filthy little critter!"

Hopper wanted nothing more. Below him he could see that Kidd and the others had made it safely to the door and were all watching this stupendous act of bravery—or was it idiocy?—with wide eyes.

Hopper was relieved that they had escaped! Now it was his turn.

Maintenance continued to stumble and stagger, swiping at Hopper. As the human danced around, shouting and flailing, his boot nearly caught on the mop handle again and again. Hopper was glad it didn't; if Maintenance fell, he would likely land face-first, squishing Hopper into oblivion.

Now Ace darted back into the room, heading straight for the mop. Clutching the handle with his teeth, he dragged it until it was directly below Hopper.

Yes! Hopper could release his grasp on the human's nose and drop unharmed into the cushiony rope head of the mop.

Hopper held his breath, then let go of the skin he was grasping. He felt himself dropping.

Pwuhmff!

The moment he landed in the softness of the mop head, Ace reached in and tugged him out of the grungy tangle.

Maintenance was sputtering in pain, crying out something about antiseptic and tetanus shots.

"Let's go!" cried Ace, bolting for the door.

He swung Hopper onto his back and took off, the basketball rats following at top speed.

Game over, Maintenance, thought Hopper. *Game over.*

Hopper, Ace, and the basketball rats managed to free themselves from the Barclays Center just before the real game let out. According to Ace, leaving with the human crowd was a good way for a small animal to get trampled.

"Thanks, Hopper," said Kidd. "You really were a team player back there. You saved my life."

Hopper shrugged, pleased. "All in a day's work," he said modestly.

"And you're one heck of a basketball star," Julius observed with a smile. But his happy expression turned worried. He looked to Ace. "Where do we go now?" he asked. "Where are we gonna live?"

Ace's reply was a big grin.

Grass.

As far as the eye could see, there was nothing but grass, slender blades looking magical beneath a sparkling coating of frost, stretching out and away toward the vast gray river.

When Ace stopped walking, Hopper did a double take and rubbed his eyes. He was so startled by the sight of all that space, he thought he might have nodded off on the ride and was dreaming again.

"Welcome to Pier One," said Ace. "Brooklyn Bridge Park, otherwise known as the grasslands. Gorgeous, aren't they? They're a lot greener in the springtime, but you get the picture." He nodded to Kidd. "These will be your new digs, if it's all right with you."

"Looks like a cool place," said Dawkins. "It's not Barclays, but I think I can get used to it."

Ace nudged Hopper toward the grass. "Let's check on Mrs. Fiorenza's mice to see if they've settled in all right."

"Okay." Hopper slid down from Ace's back and breathed deeply. Even in the winter chill, grass certainly had a wonderful scent—clean and fresh and earthy. He stepped into it and found that it came right up to the bottoms of his ears . . . and it tickled. The pointy tips of the blades only reached Ace's knees.

"How lucky these rodents are to have been relocated to such a beautiful place," said Hopper, reaching down to pick up a pebble in his path. It was smooth and shiny, with shimmering flecks. As they walked, other stones appeared in his path. Some were far too big for him to lift, so he went around them. The basketball rats followed along, taking in the vastness in silent awe.

"Well, it's not entirely without its dangers," said Ace, "but overall it's a nice arrangement." He guided Hopper toward a row of benches overlooking the water. "We can usually find some of my clients gathered over there. It's where the best human food gets left behind. It's practically a smorgasbord."

"A what?"

"Good eats. And lots of 'em."

Sure enough, as they approached the benches, the sweet smell of grass gave way to more savory smells. Crumbs, crusts, and scraps were everywhere. Several rodents were helping themselves to the bounty.

"There's someone I recognize," said Ace with a big smile. "That little white mouse over there. That's Carroll. I rescued her from an alley after she escaped from a research lab. She was next in line for some medical experimentation. Good thing she was brave enough and smart enough to get herself out of there."

"What's medical experimentation?"

Ace sighed. "I'd rather not tell you. You've got enough scary images in your little head already."

Now the little white mouse turned around to smile at them.

Hopper was sure he'd never felt anything like what he was feeling at that moment. His heart began to pound, his paws began to sweat, and there was a flutter in his belly, a bubbly feeling that reminded him of the 7UP he'd drunk. The more he looked at the white mouse—who, he now realized, had lovely pink eyes to match her petite pink ears—the more bubbly he felt. The sensation was not unlike the one he'd had at the arena; it was like eating too much candy. Or riding the subway train. No . . . it was like eating too much candy *while* riding the subway train!

And it was wonderful.

Carroll ran over and gave Ace a hug.

"Carroll," said the cat, "I'd like you to meet my new friend, Hopper."

Carroll turned her glowing smile to the mouse. "Hello."

Hopper gulped. He tried to say hello but just couldn't manage it. He wondered where all his words had gone, because none seemed able to find their way to his lips.

Then Ace spotted another acquaintance.

"There's an old friend," he said, pointing to a handsome chipmunk wearing thick-rimmed spectacles. "Hey, Valky! Over here!"

When the chipmunk saw who'd called out to him, his face lit up. "Well, if it isn't Ace the cat! Just in time for a late-afternoon nosh!"

As the chipmunk bounded toward them, Ace told Hopper and the basketball rats, "Van Valkenburgh got himself trapped in an air vent of some building over on Court Street. The human tenants were clear about not wanting him hurt. I like it when that happens. But they were having trouble coaxing him out. When I heard about the problem, I went right over and handled the job. Now Valky helps me out by looking after the newcomers."

Valky proudly puffed out his chest and his cheeks. "That I do," he said. "And speaking of newcomers..." He eyed the rats with friendly interest. "More clients of yours?"

"Yes. And you're going to love having these guys around. They're sports heroes!"

Now Valky's face became serious. "We have another new arrival," he said, motioning across the grass. "She got here this morning. Is she one of yours?"

Hopper gave a quick glance in the direction Valky had pointed, but found his eyes pulled right back to Carroll.

"I don't think so," said Ace, frowning. "I did send over a family of mice about a week ago, but that's all. Where is she from?"

Valky shrugged. "I haven't had a chance to talk to her yet. She looked exhausted and in serious need of nourishment, so I decided she should eat first and talk later. But she looks pretty worse for wear, like she's been through something rough."

"I heard her talking to a squirrel earlier," Carroll offered. "Something about coming upland from . . . what did she call it? Oh, right . . . from the subway tunnel."

Hopper was still so involved with admiring Carroll's pretty face that it was a moment before he actually registered what she'd said. When the import of her statement finally broke through the fog in his head, he whirled, training his anxious eyes on the spot where Valky had pointed.

There he saw a rat with the dainty frame, proud shoulders pressed back into an elegantly fierce posture, dressed in a white tunic with red-and-blue stripes.

And of course there was the sword. That wonderful, glittering, *familiar* sword.

Hopper could barely control the beating of his heart. He wanted to shout, to run, to sing out with joy and relief. But he didn't dare hope. Not yet.

And then the figure, as though sensing his gaze, turned slowly in his direction. Her face lit up with a smile even as her eyes filled with tears. Then she threw back her head and cried, *"Aye, aye aye!"*

And Hopper was running. Running across the grass. Running toward Firren!

MIDLOGUE

PUP DID NOT LIKE the Mūs village. Not at all.

He did not like the way the children hid their faces when Pinkie strode past, her gold-cloaked shoulders pressed back, her whiskers pricking the air.

And he did not like the way the residents muttered and whispered about her being a tyrant and a dictator. To his mind, their resentment over Pinkie's new brand of leadership was outrageously disrespectful, just this side of treason. He *understood* their complaints, of course—Pinkie was a bully of the first order who saw to it that her way was the only way. But she was a bold warrior, and a Chosen One besides, who had proved her mettle in a great battle against the loathsome feral cats and their wicked queen, Felina. Pinkie had both inherited and earned her authority, and these ungrateful Mūs citizens had no right to question it.

Pup himself questioned it every moment of every day, but that was different. He was family.

What he disliked most about living behind the gray wall was the condescending way the soldiers smirked at him, the way they glowered with mistrust and disdain whenever he was in their company. He despised how they whispered and chuckled about how small and weak he appeared, especially in comparison with his fierce and haughty sister.

Pup's goal was to be accepted by the soldiers. Feared would be better. Liked would be best of all.

Which was why, not long after their arrival in the Mūs village, he'd summoned his courage and asked his sister for a uniform. He did think the pink motif was ridiculous and not soldierly in the least, but he appreciated the shiny buttons and heavy braided trim. To him, such military trappings announced, *I am important. I belong. Pinkie values me and finds me worthy.*

A uniform did not seem like an outlandish request to Pup. After all, Pinkie the Chosen had forced nearly every other Mūs to wear one, so why not him? Joining her army was required; it was a rule.

But apparently, when it came to Pup, the rules were different.

He'd asked for a uniform. But he didn't get one.

"Are you out of your mind?" Pinkie had scoffed. "You are not exactly military material, Pup. I have enough to think about without having to worry about you playing with swords."

"Is that a no?" Pup had asked through his teeth.

"That's a never," Pinkie had replied.

Pup had said no more, but his sister's cold refusal had sparked a flame in his gullet. This was a feeling he'd known only once before—the Day of the Sweeping, as he'd come to call it in his nightmares—when he'd watched his two siblings disappear from his life without even stopping to see if he was alive or dead.

On that day he had elected *not* to nurture the feeling; he'd allowed the fear and confusion to push his anger aside. But when Pinkie had denied his simple petition, and he'd been left to slink away (with her laughter ringing in his ears and his little, un-uniformed body shivering with shame), he'd had no choice but to allow that angry flame to flare, to burn slowly and steadily of its own accord.

Then there had come the day when he'd looked up from making what he thought were some very necessary changes to one of La Rocha's prophecies—the one they all made such a fuss about—and he'd seen his brother standing there in the engine room, facing off against Pinkie, asking her for favors.

The sight of those two white circles mirroring each other had actually made him queasy. It was as though a current of power and purpose flowed between them . . . a current he could never tap, no matter how hard he tried. Seeing that matched pair of extraordinary siblings had further ignited the flicker of anger burning inside him and fanned it into a mighty blaze of fury.

Pup wanted to be like Hopper and Pinkie so badly that he'd actually adorned himself with a circle of his own. But even he had to admit that there was something desperate and fraudulent about it. The marking around *his* eye was not a sign of a proud heritage and preordained future; it was not of clean, soft fur but of chalky stone dust. And instead of bright white it was the color of gloom, of afterthought, as though he could only ever hope to be a mere shadow of his famously foretold brother and sister.

And did they care?

Well, maybe Hopper did, Pup allowed. He had seen something in Hopper's eyes on that day he'd come to appeal to Pinkie—a warmth, a longing, that had sung out to Pup. But he'd made himself ignore it. He'd loved Hopper before, and where had that gotten him? Left for dead on a pet-shop floor, that's where. Abandoned to a death camp and almost eaten alive.

And Pinkie . . . to her, he knew, he was nothing more than a glorified servant. A delivery boy to send out with food for their departing brother.

"Why are you doing this?" he remembered asking her when she'd thrust the felt-wrapped bundle of provisions into his paws.

"You don't understand," Pinkie had said, her words curt and brittle. "He's my brother."

"And mine," Pup reminded her.

"But Hopper and I share something you could never understand," Pinkie went on, although Pup suspected she was talking more to herself than to him. "The great burden of responsibility."

"Responsibility?" Pup's anger blazed. "For me?"

"Yes, for you! And also for what we lost, for what went away in the night . . ."

Pup did not know what she meant by that. Whatever was lost in the night, and however Hopper and Pinkie had been to blame for it, he did not know nor care.

All that mattered was that they considered him to be a burden, an encumbrance, a runt (as Pinkie never tired of calling him) who needed to be watched out for and worried over.

Perhaps it was time for him to prove them wrong.

It took Pup only a matter of days to plot how he would go about this. First, he would need someone to write for him, so he could he leave his sister a note, telling her of his bold, intrepid plan. He certainly could not inform her to her face, for surely she would forbid him. No, he would have someone compose a letter, outlining his objectives. This letter would be left for Pinkie to find after he'd escaped the Mūs encampment, something he'd have to do in secret, probably during the wee, small hours in order to avoid being forcibly apprehended by one of Pinkie's (uniformed!) soldiers.

Pup was actually quite eager to learn to inscribe words on paper, mostly because Pinkie herself had not yet learned to write; she dictated her words (which he supposed lent some literal truth to the widespread accusations that she was a dictator) to educated underlings she called scriveners. But learning so much would take too long, and Pup was in a hurry. What he needed was a scribe.

So he made some discreet inquiries, and the consensus was that the best Mūs for the task was the sweet old midwife. She was gifted at many things, reading and writing among them. And she was, everyone agreed, a wonderful cook.

So he presented himself at the door of the midwife's cottage. As he rapped his tiny paw against the sturdy wooden door, he had no way of knowing that this was the selfsame little dwelling where his brother, Hopper, had dined on his first visit to the Mūs village.

Of course, the cozy nest was now serving double duty as a weapons forge for Pinkie's army. By day the hearth fire was used exclusively for the casting and molding of swords. Per Pinkie's orders, during working hours the elderly midwife and her mate would surrender their home to the smithy, and thusly found themselves with only the evenings in which to enjoy their privacy. And then they were obliged to tiptoe cautiously around the ever-growing arsenal of blades piling up atop their rocking chairs and sofa pillows.

The midwife's name was Maimonides—Mamie for short.

"I will be happy to teach you the art of penmanship," she said calmly, placing a steaming bowl of stew before him.

"No thanks," said Pup. "I don't have that much time."

Mamie looked at him across her dining table (where two lethal dirks and a deadly rapier lay beside the earthenware stew pot, somewhat incongruously between a pair of filigree candlesticks). She spooned more of the hearty fare into his bowl; he acknowledged this second helping with a grunt, feeling that, somehow, showing his gratitude might be construed as a sign of weakness.

"Your brother, the Chosen One, once dined at my table," she told him proudly.

"Big deal," Pup muttered over his bowl.

"Oh, it was!" said Mamie, smiling. "You probably don't know this, Pup, but I was the midwife who delivered your own father into this world."

Pup wasn't sure exactly what that meant, but it sounded monumental. The thought of his father, who he now knew was a rebel named Dodger, made him all the more desperate to prove himself.

"And I was also the one who brought him here, for his own safety, to the Mūs village," Mamie continued. "His father had been mortally wounded, and his mother and siblings had already been taken from him by Queen Felina."

At the mention of that name Pup looked up from his stew. "She killed them?"

The midwife nodded, her eyes somber. "She consumed them, your gentle grandmother and all your tiny aunts and uncles. Your father was spared thanks to the courage of a rat you may have heard of . . . he called himself Titus."

"Titus?" Pup frowned. "You must be mistaken. Titus is a villain, a monster. He was the one who struck the peace accord with Felina."

"I am aware of that." Mamie sighed. "But I have always believed there was more to that story. Much more." Her keen eyes looked pointedly at Pup. "Perhaps you might one day find a means to learn the whole of it."

"Perhaps," Pup said dismissively.

He gulped down the rest of his meal, wondering if it might be his last for a while. He wasn't sure how he would feed himself out there in the tunnels, and he could not even guess how long his quest might take. He supposed he'd find a way to subsist, smart and determined as he was. The important thing was that he do what must be done to prove himself to Pinkie.

Mamie cleared away his bowl, then brought a slip of paper to the table and a chalky stone like the one he'd used to draw the dark ring around his eye.

"What would you like me to write?" the old mouse asked. "What is it you wish to say in this correspondence of yours?"

"We can start with this," said Pup, his voice level, his words icy. "Dear Pinkie, I have gone out to slay Felina."

CHAPTER FOURTEEN

AGAIN THE SWEET VOICE lifted in that familiar call. *"Aye! Aye! Aye!"*

Hopper's heart surged as he ran; Firren was running too, across the grass.

Part of the Chosen One was still afraid to believe what he was seeing. But with every step she took, it became clear that he was not imagining things. It was more than just the white tunic with its red-and-blue stripes that announced her—it was those keen black eyes, that strong but graceful manner. This could be no one but the powerful warrior he knew and adored.

"Firren! It's really you!"

She caught him in a hug. "You're alive! Oh, Hopper, I was so afraid the exterminators had gotten you."

"I was afraid they'd gotten you, too. I went into the city to find you, but you weren't in the trap." He gave her an astounded look. "How did you manage to release yourself? How did you escape?"

"I didn't escape. I was rescued. By La Rocha!"

Hopper sputtered and blinked. "But La Rocha is a thinker, an oracle, not a warrior. And if he's a cockroach, like everyone says, how could he possibly be strong enough to open the cage?"

"I'm not sure he *is* a cockroach," Firren said, nearly as baffled as Hopper. "He wears a cloak with a hood,

so I couldn't tell for sure what sort of creature he was." She smiled. "He was brave, though, and kind. And he led me to you."

"To me? Here? How?"

"He left a message at the Runes, just like Zucker did when he wanted me to know that Titus and his army were preparing for the rebel raid."

At this Hopper flushed; he was the one who'd given the former emperor that information. "What was La Rocha's message?"

"He wrote the name of the exterminating company on the wall, right beside my drawing of Dodger, and a note, telling me I needed to come upland and locate this Pier One place."

"Brilliant!"

"You don't know the half of it." Firren laughed. "Before I could do that, I had to escape Pinkie."

"Pinkie?!"

Firren quickly recounted the tale of Pinkie sneaking up on La Rocha and dragging the two of them from the Samsonite fortress. "Never a dull moment," she said, in what Hopper decided was one of the greatest understatements he'd ever heard in his life.

"Who else made it out?" he asked eagerly. "Who's with you?" He looked deep into Firren's eyes and whispered: "Zucker?"

"I . . ." Firren glanced away and shrugged. "I don't know where Zucker is."

"Oh." Hopper allowed the pain only a single moment to slice through him, then tamped it down. It would not do to succumb to the hurt now. He could mourn Zucker later, in private, if, in fact, mourning was what needed to be done. But for now he would cling to what hope remained.

"What of Garfield and Polhemus? And Ketchum?"

"I can't say, Hopper. I haven't been back to Atlantia . . . or what's left of it, that is. After I escaped Pinkie, I went right to the Runes. Then I came upland in search of you, because . . . well, there's a big problem, Hopper. *Another* big problem."

"What is it?"

"It's . . ." Firren broke off, her eyes narrowing. Her paw went slowly to the handle of her blade just as Hopper felt the large shadow fall across him from behind. The ground beneath them shook a bit from the rumble of a powerful purr.

"Hopper . . . ," Firren whispered, carefully withdrawing her sword from its sheath. "Be very still. I don't want to frighten you, Chosen One, but there's an enormous *cat* standing right behind you."

"I know there is," said Hopper, smiling. "His name is Ace. And something tells me you two are going to be great pals."

Despite Hopper's assurances Firren continued to regard Ace with concern.

"This is Ace," Hopper repeated. "He saved me from a tragic demise. So I guess you two have that in common. Ace, this is Firren. She's the bravest rebel you'll ever meet. She was a friend of my father's long ago, and she's a big part of the reason Titus's refugee camps were liberated and Felina's hunting ground was destroyed."

"Any enemy of Felina's is a friend of mine," said Ace. "Of course, when I knew her, she wasn't royalty. She was nothing but a stray, a common alley cat."

"He's awfully big," Firren whispered out of the corner of her mouth. "Are you sure he's trustworthy?"

"He's as loyal and reliable as they come," Hopper assured the rebel.

Ace put out a paw to shake. "Welcome to Pier One."

Firren maneuvered her sword back into its sheath and shook the cat's paw.

"Ace can tell you everything you need to know about living here in the grasslands," Hopper informed her.

"That's nice," said Firren, "but why do I need to know that?"

"What do you mean why?" Hopper was perplexed. "Because you're staying, that's why! Brooklyn is great. I like it here, and I think you will too."

The look Firren gave him was part shock, part disappointment. "Hopper, don't you understand? I had only one reason for risking my life coming up here . . . and that was to bring the Chosen One *back*."

"Back? Into the tunnels?" Hopper flinched at the thought. "Never," he said in a dull voice.

"But I haven't told you about—"

"Forget it!" said Hopper, shaking his head. "No way. Not happening. There's nothing you can say that could get me to go back into those tunnels."

He hated telling her no, but she was asking too much. Whatever this new problem was to which she'd referred, he had no intention of trying to fix it. He couldn't stand the thought of failing yet again.

An awkward silence settled over the mouse, the rat, and the cat. After a long moment Ace forced a chuckle.

"Maybe we should discuss potential travel plans later," he said cheerfully. "Firren's been through quite an ordeal, and I think she can use some rest. She and I can get acquainted while I wait for Capone. He should be by any minute now for his daily romp. Maybe Carroll can show you around the park." He waved the white mouse over to join them and told her what he was thinking.

"I would love to give Hopper a tour," said the mouse.

Carroll's arrival went a long way toward pushing Hopper's dark memories of the tunnels aside. Feeling bubbly again, he left Firren in Ace's care and fell into step beside Carroll.

As they walked along, Hopper marveled at the amount of misplaced human belongings he saw. When Carroll noticed him eyeing a collection of jagged metal objects looped together on a ring, she laughed.

"Keys," she said. "They're one of the most common sorts of lost articles we find around here. Humans seem to have a knack for misplacing them, along with coins and ballpoint pens and these strange, noisy things called cell phones. You can't imagine how many of those we come across."

They walked on until they reached a playground, which Hopper recognized immediately because it was just like the one in Atlantia, only much, much bigger. Because of the nip in the air there were only a few children present.

"My favorite kind of humans," said Carroll. "The little ones."

"They won't call for exterminators?" Hopper asked nervously.

Carroll laughed. "Hardly. Human pups are friendly. If you stand very still, one of them might even—"

"Even what?" asked Hopper, wide eyed at the sight of a chubby-cheeked little girl toddling toward them.

"Pet you," Carroll whispered. "Now just be very still, keep quiet."

Hopper looked up into the bright blue eyes of the child. A pink ribbon fluttered in her hair. She was the tiniest human he'd ever seen, but still enormous compared with him. He held his breath and made no attempt to move, just as Carroll had instructed.

The child smiled and burbled as her plump hands reached for him. Hopper muffled a scream as one little finger stretched out toward his back. But it was not a violent touch at all; it was just the slightest brush, light and gentle. The child giggled and began to stroke his fur. It was a gesture filled with love and wonder, and despite the chilly air Hopper's whole little body flooded with warmth.

"I pet the mousey," the child gurgled. "Nice mousey. I pet you."

Pet. So that's what the word meant. Hopper had heard it a million times in Keep's store—it was a *pet* shop, after all—but he'd never dreamed it could have such wonderful implications. Hopper thought he would be happy just to sit here and let this angelic little child pet him forever.

A breeze came up and the ribbon slipped from her hair. Hopper tucked it in his pocket just as the child's tiny finger touched his torn ear. Her bright eyes turned sad. "Boo-boo?"

"Uh-huh," Hopper whispered.

"Poor mousey got a boo-boo."

Hopper nodded, and gently pressed his back into the stroking of her plump little thumb. The comfort was all consuming, and for that moment the boo-boo—*all* of the boo-boos—somehow ceased to matter.

The child went on petting Hopper until her attention was caught by something moving in the grass. She laughed out loud and pointed across the park. "Kitties!" she cried. "Kitties!"

"Kitties?" Hopper turned to Carroll. "What's that mean?"

"I don't know. I've never heard it before."

"Kitties," the child repeated, clapping her hands in delight. And then she said a word that set Hopper's fur on end:

"Kitties coming. Kitty *cats*!"

Six felines were making their way across the park.

Frantic, Hopper and Carroll bolted, running back

across the grasslands as quickly as their legs could carry them. When they were close enough to see the faces of the enemy, Hopper immediately recognized the big cat whom Ace had challenged on Pilot's behalf, and his two raggedy sidekicks. It was hard to tell if the other three cats were in cahoots with the trio, but in any case the six feline interlopers had a singular purpose: to feed. They stalked like the wild, untamed things they were—heads down, fangs bared, tails swatting out an ominous rhythm.

By the time Hopper and Carroll arrived, the scent of fear had risen above the sweet, greenish smell of grass and earth as the panicked rodents scattered and burrowed, screaming out for help.

Ace was fighting madly, trying to cover all sides. Valky struggled to direct the rodents to safety. Firren was engaged in a one-on-one battle with a straggly stray. Her sword sliced the air as she struck out at the hissing, spitting cat. But she was weakening. Hopper realized that Ace had been right—after her long journey to the daylight world Firren was truly and deeply exhausted.

Well, then Hopper would save her!

But when his paw went to the place where his blade should be, he remembered his sword had been stolen by that ungrateful rat.

Now the biggest of the cats—the leader of the pack, who'd terrorized Pilot on the street—noticed Firren's fatigue and was bearing down on the warrior.

"Firren!" Hopper screamed. "Behind you! Run!"

But the fighting had taken what little strength she had left. She turned to Hopper, her face unreadable, as the cat skulked closer.

When the cat Firren was fighting saw the big, mean cat and his two sidekicks ambling toward his prey, he took off. Clearly, these three were the hooligan strays that even the other strays feared.

Hopper could see the big cat's hot breath making frosty ghosts in the chilled air as the trio stalked across the grass. Sword or no sword, he had to do something. He ran straight for the panting Firren, reaching her at the same moment the cats did.

"Well, look who it is! Ace's little buddy."

"Start crawling away," Hopper whispered to Firren. "I'm going to try to reason with them. Or at least distract them."

"*Reason* with them? But, Chosen One—"

"There's no need for both of us to die. Now go, Firren. *Go!*"

Hopper didn't look to see whether she obeyed his order or not; he was too intent on keeping his eyes locked on the three enemies who hovered above him. He was outsized and outnumbered. He could bolt, but he'd never outrun them.

Hopper never saw the slap coming. The cat's matted paw collided with him, a swift, thundering backhand that knocked him off his feet.

"I like to knock you mice around a bit before I eat you," the cat snarled. "It tenderizes the meat."

The paw smacked into Hopper again, somersaulting him sideways. Dazed, he managed to get back on his feet, but the earth seemed unstable beneath him.

So this was how the Chosen One was to die, then? On a grassy lawn, shrouded in a foul cloud of cat breath? Hopper felt his shoulders go slack, and he stared at the rocks and pebbles dotting the ground around his paws.

One of the sidekicks laughed. "My turn!"

Hopper felt the breeze of a paw swiping toward him. He tensed, waiting for the hit, but instead he heard the sidekick yipe, then howl in pain. Hopper snapped his head up to see that Firren had *not* followed the directive to retreat; the rebel had rallied, stabbing her sword into the cat's paw!

The other sidekick bared his teeth; he went on his haunches, ready to spring, when Hopper felt another presence beside him. Carroll! And she was holding something out to him.

A rock?

"What are you doing here?" he breathed. "It's dangerous. Go!"

"I'm helping you," Carroll said, pressing the stone into his paws.

"What's this for?"

"Hopper!" It was Ace's voice that ripped across the park. "Three-pointer!"

Hopper heard the words but was too scared to make sense of them. He stared at Ace, who was defending a family of squirrels against one of the strays.

"*Three-point shot*, Hopper!" Ace cried.

Realization dawned. Strength surged through him as he prepared to shoot. . . .

Wrists and knees!

The stone flew as gracefully and powerfully as any basketball ever had, and with a sickly *thwap* it connected with the sidekick's skull. He let out a shrill meow, staggered back, and crumpled into the frosty grass.

Carroll picked up a second stone; this one she hurled herself, landing it right on the cat's sensitive nose. He howled in pain.

All that remained was the big cat, who let out a shriek of fury and reached for Hopper with claws like knives. But before the claws could connect, Hopper heard a sound he'd never experienced before. The cat heard it too and jerked his paw back in terror.

Barking!

Capone was barreling across the grass, growling and snarling. His muscular form was like a cannonball.

The big cat quit his attack and took off, leaving his wounded friends to fend for themselves. Blood spurted from the stabbed one's paw and it streamed down the face of the one who'd taken Hopper's rock to the head. Dazed and terrified, the sidekicks scampered out of the park. The burly canine gave chase, his fierce bark echoing behind him.

Ace rushed to Hopper's side, and Hopper flung himself against the silky fur of the cat's leg. Then he turned a grateful grin to Carroll.

"Nice work," he said. "Good aim."

"Thanks. You too."

As the rodents slowly ventured out of their nests and hiding places, Carroll, whose time in the medical lab had taught her a thing or two about surgery, went off to assist the ones who'd been injured in the fray.

Valky and the basketball rats hurried over to join Hopper, Firren, and Ace.

"Everybody okay?" Ace asked. He had a cut over his eye and one bent whisker.

"No," Firren said curtly. "Everybody isn't okay." She brushed off her tunic and turned to the Chosen One. "It's your brother, Hopper. It's Pup. And he's definitely *not* okay."

CHAPTER FIFTEEN

"WHAT IS IT?" HOPPER asked. "What's the matter with Pup?" His stomach roiled at the very thought of his tiny sibling being hurt or in danger.

"He's run away from the Mūs village," Firren explained gravely. "Pinkie told La Rocha all about it as she marched us away from the mystic's fortress. To be honest, I think the reason I was able to escape was that she was so preoccupied with her story."

"Why did he run?" Hopper asked. "Did he go looking for me?" This possibility pleased Hopper a great deal, despite the fact that the thought of Pup traveling alone in the lawless tunnels made his blood run cold.

"No. He went looking for Felina."

"*What?!*"

"According to Pinkie, Pup was getting a little full of himself. He didn't like that everyone thought he had to be protected. He said he could be just as much a Chosen One as his brother and sister were, and if he had to slay Felina to prove it, he would."

"What did Pinkie say to that?" Hopper asked.

"Nothing," Firren reported. "He left it in a note. By the time she found it, he's already fled."

Fled. The word hit Hopper like a punch. She might as well have said "suicide."

"That's why I need you to come back with me." Firren sighed and turned up her paws in a gesture of desperation. "I can't save Pup alone, and even if I could, I doubt he'd listen to anything I had to say. You have to be the one to talk to him."

That reality scared Hopper even more than returning to the tunnels did. Pup had been so cold the last time they spoke. The memory of his little brother's contempt made Hopper shiver.

"Pup's determined to face Felina," Firren went on, "and if she gets word of it, you can bet she'll be out for blood. I certainly won't be able to keep her from going after Pup by myself, but I don't know where any of the Rangers are, and I have no idea if any of the soldiers survived the exterminators."

Last Hopper knew, Garfield, Polhemus, and Ketch were alive and tending to Beverley and Driggs. But he couldn't say for sure that they hadn't gone back into Atlantia, which was teeming with traps, after he was carried away in that infernal Windbreaker. And even if they hadn't braved the minefield that was the city, the tunnels were now an even bigger threat than ever before. Who knew what terrible fate could have come to them as they wandered in the darkness?

"You see, Hopper," Firren coaxed, "we really don't have any choice but to head south."

"South?" Valky looked at Ace with disbelief. "Did she just say she wants the mouse to go to New Jersey?"

"Not south to New Jersey," Hopper said grimly. "South." He pointed to the frozen earth beneath his paws. "Into the subway tunnels."

To Hopper's surprise, when Firren spoke again, her ordinarily brave voice trembled. "We're the only ones who can save Pup. And we have to go back to the tunnels to do it."

Hopper felt dizzy; he half imagined he could taste the dust and mildew of the tunnels on the back of his tongue. It made him queasy. What if he failed again? What if he went to save Pup and succeeded only in making things worse?

He told himself to ignore the grip of responsibility, to put the memories of being the Chosen One out of his mind forever and live happily in the warm, cozy stockroom behind Bellissimo's Deli. But he loved his brother, and he was still the son of Dodger, who had fought to make the tunnels safe and had believed so strongly in freedom that he'd made an enormous personal sacrifice in pursuit of it.

Sacrifice. Hopper understood now that sacrifice was the name given to a monumentally unselfish deed. Oddly, it was also the word used to describe what Titus had done—the act of condemning the innocent to benefit those in power. It was a single word to define two completely opposite ideas.

Hopper was starting to see that the bigger the idea,

the more likely it was to be double edged, like a rapier or long sword. Survival and justice, choice and destiny, power and responsibility—all weighty, complicated concepts, inextricable pairs in which each pivoted on the existence of the other. The result, he realized, was an intricate web of giving and taking, winning and losing, risk and reward. Nature was made up of an endless mesh of complex notions woven in and out of one another, like the strong, spidery cables that supported the majestic Brooklyn Bridge. Opposite but intertwined.

Like catch and release.

Above and below.

Hopper had never been so conflicted. His heart screamed out for Pup, but at the same time he couldn't imagine himself returning to the site of his greatest loss. He wiped at a tear that had already turned cold in the white fur around his eye.

"I can't do it," he said softly. "I couldn't bear going back to the place where Zucker died. I want to save Pup, but I don't think I could stand it if he refused my help." He looked to Firren, his whiskers quivering. "Besides, would we even stand a chance?" he asked warily. "Just the two of us?"

"It's not just you two," said Ace, a look of gritty determination in his peridot-colored eyes. "It's me, too. I'm in."

"So am I," said Valky. "Hopper, you fought those

cats to defend my home. I'd be honored to help you find your brother."

"We'll go too," said Kidd. "You saved us from the mop. Consider us part of your team."

Hopper looked from the athletes to the kindhearted feline to the warrior whom he trusted and adored as much as he loved Pup.

"But I failed," he murmured. "I failed so utterly and completely. If I were to fail in saving Pup, I truly don't think I could bear it."

"If you don't try," Ace said wisely, "then you've done something worse than fail. You've quit."

They were quiet for a long moment, with only the sound of the growing wind in the ice-crusted grass to interrupt the charged silence.

And suddenly he heard Zucker's voice in his head. *I believed you were my old friend's kid. And that was all I needed to know in order to put my faith in* you.

Zucker had believed in Hopper before Hopper had believed in himself. And now, once again, when he was suffering the pain of doubt and dread, he had others who would put their faith in him, in his mission— Ace and Valky and the basketball rats. Hopper had earned their faith by standing up to protect them, and now they were prepared to do the same for him.

Hopper still wasn't absolutely sure he deserved such kindness, but he would accept it. For Pup.

"Okay," he said. "We go back. We save Pup."

"Excellent!" Firren crooked a grin at him. "And as long as we're going back anyway . . ."

Hopper laughed. "As long as we're going back anyway . . . we continue the fight against Felina. We do whatever we can, in the absence of Atlantia, to protect the rodents who are still at the mercy of Felina and her ferals."

"Sounds like a plan," said Ace. "Let's give that white nightmare exactly what she has coming to her."

"We're going to need weapons," said Firren. "Any ideas?"

Hopper remembered the flat metal objects Carroll had called keys, and quickly explained. "If the tips were sharpened, say against a stone, they'd be terrific weapons."

He quickly sent the basketball rats out into the grasslands on a quest for as many of these jagged human articles as they could find.

Hopper felt a spark of confidence igniting deep within himself. He was ready to fight for the tunnel world he missed so much. Because although he did not have a thundering battalion of soldiers to defend him, he had something much better.

He had friends. Brave ones. Loyal ones. Friends who would stand beside him, come what may. And no army could be mightier than that.

CHAPTER SIXTEEN

Firren said, in the Samsonite fortress, that the rebel cause was back to where it had started. And now so am I ... in many ways.

I have been Pinkie's prisoner for days now, during which she has mostly ignored me. I am being held in the very locomotive where, not long past, I would come to seek refuge. But I have not been returned to my comfortable accommodations in the smokestack, the private haven where the Mūs once saw fit to house their mystical guide and spiritual leader. This time Pinkie the Chosen has chained me by my waist to the guts of the engine, with all its cranks and clockworks.

I am happy to say that I am her only captive.

On our trek from the fortress Firren the warrior ran true to form. Pinkie was distracted, telling the story of Pup's defection, and Firren, ever the strategist, took advantage of our captor's lapse in focus. She fought the members of Pinkie's personal guard and escaped them, disappearing into the tunnels, where she will ... well, I can only guess at what she will do from there. Perhaps she plans to find her band of mighty Rangers, assuming any have survived. Or maybe she will go single-handedly to find Felina's lair and face the ferocious cat alone. I do know this: she will not merely hide in the darkness and do nothing. That is not in her nature. Nor is it her destiny. Firren was designed for braver things than that.

As she sprinted away, her familiar battle call ringing in her wake, I called out to her a message:

"Go look into the face of an old friend, for it is there that your instructions await."

I can only hope she heard my words and made the connection.

Pinkie stands before me now, for the first time since our return to the village.

"Why do you wear that tattered cloak?" she demands to know. "If you are supposed to be so great and wondrous, why don't you wear a shimmering cape of gold like I do?"

"I wear this cloak to maintain my anonymity," I reply. "I work in service of the common rodent, I seek to be of solace to the lost and lowly ones, and to provide guidance to those who cannot choose the right road on their own. One does not need cloth of gold for that."

Pinkie rolls her eyes. "I think I might puke."

"I'm sorry if my mission offends you."

She reaches down to tug at the torn hem of my blue felt cloak. "It's ripped. I guess that explains the scrap I found in the smokestack."

"I found this cloth after the Atlantian exodus. I believe it was once a cherished human artifact, but it was misplaced and trampled when the rodents fled the city. I found it in the dirt and used what was left of it to make myself a hooded robe."

"There is writing on it," she observes. "'Brooklyn. 1955.' Will you interpret these words and use them as part of your teachings? Will you add them to your Sacred Book in a way that suits your purpose?"

"Will you allow me to?"

"Not on your life."

"Then I suppose I will not."

Pinkie paces half the length of the engine-room floor; her claws clack against it, the embroidered edge of her pink-trimmed gown makes a sound like whispered secrets.

"Here is what I want you to do," she says. "I have already gathered paper from the tunnel. You and I both know it is just more human garbage, but once you scrawl something on it, it will become revered as the newest prophecy from the wise and beloved La Rocha."

"What do you desire me to write upon these pages?"

"You will write that the Mūs are to follow me as their leader. What I say goes. No one is to challenge me, ever. Pinkie is the one true leader of this clan, and under my rule we will never again band with any scruffy outsiders for purposes of war or peace. Then I will enjoy complete and absolute authority."

"And what will you do with it? Commission more golden attire?"

"I will be in charge."

"Yes, but to what end?"

She gives me a scathing look. "Have you ever been powerless?" Her eyes flash with dark humor. "Other than right now, I mean."

"I have been at the mercy of forces stronger than myself, yes."

"It's not fun, is it? In fact, it's miserable, being without power. Waiting in a pile of aspen shavings, wondering which of your loved ones might be snatched away by some fat human fist, or worse . . ."

She trails off.

"Worse?" I venture quietly, although I know exactly what she is thinking. "What is worse than a loved one being stolen?"

"A loved one creeping off at dawn, taking his warmth, taking his protection, and leaving you with nothing, that's what. I was new and frightened. I begged him, 'Papa, please don't go,' but he said he had a job to do. He promised there would be great things ahead for Pup and Hopper and me when we came to live among the Mūs. But I guess he didn't plan on being part of that promise."

The hurt she feels seems to emanate from her, like the burning rays of an angry upland sun.

I hesitate before I pose my next question. "What if I refuse to write you this new prophecy you demand of me? What then?"

She glares. "If you do not make this revelation, I will destroy you."

As she makes this threat, her voice is calm, but there is something in her bearing that betrays her. A jerk of her tail, a quiver in her paws. So she is not yet the ruthless tyrant she aspires to be. She is not lost to us entirely; she only plays at brutality.

There is decency in Pinkie still. It is buried deep beneath the anger and distrust, but it is in there. She is still her father's daughter, her brother's sister. She is afraid, but she has goodness in her broken mouse heart.

And I know that there is only one way to draw it out.

If it is a revelation she wants, it is a revelation she shall have.

I reach for my hood.

CHAPTER SEVENTEEN

IT WASN'T LONG BEFORE Julius, Kidd, Dawkins, and the others returned, each toting a jangling ring of lost keys. Firren set about teaching them to hone the tips of these otherwise harmless metal objects into lethal points simply by grinding them against stones.

"How do we get into these subway tunnels?" Valky asked.

"Just like the humans do," said Hopper. "We go to the station and make our way downward."

Ace pointed out that the closest station to Brooklyn Bridge Park would be Clark Street, but Hopper decided they should travel the extra distance to Atlantic Avenue, since he knew for certain there was an easy way into the tunnels through the hole in the wall.

Easy if you didn't mind falling a zillion miles and landing hard in the dirt.

For hours the ringing of stones pounding metal filled the air. As the daylight began to fade from the sky, Valky found a book of matches and lit a small campfire. In the glow of its flickering flames Firren taught her new, upland band of rebels the basics of swordsmanship. No one was surprised when the basketball rats proved to be as gifted with blades as they were with a ball. They even taught Firren a very useful strategy called the full-court press.

At twilight the lights began to come on in the windows of the tremendous buildings across the river—a place Ace identified as Manhattan—and Hopper began to notice a change in the atmosphere. The temperature was dropping quickly, and the world took on a wintry smell, a scent that Hopper did not recognize. It made the air damp and heavy.

"Snow," said Valky. "Coming soon. Gonna be a big one."

"A big what?" asked Hopper.

"Storm," Valky clarified, his fur bristling. "The sooner we get to that subway station, the better."

Hopper looked around at the eager, determined animals who had united on his behalf. He saw their arsenal of key swords glinting in the firelight; he saw Ace's sleek black coat, which made him nearly invisible in the dusky light. And he wondered:

Would they really be able to find Pup, and possibly even defeat a vicious enemy?

He desperately wanted it to be so, but he really couldn't say for sure.

All he could do was hope.

Evening came in earnest and with it a bitter wind. Under the frosty canopy of sky Hopper sat quietly beside Ace and looked out at the East River.

More lights bloomed in the windows of the tall buildings across the water and shimmered on its cold surface.

"Promise me something, Hopper," said the cat, absently flexing his claws. "If we do get the opportunity to take down the feral queen, you'll allow me the privilege of removing that collar from around her neck."

Hopper eyed his friend curiously. "Sure," he said. "But why?"

"I have my reasons," Ace replied in an icy tone.

Behind them Firren was busy familiarizing Valky and the basketball rats with the lay of the land down below. She'd scratched a crude map into the frozen dirt and was pointing out the area where she believed Felina's lair was located and all the possible routes a determined Pup might employ to discover it. She also showed them the spot where Atlantia had once stood and, with any luck, would stand again, and marked off many of the Rangers' favorite hiding places. Hopper knew, although Firren hadn't said so directly, that she was worried for her rebel band's safety and that she hoped no harm would come to them before she returned.

Hopper's gaze was drawn upward from the river by a hazy smudge of brilliance in the sky; it seemed to be caught in the metal web of the Brooklyn Bridge. There was something awesome and ethereal about it, this round white glow, floating there in space.

"What's that?" he asked, pointing.

"That's the moon," said Ace. "It's usually much brighter. The snow clouds are hiding it tonight."

Hopper had never seen the moon when he'd lived

in the pet shop, and he found himself wishing he'd paid more attention to things like that. "How do you get there?" he asked. "To the moon, I mean."

Ace shrugged. "I don't know. By taxi maybe."

Now something else caught Hopper's eye—a white fleck, swirling downward through the dark sky. It spun and hovered and dipped and rose, weightlessly graceful, aimless and lovely, drifting and twirling. Another fleck of white followed it. Then another.

For a moment Hopper wondered if the moon was breaking into tiny pieces and sprinkling itself over Brooklyn Bridge Park. But when one of the delicate flakes landed on his nose and sent a pleasant chill through him, he knew that these icy specks were not shards of broken moon.

He reached out and caught a glistening flake. It was pure white, crystalline and cold. Lying flat, it was as big as his paw, all lacy angles and intersecting zigzags. It was stunning to look at, and although Hopper knew he should fear it, at the moment he was too awed by its beauty.

"Snow," he whispered.

The jewel-like flake melted away with the word, but when he looked down at the grass, he saw that several of them had already created a thin, sparkling white coating on the ground around his paws. So this was how snow worked—small, singular elements coming together to create a larger, powerful force.

"Look, Ace," Hopper cried delightedly, catching a second flake and holding it out to show him. "It's snowing!"

But when he looked up into his friend's green eyes, he realized that Ace was not delighted by the pretty flake.

Not delighted at all.

Hopper wasn't the only one who'd seen the snowflakes. Valky had noticed too and was hustling to get the basketball rodents moving.

"We've got to get ahead of it," the chipmunk advised. "We can't be traveling at the height of the storm."

"Wait," said Hopper. "I want to say good-bye to Carroll."

"There's no time," said Ace. "Snow is a formidable enemy. The sooner we get to Atlantic Avenue station, the better off we will be."

Looking down at the grass, Hopper saw that Ace was right; the gentle dusting was quickly becoming a heavy blanket around his paws. The sky was now filled with swirling flakes, and the wind had grown stronger.

He put his paw in Firren's and joined the small procession—Ace, Valky, and the nine Barclays rats—as they trotted down Furman Street to the intersection of Atlantic. The snow was falling faster and harder with every passing second.

"At this rate," said Ace, shouting to be heard above the howling of the wind, "I don't think we'll make it to the station before the worst of the storm hits."

"We're going to need to find shelter," Valky agreed. "Any ideas?"

"Can't go to the deli. The Bellissimo brothers wouldn't appreciate ten rats, a mouse, and a chipmunk hunkered down in their back room. Besides, they lock up at night. There's no way in."

Hopper turned to Firren, whose teeth had begun to chatter; her delicate whiskers were already coated with ice. He realized with a pang of terror that if they didn't find some place to wait out the storm, they would all freeze to death. His heart began to race, like it had so many times before, beginning on the day he and his family escaped their cozy cage.

The cage . . .

"I know where we can go!" he cried, galloping up to the front of the line. "Everybody follow me."

Without so much as a moment's hesitation, they did.

They didn't stop running until they reached Keep's shop. The red-and-gold letters on the window were nearly obscured by the snow, but Hopper recognized the place instantly. "We're here!" he announced.

Valky looked up at the tall glass door with a forlorn look. "How will we get in?" she asked.

Hopper went to the place in the wall where he remembered seeing the crumbling mortar. It was only partially blocked by the snow that had fallen, but with so many paws digging together it wasn't long before the gap between the bricks was visible.

"Who says you can't go home again?" Hopper quipped.

Shivering, the rats began to squeeze one by one through the tiny opening.

"Uh-oh," said Hopper, looking up at Ace. "I think we have a problem."

Ace laughed. "I was wondering when you were going to figure that out."

"What are you going to do?" asked Hopper, panic rising in him like the growing drifts of snow sweeping up against the outer walls of the shop.

"Don't worry about me," Ace assured him. "I'm a Brooklyn cat. I'll find someplace warm for the night and I'll meet you at the station in the morning."

"Be careful," said Hopper. His voice cracked when he added, "And say good-bye to Capone for me."

"How about I just tell him you'll see him next time you come upland for a visit?"

Hopper gulped and smiled. "Yes. Tell him that."

"I'll see if I can gather some provisions from the deli when they open at sunrise," said Ace with a grin. "Think you can fight with a belly full of eggplant?"

"I think I can *win* with a belly full of eggplant!"

Ace gave him a wink, then ducked his pointy ears into the wind and took off, his black coat a shining shadow against the growing expanse of white.

Hopper watched until his friend disappeared

around the corner, then took a deep breath and crawled through the gap in the mortar.

Into the pet shop.

Into his past.

Even empty, the place was filled with the lingering scents of birds, reptiles, and rodents. Hopper breathed deeply, his mind swimming with the earliest recollections of his life.

"What is this place?" Julius asked.

"I lived here once," Hopper explained. "With my mother, my brother, and my sister." He closed his eyes to conjure a memory of a furry white circle and a softly thrumming heartbeat. "And my father," he added in a whisper.

A few half-crushed boxes littered the space; a forgotten housebreaking pad, a squeaky toy, and an electrical extension cord. For all Hopper knew, it was the same one he and Pinkie had skittered down on their flight from Keep's counter the night they escaped.

Chilled and exhausted, Valky quickly found a spot away from the draft coming through the gap in the wall and snuggled into a little tan-and-black ball. The rats settled themselves into nooks and corners, and soon the shop fell silent but for the sound of the rodents snoring softly.

"I'm going to turn in too," said Firren. "Big day tomorrow."

"Yes. Big day." Hopper was about to curl up himself when he spied a plaid scrap of material on the floor. He moved toward it and his nose twitched. He could smell Keep's human scent on it; it was the pocket that had gotten torn off his shirt the day Hopper and his cagemates climbed out of their cage using the shopkeeper's pudgy arm.

He picked up the fraying square of material and tucked it into his own pocket. Of all the scraps he'd collected so far, he knew that this one, above all, was the most meaningful. Because this scrap represented the first time that Hopper had dared to believe in himself. Even if he hadn't understood it at the time, that rainy morning when he and Pinkie toppled their cardboard prison was the day a great change had begun.

The day his tiny mouse heart had felt the very first stirrings of courage.

Hopper crossed the cement floor, the scraping of his claws echoing into the emptiness. As he snuggled beside Firren, he knew that there would be no sound of coins in the money machine to break the silence tonight, though Keep's voice still seemed to whisper through the gloom.

Birds . . . check. Felines . . . check.

Tonight Hopper would not drift off to the soft tweeting of the canaries in their cages.

Reptiles and amphibians . . . check, check.

Nor would he be lulled by the soothing rhythm of bubbling aquariums. Tonight he would simply be pressed into a deep, dreamless sleep by an exhaustion that threatened to overwhelm him.

Outside the wind howled and hollered and the snow pattered against the window. Hopper closed his eyes and felt his own history enfold him. Moments, good and bad, came out of the past to welcome him home, and to wish him luck on his journey; to remind him of where he had come from and to urge him onward to wherever his heart would take him.

It was a bittersweet peace that settled over Brooklyn Small Pet Supply as the Chosen One yawned and sighed.

Seconds later he was fast asleep.

Rodents . . .

Check.

Hopper awoke to a loud, metallic scraping sound. At first he imagined it was the scream of metal subway wheels braking on the track. But when he opened his eyes and saw the sunlight filtering through the big window, he remembered where he was.

"Look how deep it is!" cried Dawkins, who'd climbed onto Keep's counter and was pressing his nose against the window glass.

The others joined Dawkins on the countertop to see the snow for themselves. Hopper's eyes went round at the sight of so much dazzling, frosty white. Last night the surface of the snow had been powdery, but this morning there appeared to be a crisp glaze of thin ice everywhere. It glistened under an endless sky of pristine blue. He was sure Brooklyn had never looked more elegant. Looking down, he saw that the snow had drifted as high as the mail slot in Keep's front door; it sloped in a steep curve from the bottom edge of the brass flap all the way to the far side of the sidewalk.

"How are we going to get out of here?" asked Kidd. "We can't go out the way we came in. The snow's all piled up against the wall, and it's blocking the broken place."

"Could we tunnel through?" Valky suggested.

"Doubt it," said Julius. "We'd either freeze or suffocate before we got very far."

Outside the wind swept along the sidewalk, causing the metal flap of the mail slot to swing back and forth; the hollow clank it made echoed through the shop as the flap flew open, letting the cold air in before banging shut again.

Hopper's eyes shot to the mail slot, then moved down the glass door to the sloping drift outside.

"I have an idea," he said.

At first the rodents looked as if they were afraid he'd lost his mind.

"You want us to jump through that little slot in the

door and slide down that snowdrift?" said Julius.

"Yes," said Hopper.

"I think it could work," said Valky. "I've seen the humans do it. They call it sledding." He frowned. "Of course, the humans actually have *sleds*."

"What if we sink into it?" Dawkins reasoned. "Last night it seemed lighter than air. Fluffy. What if it won't hold us?"

"It's iced over now," Hopper pointed out. "I'm sure it will support our weight if we go one at a time. Besides, we'll be moving so fast we won't have time to fall through."

"*That* fails to relieve my concerns," grumbled Julius.

"I like the sliding plan," said Firren, "but how do you propose we get up to the slot? Climbing a flat glass surface is impossible."

Hopper grinned; he'd already thought of that. He pointed to the broom propped in the corner. It was the same broom that had facilitated his first exit from Brooklyn Small Pet Supply . . . with a little help from Keep.

"We can drag the broom to the door and stick the wooden end through the slot. Then we can climb up the handle and jump."

"Jump," Julius said with a sigh. "Wonderful."

"It's our only option," said Firren. "I say we give it a try."

Even with all twelve rodents working together,

dragging the broom across the shop was difficult. It was heavy and cumbersome, and since the brass flap opened in, they had to time it just so with the gusting wind in order to poke the tip of the handle through.

The rats grunted and heaved, and Hopper's muscles burned as he used all his strength to push the weighty handle upward. After a few near misses they were able to balance the broom on the rim of the slot. The handle rose up to the center of the door in a gentle incline.

"Now listen," said Hopper. "If for any reason we get separated, we'll meet at the subway station. Ace might already be waiting there when we arrive."

He gave them directions to the Atlantic Avenue Barclays Center stop.

"Who's going first?" asked Firren.

"I will," said Valky, positioning himself carefully on the narrow wooden handle. It wobbled, but the chipmunk remained undaunted. He scrambled quickly to the top, then squeezed under the brass flap. "Here goes!"

The others looked up from the floor, holding their breath as Valky pushed off the rim of the mail slot with his hind paws and sailed outward into the atmosphere.

"Wooooooo-hoooooooo!" cried Valky when his striped bottom landed on the frozen surface of the drift. He was off, sliding and swooshing. The wind whipped his tail and blew his tiny ears back. Seconds later he was spinning to a stop, safe on the snowy sidewalk.

"I'm next," cried Kidd, scampering up the broom

handle. He ducked under the flap and sprang forward, pumping his paws happily above his head as he swooped down the slope.

Julius actually did a front somersault in the air and slid down on his belly.

Hopper watched as rat after rat scrambled up the wooden ramp and launched himself out into the cold. And with each exhilarated leap, with every gleeful ride down the icy drift, Hopper began to feel smaller.

And more afraid.

His stomach churned as he listened to the muffled shouts of joy through the glass door. His friends cheered and celebrated, but he shared none of their excitement.

What had he been thinking? How could he possibly go back to those sinister, unforgiving tunnels? He loved them and hated them, yearned for them even as he loathed the thought of setting one paw back into that gloom. Down there, in the hole in the world where Atlantia lay in ruins, was where Hopper had failed to save Zucker. What in the name of La Rocha could ever have made him think he would have any better luck with Pup?

Now Firren was scrambling onto the straw head of the broom, preparing to climb the handle for her jump. She moved gracefully, with skill and agility, every step bringing her closer to the mail slot.

Closer to the Atlantic Avenue station.

Closer to the tunnels.

CHAPTER EIGHTEEN

"NO!" HOPPER SHRIEKED.

Firren was so startled by this unexpected outburst that she lost her footing and bobbled. Her struggle to hang on set the precariously placed broom bouncing, until finally it slid from its perch on the edge of the opening. The handle clattered to the floor, taking Firren with it.

Hopper gasped.

But Firren had already sprung to her feet and was brushing the dust from her tunic. She gaped at Hopper. "What was that all about?"

"Are you all right?" he asked sheepishly.

"I'm fine. I've fallen from much greater heights than that." Firren cocked her head. "But why did you shout like that? Why didn't you want me to go?"

Hopper buried his face in his paws. "Because I'm terrified," he said.

Firren said nothing for a long moment. Then Hopper sensed her making her way to the glass door. He heard her tap on it to get the attention of the rats outside. "Go ahead," she called loudly. "We'll catch up."

"No we won't," came Hopper's voice through his paws as Firren returned to put an arm around him.

"You're remembering it all, aren't you?" she whispered.

"Yes." Hopper stayed hidden behind his paws and nodded. The images of bleeding rodents and burning barracks and exterminators in pounding boots had all come flooding back to him. "I don't want to go back to the scene of my failure," he confessed. "I don't want to fail all over again."

"You think you failed?"

"Don't you?" Hopper lifted his face and blinked at her. "You do recall the part about Zucker dying and the city being decimated, right?"

"First of all," said Firren, "we don't know for certain that Zucker is dead."

"He's dead." Hopper sighed. "Oh, he's dead. Dead!"

"Stop that," said Firren, giving him a shake.

Hopper stopped.

"The answer is yes," said Firren calmly. "I *do* recall the downside of our plan. But I also recall the part about you making it possible for all those imprisoned rodents to escape the camps. You were the guiding force that brought down an evil regime."

"Yes, I know that," said Hopper. "But I'm talking about the part that came after. The exodus and Pinkie refusing to grant us her protection."

"None of that was your fault," Firren assured him.

Hopper scowled. He still wasn't convinced.

"Did you notice I said 'our plan'? You were counting on us—Zucker and the soldiers and me—as much as we were counting on you. You can't shoulder all the blame yourself. I'm a far more seasoned rebel than you are. I should have foreseen that the rodents would panic and run, and the city would get looted and Titus would escape."

"How could you have foreseen that?"

Firren smiled. "I couldn't. See? That's my point. No one could. Not me, not Zucker, not Garfield or Pritchard or Marcy's brothers. And not you. We acted with pure hearts. And we did achieve some good. We just aren't finished yet." She patted his back. "I know this must be scary for you."

"It's more than scary," grumbled Hopper. "It's sickening. I risked my life, and what did I get? Pinkie hates me, and Pup is a lost cause, and Zucker is probably gone forever."

"If he is, staying upland won't bring him back." Firren gave the Chosen One a patient smile. "I know you, Hopper. If you give up now, if you don't at least try to save Pup from this crazy scheme of his to fight Felina, you'll never forgive yourself."

"I know," Hopper muttered. "But why did I have to be the one with a destiny?"

Firren laughed. "Hopper, everyone has a destiny! Yours just happens to be a little more exciting than most. I think you know what you have to do, and I believe if we all work together, it will all be okay in the end."

"And what if it's not okay?"

"Then it's not the end." Firren clutched his paw in

hers. "That's the thing about destiny, Hopper. There's no deadline, no expiration date. You just have to keep trying until you make the difference you hope to make . . . until you make things turn out the way you know in your heart they should."

Hopper closed his eyes and pictured Zucker. He wished he could picture his father beyond the white circle of fur, but all he could manage was the memory of a warm pelt and steady heartbeat.

It was enough.

He took a deep breath. "I'm ready," he said, his voice clear and confident in the empty shop. "Let's go."

"Uh, yeah . . ." Firren wrinkled her nose. "About that . . ."

Hopper followed her smart black eyes to where the broom lay on the floor. He understood that they'd never be able to lift it themselves.

They were stuck.

It was all he could do to keep from screaming. To have come this far—only to see it all end here, back where he started . . . a prisoner in Keep's shop . . . it was infuriating!

He scanned the shop for something else that might work. Not the housebreaking pad, and certainly not the squeaky toy.

Then his eyes landed on the extension cord and an idea began to form. The cord was plenty long enough to reach the slot. As with the broom handle, if he timed it properly, when the next gust of wind opened the metal flap, he might be able to toss the plug end as high as the slot. If the flap closed on it, it might hold tightly enough for him and Firren to shinny up the wire.

He dragged the cord to the door, cocked his arm, and fixed his gaze on the narrow slot. When the metal flap rattled open, he sent the plug sailing. But the flap banged closed and the plug pinged off it, dropping back to the cement floor.

Hopper grumbled and picked it up, waiting for another gust. It came soon enough, and once again he tossed the plug.

This time the flap bit down on it and held it in place. Hopeful, Hopper reached for the dangling cord and gave it a firm tug. Unfortunately, the cord came away and dropped back to the floor.

"You can do it, Hopper," said Firren. "Just throw a little bit harder, so the end falls over the outer edge. If it catches right, it'll anchor itself in place."

Inspired by her confidence, Hopper again bent his elbow and gripped the plug. He held it poised above his shoulder, listening to the howling of the wind.

When the flap again blew inward, Hopper sent the plug flying. . . . It zoomed up, through, and out the other side! The metal prongs caught on the outer lip of the slot and stuck there.

He tested its hold with a couple of firm pulls on the cord. Sturdy.

"You go first," he told Firren. What he didn't mention was that he wanted to be there on the floor to catch her if the prongs gave way.

Firren took hold of the cord to begin her climb. Every time the wind blew, the wire trembled violently, but she held fast and made it to the top. She flung her hind legs over the side and waited.

Hopper took a deep breath and grasped the cord. He made quick work of pulling himself up the length of it, grasping and climbing, jerking and rising. He reached the top just as an enormous, growling monster lumbered up the snow-clogged street. It had a single orange claw where its snout should be, and Hopper realized this was the beast that was responsible for the scraping sound that had awoken him. It had blinking yellow eyes and a logo painted on the side:

BROOKLYN PLOWING
"SNOWBODY" DOES IT BETTER!

He also realized that Firren was shivering.

"You okay?" he asked.

"Just a little ch-ch-chilly," she said, forcing a smile. But Hopper knew that she wasn't used to the winter elements, having lived her whole life in the tunnels. For that matter, neither was he. He was beginning to dread the long, icy walk to the subway station.

Now the clawed creature pulled over to the curb,

where it ground to a halt, spitting out dark clouds of smoke from its hindquarters as it idled.

Hopper was suddenly thinking back to the first time he had ridden a speeding subway train. It had been dangerous and terrifying.

And it had been the ride of a lifetime.

Maybe he and Firren could shorten their cold journey by taking a similarly dangerous and terrifying ride . . . on that growling, yellow-eyed monster.

"Do you trust me?" he asked.

Firren's answer was immediate. "Implicitly."

"Good." He grasped her trembling paw, sent up a silent prayer to La Rocha, and pushed away from the mail slot. They flew down the snowdrift together, crying out with delight the entire way.

"That was exhilarating!" Firren said breathlessly. "Now what?"

Hopper pointed to the snowplow. "We ride."

There was a built-in ledge, like a step, beneath the door of the truck. They climbed onto it just as the monster roared to life.

"La Rocha, if you're watching . . . ," called Hopper, "protect us on this ride!" He gave Firren a quizzical look. "He does that sort of thing, right?"

"Let's hope so," said Firren, grinning, as the plow pulled away from the curb.

They were off!

Hopper and Firren arrived at the Atlantic Avenue station chilled but unharmed. They jumped off their perch just as the slow-moving beast plodded its way past the street-level entrance to the subway terminal.

Dashing across the sidewalk, Hopper was relieved to find there were very few humans about. He was even more relieved to see several familiar faces waiting for them. Valky and the Barclays rats were huddled against the outer wall of the station, looking weary and cold.

"What's wrong?" asked Hopper when he saw the harried expression on their faces.

Valky explained that although the slide down the snowdrift had been fun, the ensuing trek through the snowy streets had been grueling and fraught with all manner of peril. Frankly, the chipmunk was surprised they'd all arrived in one piece. There had been several moments when he doubted they would.

"And there's something else . . . ," Dawkins broached.

It took Hopper only a second to understand the inference. His stomach plummeted. "Where's Ace?"

Valky replied with a grim shrug.

Hopper gulped, eyes searching, heart thudding. "What happened?"

"We don't know," said Kidd. "He was traveling when the storm was at its worst."

The blood drained from Hopper's face. "So he could be lost . . . or stuck in a drift or . . ."

Hopper felt instantly sick. Last night the snow and the wind had been brutal. How low had the temperature dropped during the night? Surely, a cat could not endure such a deep freeze! And even if he had made it through the night, this morning there would have been shovels to dodge and towering snowbanks to navigate. Trembling, Hopper thought of his recent snowplow ride, picturing the way that claw had pushed the deep snow into densely packed mountains. If some small animal had accidentally stumbled into its path . . .

He shuddered violently, willing the image out of his head. Then he began to shout. "Ace! Ace, where are you?!"

"It's no use," Julius said with a sigh. "We've been calling for him since we got here. He isn't nearby."

"But we have to find him!"

"I don't see how," said Valky, his voice cracking. "It would be madness to venture back out into that snowy mess."

Hopper's mind reeled. He knew Valky was right. They couldn't go back into the snow to search for Ace without endangering their own lives, and although he was willing to do that himself, he couldn't ask his new friends to do the same.

He turned to Firren, to see if she might have an idea, and immediately shaded his eyes against the blinding glare of the sun reflecting off her sword handle. The reflection of light threw shimmering, trembling prisms across the white snow.

Hopper had seen colors shimmer like that before.

On Pilot's feathers.

Surely, Pilot would be more than willing to help their friend. He'd even said as much to Ace: *I owe you one.*

And Ace had said, *You know the signal, right? Three short, three long, three short.*

Hopper took a deep breath and began to whistle with every ounce of air in his tiny lungs. He whistled as loud and as hard as he could—three short blasts, three long ones, three short again.

"What's he doing?" asked Julius. The other rats were looking at Hopper as though he were insane.

But Firren, the warrior, understood. "He's sending out a call for help," she explained. "An SOS."

"To whom?" asked Kidd.

"I have no idea," said Firren. "But let's hope it works."

Once more Hopper filled his chest with oxygen and whistled, pushing the piercing, high-pitched sound out into the world with all the might he could muster. Three short, three long, three short.

This time the effort left him dizzy and light-headed.

Valky noticed and immediately and took up the cause, sending his own powerful whistle slicing into the atmosphere. *Fwee, fwee, fwee. Fweeeeee, fweeeeee, fweeeeee. Fwee, fwee, fwee.*

Hopper cocked his ear toward the vast blue sky. He heard a ruffling sound, a ragged flapping, a beating of feathers against the wind.

In the next second Pilot swooped down to join them on the sidewalk.

"Your wing!" cried Hopper. "It's healed."

Pilot grimaced. "Not completely, but it works. What do you need?"

Hopper quickly explained that Ace had gone missing and they hoped Pilot would be willing to execute an aerial search.

"Anything to help Ace," Pilot said, his head bobbing, his tone determined and sincere. "Anything."

Hopper told the pigeon that if he found Ace—*when* he found him—he should report that Hopper and the others were safe and heading into the tunnels. "And please ask him to join us there. That is, if he's . . ." Hopper gulped and chose his next word carefully. "Able."

They all watched as the half-healed bird lifted off into the bright blue sky.

"If anyone can find him," Valky assured Hopper, "Pilot can."

If anyone could find him.

Still, Valky's optimism made Hopper feel a little bit better, and he was further encouraged when he recalled how Ace's black coat had made him nearly invisible at dusk. Like two edges of a single sword,

Ace's dark fur would have the opposite effect against the pure-white snow, making him that much easier to spot from the air.

Hopper kept his eyes on the sky until Pilot's gray tail feathers vanished into the infinite sweep of brilliant blue, and sent up a whispered request for any mystical, magical assistance La Rocha might be able to offer.

Then he led the rodents down to the platform and headed for the gap between the wall and the floor.

They would drop themselves through that portal, from the above to the below, out of the daylight and into the darkness.

And they would continue their journey onward, to whatever remained of Atlantia.

CHAPTER NINETEEN

HOPPER THOUGHT HE MUST be dreaming.

As they reached the rolling crest from which Zucker had given him his first glimpse of Atlantia, he'd prepared himself to look not upon the stunning spectacle of spires and rooftops he'd marveled at then, but rather to view only a desolate wasteland left behind by war and exterminators.

What he saw was the beginnings of a whole new skyline—a new Atlantia rising up from its own ashes. Hopper blinked hard in an attempt to dispel the image he was sure was a mirage. But when he looked again, he was met with the same incredible scene.

The city was sprouting up before his eyes.

"What in the world is going on down there?" he asked breathlessly.

Firren shook her head. "I have no idea. It looks as if someone's rebuilding the city."

It had been only a short time since they'd landed in the tunnels. As Hopper had expected, the uplanders had been rendered speechless by their first sight of the endless darkness, by the thickness of the air and the smells that seemed to cling to the walls and rise up from the dirt and stones. It wasn't long before a familiar rumble began to shake the planet, and Hopper and Firren quickly directed the rodents off the metal rails of the tracks. When the subway train came screaming past, they were, of course, terrified and amazed. Hopper took a mischievous sort of pride in their shock. The power of the serpentine machine and his understanding of it were just part of what made the tunnels home. He knew his friends were used to the fresh breezes of Brooklyn Bridge Park and the glittering lights of the Barclays Center. But to him the subway tunnels were just as inviting.

"Welcome to my world," he'd said with a grin as they set out on their march.

But now he could only gawk in amazement himself at the sight of new rooflines and nearly repaired chimneys. Someone was rebuilding! And it seemed a great dealt of progress had been made in a relatively short period of time. Thrilled and curious, Hopper took one eager step forward, but a firm paw on his arm jerked him back.

"Wait," said Valky. "What if it's that nasty white cat you told us about? What if she's in there right now, reclaiming your Atlantia for her own diabolical purposes?"

"He's right," Julius agreed. "The place could be crawling with ferals."

Hopper considered this. It was possible that Felina had seen the fall of Atlantia as her opening to take over the once-thriving metropolis. After all, it was a fabulous location, with a solid infrastructure. Even following the raid and the exterminators' wrath, the shell of a beautiful city remained, filled with potential. All Felina would have had to do was bring in her minions to repair the structural damage. That accomplished, she could simply move in, claim Atlantia's magnificent buildings and parks, and of course Titus's opulent palace, as her own. And oh, wouldn't Felina just love *that*? What a fitting symbol of her ultimate victory that would be.

"I guess it could be Felina," Hopper allowed, his eyes suddenly drawn to a flicker of movement in the shadows along the tunnel wall. But his hope outweighed his fear, and he ignored the motion. "But what if it isn't?"

"Isn't Felina?" Firren knit her brow, wary. "What are you thinking, Chosen One?"

"Just that it could be someone else leading the reconstruction."

"Who?"

There! By the wall. A flick of a tail. Someone was approaching. Hopper squinted into the gloom and his heart leaped.

A flash of purple, a silvery embroidered *Z* . . .

The word sprang to his lips straight from his pounding little mouse heart.

"Zucker!"

The prince's name rang through the air as Hopper galloped in the direction of that unmistakable uniform. He could see, as he drew nearer, that the rat was limping badly, his left hind leg dragging. So the prince had been wounded. But he'd made it out of Atlantia alive, and that was all that mattered.

"Zucker!" Hopper called out again.

But when the broad-shouldered rat in the purple vest stumbled out from the shadows, Hopper stopped in his tracks. He felt as if he'd run headfirst into an oncoming subway train. Because while the dark eyes that met his were keenly intelligent and familiar, they were not Zucker's.

"Ketchum?" The name was a hollow croak in Hopper's throat.

The soldier looked at first surprised, then thrilled at the unexpected sight of the Chosen One, safely returned to the tunnels. "Hopper! You're alive."

Despite his injury Ketch caught the stunned mouse in a powerful embrace; the silvery stitching of the *Z* on his tunic pressed against Hopper's cheek.

It took Hopper a moment to collect himself. He'd been so sure it was Zucker that realizing it wasn't nearly cracked his heart in two. It was like losing him all over again. Shaking off his disappointment, Hopper smiled at his friend, glad to see that no truly great harm had come to this valiant soldier.

"I thought you were lost forever," Ketchum gushed.

"So did I," said Hopper. "And I'm so happy to see that you're okay too." His eyes went to the rat's crudely bandaged limb. "You *are* okay, aren't you?"

"Took a cat claw to the leg," said Ketch. "Could probably use some medical attention, but I'm fine."

Hopper frowned at the bloody crust caked on the makeshift bandage and hoped Ketchum wasn't just putting on a brave face.

"What's going on in the city, Ketch? *Who* is rebuilding Atlantia?"

The rest of Hopper's traveling party had joined them now, and Firren stepped forward, her eyes shining with hope. "Is it Zucker? Is the prince alive?"

Ketchum turned away and gave a small shake of his head. "It's difficult to guess. If he were, I'm fairly certain he would have come looking for me."

"True," said Hopper. "What are you doing out here in the tunnels, anyway? Alone!" He dearly hoped the reason wasn't that Garfield and Polhemus and the others had been lost.

"Well, it's all a bit hazy. But I'll tell you what I remember." He turned to face Firren, wincing at the pain in his leg. "When the exterminators left, the other soldiers and I went in to find you and the prince. When we saw neither hide nor hair of either of you, we hoped you two had somehow saved each other."

It was Firren's turn to look away.

"As I said, when the exterminators were gone, the

other soldiers and I went back in on a search-and-recover mission. But the ferals returned. They were wild, half crazed with starvation, and more vicious than ever. Without the hunting ground they aren't enjoying half the amount of food they'd grown used to. They prowl the tunnels more savagely than ever now, but they still aren't satisfied."

Hopper thought of Pup, on his ill-advised quest, and shuddered. It was all he could do to keep from interrupting Ketch and asking if he'd seen him. But Hopper sensed this was a story the soldier needed to tell, so he held his tongue.

"We fought as long as we could," Ketch was saying. "Some tabby got his claws into my leg, but I managed to get away."

"Thank goodness," said Hopper.

"Yes." Ketchum sighed. "But it quickly became clear that continuing to engage would mean certain death for all of us, and we were forced to retreat. We left the cats to do what they would with the dead and those who were nearly thus, because we knew Zucker would want us to see to the safety of the rodents who'd escaped. So we took cover and waited out the massacre."

Hopper closed his eyes. The images that spun in the darkness behind his eyelids were gruesome and nightmarish. He saw the cages as though they were still right there in front of him . . . the torn pelts, the broken paws, the vacant, lifeless eyes.

"One of the cats saw us retreating," Ketchum continued, his tone darkening. "He followed us outside the walls."

"Oh no," Firren gasped.

"What did you do?" asked Valky, mesmerized.

"We scattered. I took the old lady mouse with me. . . . You remember, Beverley? The one who wore that old apron all the time?"

Hopper nodded, glancing again at Ketchum's bandage, with a knot of dread forming in his gut.

"I was bleeding pretty badly, so I could do little more than hobble. And Beverley wasn't much faster. Didn't take long for the cat to realize we were the easy prey. So he came after us. I fought him as best I could, but the pain in my leg was unbearable. The animal had disarmed me and I was helpless. I knew it was the end for me, that the cat was about to devour me, and then . . . then . . ." His voice caught.

"Then what?" Firren prompted gently.

"Beverley threw herself in front of me, shielding me from that monster with her own frail body."

Hopper gasped as he imagined the old mouse in her tattered apron performing such a courageous act.

"I begged her to run," Ketchum said with a haunted look. "But she just smiled and pressed her fragile paw to my shoulder . . . pushing me away!"

How selfless, thought Hopper, brushing the tears from his eyes. *How heroic.* He bowed his head and found himself whispering to La Rocha, asking for his mystical blessing upon the old mouse.

"The cat was utterly perplexed," Ketchum recalled. "This unexpected turn of events threw him for a moment."

"And that gave you time to escape," whispered Julius. "Wow. Talk about teamwork."

Ketchum nodded. "I suppose to him, when it comes to supper, one rodent is as good as another. He was tired from the battle and from what meager fight I had been able to give him, so as I staggered to safety, he didn't chase. He had a perfectly good meal option standing right in front of him, offering herself up without a struggle." Here Ketchum paused to slowly shake his head, then turned a look of bemusement to Hopper. "It was the strangest thing, Chosen One. Beverley was perfectly calm. And I'll never forget what she called out to me as I escaped."

Hopper swallowed hard around the lump in his throat. "What did she say?"

"She said, 'I make this sacrifice with a pure and happy heart. I've lived a good long life. Save yourself.' Then, in one swift movement, the cat dipped his head and Beverley was gone."

Hopper could almost feel the points of the feral's razor-sharp teeth sinking into his own skin. And suddenly Ace's words were repeating in Hopper's mind: *A larger chain of events.*

"When the feral at last took his leave," Ketch went on with a heavy sigh, "I came out of hiding, back to the place where Beverley had given her life in exchange for mine. All that was left behind was this." He reached into his purple vest and withdrew a piece of fabric—it was half of Beverley's familiar apron. "I tore it in two and used some to wrap my wound." He shrugged. "I kept this half too. . . . I really don't know why."

"I do," said Hopper. "May I have that?"

Reverently Ketchum handed him the scrap of material, and Hopper slipped it lovingly into his pocket, beside the pink ribbon, the torn piece of Zucker's tunic, and the rest.

To keep.

To cherish.

To remember.

They allowed a moment of silence for Beverley, then Valky piped up in an optimistic tone. "The good news," he said, "is that *someone* is rebuilding the city."

"But who?" asked Hopper.

The soldier shrugged, taking a cautious step on his wounded limb toward the city. "I don't know," he admitted. "But I'm just as eager as you are to find out."

As they made their way onward to Atlantia (slowly, to accommodate Ketchum's limp), Firren kept sneaking worried glances at his wound.

Hopper was now prepared to ask the question he'd refrained from posing during Ketchum's heroic tale.

"Ketch, do you by any chance happen to know anything regarding my brother Pup's whereabouts?"

The soldier shook his head. "I'm sorry, Chosen One. But I've been in and out of consciousness since the battle, and I've neither seen nor interacted with anyone. I'd only just begun contemplating a trek back toward Atlantia when I noticed your little band approaching. As far as Pup goes, the last I heard, he was in the Mūs village, doing Pinkie's bidding." Ketch gave Hopper a confused look. "Is that no longer the case?"

"The situation has changed dramatically," Firren said, then went on to explain about Pup's plan to face Felina on his own.

They trudged onward, stopping occasionally to allow Ketch to rest, and peering into the dusty gloom for signs of Pup, renegade rodents, and of course lurking ferals. The rats showed Ketchum their newly forged weapons—swords fashioned from car keys and apartment keys and safe-deposit box keys.

The soldier was both amused and impressed. "Once in my younger days I made a staff sling out of a toothpick, some dental floss, and an aggie marble."

A short distance before they reached Atlantia's iron gate, a burly black squirrel stepped out of the darkness wielding a blade. Hopper let out a squeak of alarm, but in the next heartbeat he recognized the shadowy figure.

"Garfield!"

Garfield blinked, then his face lit up. "Chosen One? Firren! Ketch, you're alive."

"Every one of us," Firren confirmed.

Hopper accepted the lieutenant's paw for a firm shake, then choked up when Garfield turned to Ketchum, eyes filled with relief at seeing the friend he feared had been lost. The squirrel offered his comrade a salute, which Ketch returned, swaying on his injured leg. When Garfield noticed the bandage, he immediately placed his shoulder under Ketch's arm and made of himself a crutch to support his fellow soldier.

"Let's get you inside the walls, brother," he said.

"Yes," agreed Ketchum. "Let's."

Hopper swallowed hard and sniffed. This was one of the things he'd missed in his time away from the tunnels. This sense of connection, the unqualified devotion.

Zucker...

"Wait!" Hopper cried. "We're going in? Does that mean it's safe? Felina and her ferals aren't the ones who've commandeered Atlantia?"

"Not by a long shot, Chosen One," said Garfield, a grin appearing on his ordinarily steely face. "Not by a long shot."

It wasn't far now, and as they made their way to the gate, Firren asked about Leetch and her Rangers. "Have you seen them? Are they okay?"

"Well," said Garfield, attempting to sound hopeful, "we have no proof that they *aren't* okay."

It wasn't the answer Firren wanted.

"As I'm sure Ketchum explained, after the exterminators' blitz and the ferals' attack we scattered. Among those who returned were two of your Rangers. They reported that although they did not know for sure, they suspected most of their brethren had gone off into the tunnels to do what they could about protecting any wandering rodents."

This had Firren smiling with pride. "That's what they have been trained to do," she said. "Under current circumstances it's more risky than usual, but with any luck they've been holding their own out there."

She didn't say so, but Hopper was fairly certain that Firren would set out on a mission to locate them, first chance she got. "What of the rest of Zucker's soldiers?" he asked. "And Marcy? Did Marcy survive?"

"Marcy is safe," Garfield assured him. "Although she's been a bit hard to pin down. Occasionally I've seen her with her brothers, patrolling the outer boundaries of the city. Other times"—he shrugged the shoulder that wasn't supporting Ketchum—"she's gone for days. Where she goes and why, I do not know, but this much is clear . . . she's as brave as they come and she's becoming quite the warrior."

Hopper was beyond pleased to hear this. He couldn't imagine where Marcy would be taking herself off to, especially given the state of unrest in the tunnels at the moment, but he knew that she'd always been much tougher than she looked. And smart! He put aside his worry with a fond thought for the pretty maid who'd once taken such good care of him and Zucker. Whatever she was up to, he was sure it was worthwhile, and he wished her well.

The sounds of construction reached them through the open gate. The gate Hopper had first walked through as Prince Zucker's royal guest. Cyclops, the one-eyed wastrel, had been in charge then, and Hopper had been terrified to the depths of his soul. But today the iron gate—which had been scrubbed and polished to a midnight gleam—stood wide and welcoming.

Still, Hopper hung back, unable to step through it. His mind flashed back to his last image of the place. Zucker unconscious on the ground, blood everywhere. Stinking humans, tromping around with only one goal in mind—destruction! He imagined their footprints like scars in the dirt. He could not bear to look upon those again. Ever.

"It's okay, Chosen One," said Garfield, noticing the mouse's hesitation. "I promise."

Hopper relaxed and followed the others through

the gate. He was immediately relieved to note that the sooty smell of burned-out buildings had been replaced by the clean and promising scent of fresh sawdust and the indescribable aroma of newly appropriated human castoffs that had been gathered in the name of repurposing. As they made their way through the streets, Hopper heard tools banging and clunking, as well as the rumbling wheels of carts piled high with building materials. To his ears it was like a symphony of possibility.

The last banging he'd heard inside these walls had been that of steel traps being laid, their metal doors slamming shut on innocent rodents. He much preferred the noisy buzz of carpentry and construction.

Garfield led them all to the top step of the palace, where Hopper and Firren and the uplanders were afforded an eye-popping view of the industrious rodents toiling happily below.

Hopper recognized some of them as former residents of the city and others as camp refugees, but there were also a number of rats, squirrels, and chipmunks he'd never seen before. And mice! *Mice!* Too many to count. As far as he could tell, none of these were of the Mūs tribe (whom Pinkie presumably still had under lock and key behind the gray wall), but their mousely presence was particularly gratifying to Hopper, since on his first visit to Atlantia no mice of any variety had been allowed inside the city. Titus had intentionally vilified the entire species because he lived in fear of a Mūs Chosen One coming to finish Dodger's mission, to remove him from his throne.

"Funny how things turn out," Hopper muttered wryly.

"What's that, Chosen One?" asked Garfield.

"Never mind." Hopper sighed. He intended to ask where all these new rodents had come from, but his mind was too preoccupied with thoughts of Titus. Only now did he begin to wonder if the old rat's feelings about Dodger and the Mūs and even Hopper himself had been far more complicated than anyone had ever known. Feelings that had nothing to do with politics or military power. He thought back now to the day the emperor had stood in the square and humbly but fiercely retracted all the horrible things he'd taught his people about the Mūs. Hopper realized now how genuine Titus's remorse had been, and he suddenly wondered what it was he didn't know about the emperor's past that might account for his complex attitude about the Mūs and the hunting ground and life in the tunnels. . . . Perhaps *no one* knew exactly what had happened in Titus's youth to make him what he was. But Hopper was suddenly gripped with a very strong hunch that there was a much deeper story behind all of it.

His ponderings of Titus were forgotten when he

saw another familiar face. A soldier rat was bounding up the palace steps to greet him.

"Polhemus!"

"Isn't this amazing?" Polhemus cried, taking the steps two at a time to clap Hopper on the back. "Atlantia will thrive once more!"

"It is amazing," Hopper agreed. "And wonderful. But where did all these rodents come from?"

"They were led to us," Polhemus replied with a nod toward the towering palace doors directly behind Hopper.

Curious, Hopper turned his gaze to the doorway, and a flash of gold caught his eye. A tiny robed figure was approaching him. Hopper tensed, fearing it might be Pinkie. It would be just like her to storm the fallen city and claim it as her own. He doubted Garfield and Polhemus would be so cheerful if that were the case, but he reached for his sword nonetheless. Of course, his weapon was long gone.

He raised one clenched fist, prepared to strike if the robed creature was, in fact, his loathsome, heartless sister about to attack.

But as the gold-clad figure drew closer, Hopper could see that the Mūs face peeking out at him from the shadow of the glimmering hood was not the tyrannical Pinkie.

It was Sage.

Chapter Twenty

Emerging from the palace right behind him were Christoph and Temperance.

Hopper's mouth dropped. "I don't understand! *You're* responsible for all this rebuilding? I thought you three had gone off on an infinite journey, riding the train to wherever it might take you."

"As it happens," said Sage, "it took us back here."

"You told us the means by which we could return to this place, should we ever need to find you," Christoph reminded him.

"We did precisely as you said." Temperance nodded. "We took the two train."

"But we found you gone," said Christoph, his tone solemn. "Nothing remained but destruction."

"We are not fond of destruction," said Sage. "We knew this place had once known greatness. And so we set about rebuilding."

Christoph swept a paw to indicate the busy rodents working below. "On our train journey we met many rodents who were lost and alone, near to starving out there in the tunnels."

"We brought them all here with us," said Sage. "We had hoped to find you and the prince, but of course all we found was wreckage and ruin. Since we needed a place to set down roots, we chose this one. And soon many who had fled Atlantia—Garfield and Polhemus and the swordsmith, Fulton, to name a few—returned. We joined forces in the hopes of becoming the next generation of Atlantians. The rodents we brought here with us are all hard workers, as you can see. Look how much we've accomplished in just a short time."

Sage was not exaggerating. From his vantage point on the palace steps Hopper could now see just how much progress had been made by these rodents who were working together to repair their adopted city. Some were hauling away the wreckage left by the battle and the exterminators, others were dragging in all manner of human artifacts to use as building materials, and still others had assembled in the town square to discuss the exciting future of Atlantia.

Hopper remembered the last such meeting that had taken place in the square, and again he thought of the emperor. "What of Titus?" he asked. "Has he turned up?"

"No sign of him," Polhemus replied with a shrug. "But he's not likely to have lasted in the tunnels this long. The pampered ones don't know how to fend for themselves, and there was none more pampered than the emperor."

Except maybe me, thought Hopper, remembering the royal banquet the emperor had held for him and all the luxuries that had been showered upon him during his time in the palace. He expected to feel relief in knowing that Titus was no more, but instead he was filled with a powerful sense of regret. Titus had done evil things, it was true, but he had been brilliant in his way. If only he had used his wiles in the name of goodness. It was this potential that Hopper mourned.

Now Firren excused herself to go find those of her Rangers who were already here among the next generation of Atlantians. "I'll take them with me to make a sweep of the tunnels," she told Hopper. "I want to see what's going on out there, perhaps locate the rest of my Rangers and bring them back. I'll be on the lookout for Pup, of course."

Hopper smiled his thanks. "Be careful, Firren."

She gave him her word that she would, and she was off.

"What did she mean by that?" asked Sage. "Why would she keep a lookout for Pup?"

"Isn't he still back at the Mūs village, enjoying his part in Pinkie's reign of terror?" asked Christoph.

"If only he were," said Hopper with a long sigh. "But Pup's decided that the only way to prove his worth to our sister is to take down Felina himself. That's why I came back. To stop him from confronting her. I just hope I'm not too late." He frowned. "Does anyone know where Felina is? Have you located her lair?"

"We have some educated guesses, and I've got scouts searching," Garfield said grimly. "But so far nothing. Perhaps Firren will have better luck. In the meantime we've posted soldiers around the perimeter as a precaution. I believe that for the moment, at least, we are safe."

Hopper was glad of that, but he also knew they could not rely on such good fortune forever. Sooner or later Pup would manage to hunt down the white cat, or Felina would learn of the resurrection of Atlantia and she would be back. With a vengeance.

He was going to have to find Pup quickly, before either of those things could come to pass.

"I wonder what La Rocha would advise," said Sage. "What I wouldn't give to be able to consult the mystic or read a passage of his sacred writings."

Hopper's paw went deep into his pocket, where the crumpled note still sat beneath his collection of fabric scraps.

"*I shall come for you*," La Rocha had promised.

Hopper was suddenly angry . . . or perhaps just deeply disappointed. The great mystic whom Sage and the others trusted so much had failed the Chosen One by not keeping that very crucial promise. He'd never come for Hopper. In fact, Hopper had never laid eyes on him.

But then, with a jolt, he realized that La Rocha *had* come for him . . . in a manner of speaking. Not in person. But the elusive cockroach *had* left the message for Firren among the Runes, and that had led Firren upland to find Hopper. He'd been looking out for the

Chosen One, even if it had been from a distance.

Yes. La Rocha *had* kept his promise. After all, it had been finding La Rocha's note in his pocket that had inspired Hopper to speak so confidently to the assemblage in the town square. And when he'd heard how Beverley had given her life to save Ketchum, he'd comforted himself with a wish for La Rocha to bring her peace. After he and Firren had made their treacherous slide down the snowdrift and jumped onto the snowplowing beast, he'd invoked La Rocha's protection. And when Pilot had soared away in search of Ace, Hopper had silently requested any aid the mystic could provide.

So La Rocha had not physically *come* to Hopper, but he'd been with him all along; he'd been present always, in the form of the wisdom and courage Hopper felt when he thought of La Rocha.

Hopper turned to Sage. "La Rocha would want us to be brave," he said, his voice filled with confidence. "He would tell us we must continue our quest to rebuild Atlantia, and to try and save Pup from himself. He would tell us the odds are with us because we are fighting for what's right."

"Yes," said Temperance. "This is true."

"Of course," said Christoph.

Sage nodded.

Hopper noticed that his words had caused the former Tribunal members to puff out their little chests and stand a bit taller. Despite all that they had lost, and the dangers that still lay ahead, there was a proud gleam in their eyes and no trace of doubt in their expressions.

And in that moment Hopper understood: *this* was the power of faith. Faith made it possible to face the unknown. Faith brought hope, and hope brought strength. What La Rocha provided—to the elders, to the wanderers, and to Hopper, too—wasn't magic or supernatural power . . . it was inspiration. And inspiration was just another word for the desire to do something good and noble and important . . . and believing that you could.

La Rocha's gift had been allowing Hopper to believe in his own worthiness, in the value of his pursuits. From that came fortitude, and from that came resolve.

But Pup did not believe. He feared and he doubted, and from this came his anger and his need to be recognized. This, Hopper realized, was why Pup needed to prove to Pinkie that he could accomplish something enormous. But it would never matter whether Pinkie believed in him or not. First Pup had to believe in himself.

Unfortunately, his crazy quest to slay Felina was not the way for Pup to achieve that or to earn Pinkie's respect.

It was, however, an expeditious way to get himself killed!

Hopper could not waste another moment. He had to begin planning his quest immediately. And although he had Firren and Valky and the basketball rats behind him, he knew that his chances of defeating the ferals would be far greater if he had what Pinkie had . . . an army!

Seeing all these new citizens of Atlantia united in their efforts to repair the city gave him an idea.

"Do you think these rodents will fight with me?" he asked Sage. "Do you think they will put down their tools and take up weapons so that I might defeat the feral queen before any real harm comes to my misguided brother?"

Temperance and Christoph exchanged glances, and for one disheartening moment Hopper was afraid they would say no.

At last Sage spoke. "It's hard to say, Chosen One."

Christoph nodded. "All these rodents have lost loved ones along the way," he observed. "Some lost them in their upland homes, before descending into this underground world. Some have lost family members right here in the tunnels, to those hunting cats with their insatiable appetites. So it is possible."

"They understand loss, and they understand the need to stand against tyranny," Temperance added. "But this is a lot to ask. It is dangerous—deadly, even. I would hope they would join you in your quest, but I cannot say for sure. I suppose all you can do is ask."

"Many of these rodents told us that they'd long heard the rumors of Titus's peace accord and of Felina's blatant disregard for nature's justice," Sage explained, "but most had refused to believe these grisly tales. When we came along and confirmed that they were, in fact, true, the rodents were both disgusted and enraged. They toil so determinedly now because they believe that starting fresh is the only way to erase the ugliness of the past." He reached into his cloak. "Speaking of Titus . . . we have something to show you, Chosen One."

"Please . . . call me Hopper."

Sage had removed from the folds of his cape a golden chain dotted with sparkling blue stones. He handed it to Hopper. "We found this hidden in Titus's bedchamber. It appears to be a priceless human relic and therefore a suitable bauble for the Chosen One."

Hopper took the shining circlet of precious metal and glittering gemstones from the elder and sighed. "Yes, Zucker mentioned we'd probably find treasure stashed all over this palace. I can't imagine where this came from or what it might have represented to Titus, but for us let it be a symbol of our unity. The future of Atlantia will depend upon all of us working together, like the links in this chain. And these twinkling blue objects shall symbolize the peace that will result from such unity."

"So it shall be," said Sage with a nod.

"Come now," said Temperance, taking Hopper by the arm. "Let us show you what we have done inside the palace."

"Although it suffered the least of all the buildings, we decided to redesign the emperor's quarters," said Sage, smiling at Hopper. "It is a symbolic gesture more than anything else. And we plan to commission a beautiful gilded chair to install in your throne room, Chosen One."

Hopper shuddered. "I think you've got me confused with my sister," he said. "I don't want to have a throne in the throne room at all. Instead I'd like . . ." He stopped midsentence and blinked. "*My* throne room?"

"Of course," said Temperance. "In the absence of royal blood we thought it only natural that you become the new ruler of Atlantia. *You* shall be called Emperor now. Or perhaps you prefer King?"

"I prefer Hopper," said the mouse, shaking his head. "And if I am going to rule Atlantia, it will not be as the king or the emperor or the exalted Chosen One. It will be as part of a team. A big team."

"So . . ." Sage knit his brow in confusion. "No throne, then?"

"No throne, no crown, no lofty titles. No pampering, no excess."

"I don't understand," said Christoph, looking perplexed. "A leader should be exalted. We would have provided the same for your father, had he returned to us."

"Had he returned to you, he would have refused it," said Hopper, confident that this was so. "Dodger would not have expected special treatment."

"But you are our Chosen One," Sage reminded him. "You should walk in nothing less than glory! Magnificence."

"I don't want glory," Hopper assured him. "And I'm not even sure what magnificence is. If I am to lead, I will not require exaltation. Respect and honesty will do just fine. I shall see to it that the rodents of this new and improved Atlantia will have all that those who lived under Titus enjoyed—prosperity, comfort, peace of mind—only this time without the refugee camps and sacrifices making it possible. And when it comes to furnishing the *former* throne room, here is what I would like to see: as many sturdy, comfortable chairs as we can fit into the space, to accommodate any and all Atlantians who might wish to gather there and discuss the concerns of government. Their presence, as well as their ideas, will always be welcome. We will rule the city together, or we will not rule it at all."

"Revolutionary!" said Christoph.

"Not really," said Hopper, blushing. "Just reasonable. And fair."

"I think fairness will be a most appreciated change of pace," said Sage.

"So it shall be," said Temperance, smiling. "So it shall be."

With that, Sage turned to the multitude spread out around the steps of the palace and called for their attention. Then he told them of Hopper's new vision for the Atlantian government. Then he explained the urgency of Pup's rescue and Hopper's request for their assistance. He implored these rodents, many of whom were perfect strangers to Hopper, to become part of a new Atlantian army, an army that would march out in the name of justice to bring the evil white cat and her band of gluttonous ferals to their knees once and for all.

"Will you help me?" Hopper asked, his voice rolling out over the city. "Will you stand beside me to save my brother?"

There was a long silence, during which the Chosen One held his breath. If they said no, he would understand. They had all been through so much uncertainty and suffering already. They had seen how even the best-laid plans could go awry, so he would never resent anyone who elected not to fight. Unlike Pinkie's army, Atlantia's would be optional, a matter of choice.

Hopper looked out over the workers, who had begun to whisper to one another, and felt his hopes dissolve. He was about to accept that he would be fighting only with Firren, the soldiers, and the uplanders who had joined him on his return. But then . . .

A paw went up.

And another.

And still another followed that one. Brown fur, gray fur, black fur . . . large paws and tiny ones, paws of every shape and color were being lifted into the air as the rats and mice and squirrels and chipmunks volunteered to fight. Hopper beamed at the sight of so many outstretched paws.

When all was said and done not a single rodent had declined to join the fight.

Atlantia's new peacekeeping force had been formed.

And something told Hopper they would be unstoppable.

Construction ceased.

Garfield called in Fulton, who had been Zucker's personal bladesmith, and charged him with the task of forging as many broadswords, rapiers, and daggers as he could produce. A few rodents were assigned to aid him in this chore, while the rest were gathered in the market to be taught the art of warcraft.

Hopper had one small, strange request for the smithy.

"I already have a new sword, made from a key," Hopper said, "but I would ask that you make me something smaller."

"Anything you ask," said Fulton. "What weapon would you like?"

"A needle," said Hopper. "Like the ones the royal tailors employed in sewing the palace livery and the vests and tunics worn by Zucker's soldiers . . . yourself included."

"A *needle*?" Fulton repeated.

"Can you do it?"

"I'm sure I could," said the smithy, baffled by the odd request.

"Good. Make it slim, please, with a narrow eye and a sharp point. And thank you."

As the swordsmith went off, shaking his head, Hopper took Valky and the basketball rats to join the officers and the elders who had assembled in the large space Titus had once called the Conflict Room. Garfield had taken to calling it the Strategic Planning Area, and Hopper liked that much better. The name had a far more positive ring to it.

There they went over numerous maps and diagrams, including a quickly sketched re-creation of the map Firren had drawn in the dirt for Valky back in Brooklyn Bridge Park. After much careful analysis they had narrowed down their options and determined that Felina's lair might be in one of three possible places.

Might be.

Possible places.

Needless to say, Hopper was not entirely satisfied with this conclusion. The calculations were all very vague, and based mostly on conjecture, not fact. Simply put, what these likely locations represented were really just three strong guesses. But as far as Hopper was concerned, following these hunches was much better than doing nothing.

All day the rodents prepared for battle and the officers strategized. Hopper hustled back and forth between the training ground and the Strategic Planning Area, offering his best advice and input on swordsmanship and tunnel geography, respectively.

By nightfall he was exhausted, but their plan was in place. They would march out of Atlantia as a single army into the Great Beyond. There they would divide the troops into three separate battalions, each led by an experienced soldier. As time was of the essence, these separate forces would strike out in different directions (based on the three potential locations their analysis of the maps had indicated) in hopes of discovering Felina's lair. Along the way they would search diligently for Pup, who it was assumed was in hiding somewhere in the tunnels, biding his time, hunting Felina and possibly forming an army of his own. If Pup was found, he would be taken captive—not harshly or violently—and brought directly back to Atlantia by armed escorts, and Ketchum would be waiting to debrief and reindoctrinate him.

Even if they failed in their efforts to contain Pup, the divided army would not give up until Felina's lair was found. Thereupon they would execute a siege, a battle, and with any luck a victory. Because one thing was certain: Pup could not face off against Felina if the Atlantian army beat him to it and destroyed her first.

Which was why Hopper's orders to Garfield and Polhemus regarding their attack on the ferals were simple:

Take. No. Prisoners.

Pup's future . . . and his *life* . . . depended on it.

CHAPTER TWENTY-ONE

THAT NIGHT HOPPER IGNORED Titus's redecorated apartment and took for his own room the royal bedchamber that had belonged to Zucker.

Not because he thought himself princely or important. But to remember. To feel closer to his fallen friend.

The room looked remarkably the same as it did the first time he'd seen it. Thanks to the protection of the crickets, much of the palace had been spared from ruin in the aftermath of the camp raid. But for Hopper this was bittersweet. The room still had an air of Zucker about it . . . an energy. It was a sensation of warmth and strength and humor.

Hopper could almost picture the prince propped against the pillows after he'd sustained a wound fighting Firren and the Mūs soldiers; Marcy had fed him hot broth.

Odd it was to think of Zucker fighting *against* Firren. But there had been so much confusion then, so many secrets and misunderstandings.

Zucker had pulled through, of course. Hopper had begun to believe then that there was nothing from which his friend the Zuck-meister could not recover.

Maybe he had been wrong.

A few hot tears bubbled out of his eyes, dampening his whiskers.

There was a knock on the chamber door, followed by a voice. "Hopper? May I come in?" It was Valky.

Hopper wiped at his eyes. "Of course."

Valky stepped in, looking troubled. "I was just wondering . . . if you thought Pilot's found Ace yet?"

It was a thought that had been gnawing at the back of Hopper's mind all day. His preoccupation with the battle plans hadn't succeeded in driving off his worry for the courageous tuxedo cat whose whereabouts remained unknown. Brave and good-hearted as he was, Ace was still a relatively small and fragile animal, and the storm had created more dangers than Hopper cared to think about: drifts and plows and freezing temperatures.

But Hopper forced a smile. "I'm sure Pilot found him," he replied. "In fact, I'll bet they're both safe and sound right now, back at the deli, feasting on eggplant parmigiana."

Valky grinned, relieved.

"How are your accommodations?" Hopper asked, wanting to change the subject.

"Very comfortable. I'm in a room near the kitchens. The rats opted to bunk with some of the other new Atlantians. Seems there are a couple of squirrels who once spent a winter in the dugout at Yankee Stadium, and they've all become fast friends."

Hopper laughed.

"Well," said Valky. "Good night, then."

Hopper wished the chipmunk a restful night's sleep and Valky was gone. But the moment he closed the door, it opened again.

Hopper actually gasped at the sight of the rat standing in the doorway. Then he beamed. "Marcy!"

"Hello, Chosen One! It's lovely to see you."

"And you," said Hopper. "I was so worried about you."

Marcy gave him a demure smile. "You of all rodents should know better than to worry about me. I can take care of myself."

"I suppose that's true." Hopper grinned, recalling the way she'd slapped him (hard!) to prove to Titus that she was loyal to the throne, when she was really as much a rebel as Firren and Zucker. And every bit as impressive as her physical strength had been the speed with which she'd crafted such a clever plan.

"Where have you been?" Hopper asked. "They tell me you come and go with some frequency. Are you a soldier now?"

"I'm many things," she said, her eyes twinkling. "But I'm always careful."

Hopper was glad to hear it. "How are your brothers?"

"Bartel and Pritchard are quite well." Marcy swept across the room in her full skirt to where Zucker's writing desk stood, gleaming in the pale light. She leaned against the edge and smiled at Hopper. "They are ready and willing to fight with you tomorrow."

"And you?" Hopper asked. "Will you march as well?"

A look of hesitation flickered across the pretty rat's face. Hopper watched her, her paws fidgeting behind her skirts, and immediately felt bad for making her nervous. "You don't have to fight," he said quickly. "I'll understand if you don't."

"I can't say for sure if I will be there," she said at last. "But I will try to join you in your quest. If you don't see me there among the troops, please know that I'm there with you . . . if only in spirit."

Hopper gave her a grateful smile; that was plenty good enough for him.

Abruptly Marcy pushed away from the desk and strode across the chamber to throw her arms around Hopper. "I have to go now," she whispered in his ear—the bitten one she'd wrapped in gauze the day they met. "Always know that I have faith in you."

With that she hurried to the door, her dainty paws skipping, her skirts rustling.

Hopper stared after her, trying to make sense of her odd behavior. But then, the battle had everyone on edge.

Hopper sat down on the plush bed and carefully emptied his pockets, arranging the scrap of blue felt fabric, the pink ribbon, Keep's shredded pocket, the piece of Beverley's apron. Lastly, he withdrew the purple fragment that had torn away from Zucker's sleeve in his attempt to free Firren from the exterminators' trap.

He smoothed this piece lovingly as he placed it among the others.

Before Hopper lay a patchwork of his past, and despite the shabby appearance, every scrap he'd collected told a story, taught a lesson . . . made a promise.

Hopper picked up the tool he had personally requisitioned from Atlantia's best swordsmith: a sewing needle.

With a deep yawn and a heavy sigh he set to work.

"Aye."

The whispered syllable floated across the room and into Hopper's dreams. His eyes fluttered, but he was reluctant to open them because in the dream he was once again with Zucker; they were hunched over the gleaming desk in the prince's chamber, and Zucker was teaching Hopper how to write. In the dream Zucker appeared as an ephemeral presence hovering beside Hopper like a ghost. But deep within the peacefulness of his slumber Hopper could hear the prince's voice as plainly as if he were really there beside him:

"These are the letters, kid. Put 'em together, they make words. Words have meaning. We use them to send messages. . . ."

In the dream Hopper was writing a message. A note to himself. Or maybe the note had already been written by someone else. Perhaps he was only reading it. Or dreaming it. It was difficult to be sure; he was lost in his slumber, which made the images all very hazy and indistinct.

In the dream Hopper could feel the crispness of the paper. Shiny paper, tattered at the edges. He could see the specific lines and squiggles of each individual letter but could not make out what the note said. Still, it seemed terribly real.

"Hopper . . ."

Zucker?

Startled, Hopper opened his eyes, blinking out of the dream even as his mind reached for it. It was still nighttime. He lifted his head, surprised to find that it had been resting on the desktop. Then he remembered . . . he'd been half asleep when he moved his sewing project from the bed to the desk to take advantage of the better lighting; he must have nodded off in earnest sometime after that.

The voice came again: "Aye."

Not Zucker.

"Oh." Hopper shook off his drowsiness to smile at Firren. "You're back. Did you find the missing Rangers?"

"Every last one," Firren said with a triumphant nod. "All unharmed."

"I'm so glad."

"So am I."

"Have you met with Garfield and the others?" Hopper asked with a yawn.

"Yes, I went directly to the Conflict—I mean the Strategic Planning Area as soon I got back. They've filled me in on your arrangements for tomorrow. The Rangers and I will be ready to march out in the morning, spread out among the three battalions."

"I wish we knew the precise location of Felina's lair," said Hopper. "That would certainly make things easier."

"It would," Firren concurred. "It's hard to believe that no one but Titus and his nasty goon Cassius ever knew where it was. I suppose Felina was smart enough to recognize there was always the chance the rodents would turn on her."

"I guess I'd hide too," said Hopper, "if I had as many enemies as she does."

Firren motioned to the fabric spread across the desktop. "What's that you've got there?"

"Oh. I was sewing," Hopper explained.

"Really?" Firren laughed. "I never thought of you as the domestic sort."

"It's a flag, actually. A banner, like the ones in the Runes, where the rodent armies are marching out, proudly flying their colors and . . ." He blushed when he realized she knew exactly what he was describing. "Well, you know . . . because you drew them."

"Yes, I did."

"See, I've been collecting these scraps of material," said Hopper. "Each one reminds me of something important. Some of those things were exciting, others were sweet, but most were just plain scary. When we march against Felina, I want to do it under this banner because it's a symbol of how far this journey has brought me—how far it's brought all of us—and of the many examples of selflessness and courage that have been shown by so many along the way."

"By no one more than you, little one," Firren whispered. "Remember that."

Hopper accepted the praise with a grateful smile as he ran his paws over the banner, smoothing out the crooked seams and wishing he were better with a needle. He'd tried to form the scraps into a tidy rectangle, but the edges were lopsided and the center had turned out lumpy. His stitches were uneven—too big and loose in some places, small and tightly gathered in others. All in all, though, he thought it was quite a beautiful thing. There was a humble, unassuming quality to it that was in keeping with what he stood for.

"May I see it?" Firren asked.

"Sure."

As Hopper lifted the patchwork flag from the desktop, a slip of paper fell off the desk and onto the floor.

Firren bent to retrieve it. "What's this?"

"I don't know," said Hopper. "I don't remember

seeing it there before, but then, I was awfully tired."

When Firren read what was written on the paper, her eyes went wide.

"What?" cried Hopper. "What does it say?"

The rebel handed the note to Hopper.

> HERE IS THE LOCATION OF FELINA'S
> LAIR. YOU WILL FIND YOUR BROTHER
> CAMPED OUT IN AN OLD SHOE JUST
> WEST OF THERE.
> LA ROCHA

Below the signature script was a crudely sketched map with a large *X* indicating the precise spot where they would find the feral queen's encampment, and slightly to the left of it a smaller one, presumably marking Pup's hideout.

Hopper noticed the paper was shaking; he realized this was because the paw in which he clutched it had begun to tremble. His eyes bored into the paper so intensely he was surprised it didn't go up in flames.

A message. And a map. Pup's location.

"I thought it was a dream," he murmured. "I thought I'd dreamed of a note . . . but it was real."

Hopper shook his head in amazement. "Firren, do you really think La Rocha was here? Do you think he actually snuck into my chamber to leave me this message?"

Firren was equally perplexed. "If he did, perhaps someone saw him. Has anyone else been here besides you?"

Hopper thought back. "Well, Valky came to ask if I thought Ace would be all right. And Marcy." He smiled. "She just popped in to welcome me back. And now you. But I've seen no one else. Certainly not a mystical cockroach."

Firren's brow was knit low in concentration. Hopper could see that she was allowing herself to wonder, she was daring to believe. . . .

If this message was true and the information accurate, they were halfway to their goal. They could save Pup and defeat Felina.

And why wouldn't it be true? Why would La Rocha lie?

Hopper looked at the note again, wanting to trust it.

But something was wrong.

Something about the writing . . . the curve of the letters, the slant of the words. And La Rocha's signature . . .

He reached into his pocket and pulled out the crinkled slip of paper he'd been keeping there with the fabric scraps. The note that had been delivered to him on the steps of the palace following the raid on the camps and the fall of the city.

First he compared the two pieces of stationery. The original note was scrawled on a flimsy piece of yellow paper with pale gray-blue lines across it. He'd seen plenty of scraps like this one fluttering around the tunnels—always with human notations about court appearances and cross-examinations written on them.

The new note was written on a much heavier stock of paper. It had one rough edge, as though it had been torn out of a book's binding, and a glossy sheen. The page looked old to Hopper, brittle and discolored, as though it had been blowing around the subway tunnels for quite some time. Hopper knew that La Rocha's Sacred Book contained several pages of varying quality and condition. So although this disparity was significant, it proved nothing.

The map, along with La Rocha's message about Pup, appeared in a wide margin surrounding a block of uniform text—lettering that looked as though it had been printed not by a person or a rodent, but by a machine. These words told of an empire in a place called Rome, of gladiators fighting in a building called the Colosseum.

Now he compared the penmanship, holding the notes side by side and examining the writing.

All the wind went out of him. His throat tightened and his eyes burned.

"It could be a hoax," he said softly.

"What do you mean?" Firren demanded.

"It's possible this note is a fake." Hopper showed her the old, crinkled note and then the new one. "This might not be La Rocha's penmanship. It could be someone else's writing."

Firren considered this. "Okay, well, perhaps the information is good, but whoever sent this message assumed you would believe it only if you thought it came from La Rocha." Absently, her paw went to the handle of her sword. "So they forged the note in an effort to get you to take it seriously."

It wasn't a bad theory. Still, Hopper's head swam with possibilities. There were so many new rodents in Atlantia. One of them could certainly be a spy working for Felina, in which case this could be an evil ploy designed to bring Hopper and his army directly to her lair, where, instead of being caught off guard by their invasion, Felina would be poised and ready to counterattack. It could be a trap.

Or it could be nothing more than a mean trick designed to raise his hopes. He couldn't imagine who would be so cruel, but he had to allow that it might be the case.

"What are your instincts telling you?" Firren asked.

Hopper closed his eyes and searched within himself. He let his faith take hold and listened to his heart. "I have a hunch it's real. I think La Rocha really did send this message."

Firren brightened. "So we're going to use the map?"

"Yes." Hopper folded the two notes and slipped them into his pocket. "But just to be on the safe side, we will also continue with our plan to set out for the three other locations the soldiers identified. We'll just add a fourth battalion—one that will consist of you and the Rangers, my upland friends, Garfield and Polhemus and me—to investigate the place marked by that big *X*. We won't be a big army, but we will be a strong one. If this little map does bring us face-to-face with Pup and Felina, I want my best soldiers by my side."

Firren nodded. It was a moment, though, before she let go of her sword. In spite of himself Hopper began to smile. Then laugh.

"Is something funny?" Firren asked.

"You reaching for your sword like that," said Hopper. "It reminds me of the first time we met. It was right after the raid, remember? You landed on me after we dove through that hole, and I begged you to run me through."

"Right! How could I ever forget?" Firren was laughing now too. "I thought I was seeing a ghost when I spotted that white circle around your eye."

"That was when you told me that you would protect me," Hopper said. "In fact, you said you'd sworn to protect me long ago. I've always wondered what you meant by that."

Firren sat down on the edge of the bed and patted it, inviting Hopper to come and sit beside her. When he did, she took his paw and gave it a squeeze.

"It broke my heart when I failed to protect my friend Dodger," she said quietly. "I wasn't there to defend him from Cassius. Dodge was an excellent fighter and an even better leader. But when it came to swordsmanship . . . well, let's just say things went better for him when I was around."

Hopper smiled. He liked finding out new things about Dodger, even if it was simply learning that he was lousy with a sword. Firren continued.

"When La Rocha's prophecy of a Chosen One appeared, foretelling of Dodger's son . . . well, to be honest, I only half believed it. I had my theories, as you know, about him heading up to the daylight world, but since I didn't have proof, I was never sure what to think. Nevertheless, I vowed that if a Chosen One ever did reveal himself, I would do everything I could to keep him safe, to defend him to the death if it came to that, and to make up for not having been able to do the same for his . . ." She paused, then grinned as she corrected herself. "For *your* father."

"Thank you," said Hopper. "And may I say, you're doing an awfully good job so far."

But Firren's smile quickly vanished.

"What's wrong?"

"I miss Zucker."

"So do I." Hopper swallowed hard. "Do you really think he's dead?"

Firren shrugged. "It stands to reason. But then, there are times when I get this feeling in my heart. This little flutter that tells me there's still hope. If only we knew where to look, we might find him. Alive." A tear spilled out of her eye and rolled down her delicate face. "There are so many things I want to tell him."

"Like what?" Hopper cocked his head. "What things?"

The rebel let out a long, weary sigh. "I would tell him I'm sorry for not trusting in him. I want to apologize for ever believing he could have betrayed me and Dodger and all we had fought for. I kept meaning to mention it, you know, after the battle, but it was all so chaotic with Atlantia falling and Titus being held under house arrest and the exodus and all. Then, even after things calmed down a bit, every time I tried to talk to Zucker . . . well, I guess you could say that by that time the situation between the prince and me had gotten a little . . . well, weird."

"A *little* weird?" Hopper raised an eyebrow. "Please! You two were a couple of blithering idiots."

"Excuse me?" Firren scowled. "We were not."

"You were too!" Hopper shot her a grin. "And I know why."

"You do?"

"Yes, I do."

"Okay." Firren gave him a sideways look. "Why?"

"Because you and the Zuck-meister are mad for each other, that's why."

Firren blushed. "We are not!"

"You are too! Totally and completely mad. And I know this because . . . because . . ." It was Hopper's turn to blush.

"Because why?" Firren prompted.

"Because it's exactly how *I've* been feeling lately . . . about Carroll."

"Yeah, I kind of had a hunch," said Firren, her eyes sparkling.

"Do you think I'll ever see her again?" Hopper wondered out loud. "Do you think—"

"Let's stick to one life-changing event at a time, shall we?" Firren teased. "Let's focus on the battle for now and plan your romantic future later, after we've defeated Felina and rescued Pup."

"Good idea," said Hopper.

Firren stood and crossed the room to where the homemade banner still lay on Zucker's desk. In one elegant movement she unsheathed her sword and neatly cut away two of the stripes that were sewn to the front of her tunic, first a red and then a blue one.

"Would you mind," she began, putting down her sword and picking up the needle, "if I added these to our flag?"

Hopper's voice caught when he replied, "I would be honored."

Firren sat down in Zucker's old chair and picked up the banner. "Better get some sleep," she said, expertly slipping the needle into the fabric and pulling the thread taut. "Tomorrow is going to be a very big day."

Hopper crawled under the blankets of the prince's bed and snuggled into the mound of pillows.

"Good night, Firren."

"Good night, Hopper."

And although neither of them said it out loud, each knew what the other was thinking in the silence that followed.

Good night, Zucker. Wherever you are.

CHAPTER TWENTY-TWO

La Rocha's journal—from the Sacred Book of the Mūs:

> To her credit, Pinkie does not scream. She does not call for her private guard or bare her teeth, nor does she throw herself across the engine room to plunge her dagger into my heart.
>
> Instead she does something of which I would not have believed her capable.
>
> She weeps.
>
> I would go to her were I not still chained to the metal mountain. Hearing her cry is a far worse punishment than these shackles. At last she quiets with a sniffle, then a deep, shuddering sigh. When she wipes her tear-streaked face with the back of her paw, I am struck by how innocent the gesture seems and how very young and fragile she appears.
>
> "You're supposed to be dead," she says at last.
>
> "I don't have to remind you that you can still arrange for that to be the case."
>
> Pinkie frowns. "Why now?" she asks. "Why reveal yourself at this point, when so much has gone wrong? Titus killing refugees . . . Atlantia

being destroyed . . . the chaos in the tunnels." Her whiskers twitch. "Mother being taken from us."

"You must know I would have given anything to save her," I say, hearing the tremble of grief in my own voice. "The loss of her changed everything for me. I had planned—"

"Planned what? Planned to bring us all down here into these godforsaken tunnels to fight for the rebel cause?"

"Yes. That was your birthright. And wouldn't that have been better than being snatched from a cage yourself, only to make your way whole through the slimy bowels of a boa constrictor?"

Pinkie toys with the pink fringe on her gilded cape. "You left me behind. Do you understand how much that hurt?"

"You will never know how sorry I am for that," I tell her.

She is silent for a moment, then crosses the room and looks me squarely in the eyes. "Tell me everything," she says. "All of it."

But this is not the command of a vicious captor to her prisoner. It is the simple and heartfelt request of a daughter to her father.

And so I honor it. And tell her all.

She listens as I recount my fight with the brutal General Cassius and describe the brain-rattling blow to the head I suffered at his hands. I tell her how he abandoned me for dead and that to this day I do not know how long I lay there unconscious. But when I did awake, I knew that I had been given a grand opportunity. I could vanish, disappear. Invisible, I would become an even greater threat to Titus than I ever was in plain sight.

"It is easy to attack the adversary who stands before you," I explain to my child. "It is far more difficult to defeat an enemy who is everywhere at once."

"So you went upland and met Mother," she says. "Tell me about that."

"That is a story for another time," I say. "One I will share with you and your brothers when we are all together. It is a beautiful tale, and I would just as soon save it for a less troubling moment."

Pinkie huffs but doesn't argue.

I go on to tell her how, upon my return to the tunnels, I met La Rocha.

"The cockroach."

"Well, no . . . not exactly. The La Rocha I met was a chipmunk. The La Rocha before him was a spotted salamander, and the one before him was a rat—a three-legged one, as the story goes, thanks to an unfortunate incident with a slow-moving subway train. It was the one before the rat that was a cockroach."

"I don't understand."

"Neither did I until the chipmunk explained it to me. You see, the first La Rocha was, in fact, an insect—a cockroach. He was brilliant and wise because he'd lived for many seasons both in and out of the tunnels. The species has an exceptionally long life span, you know. Some say they can live forever."

"I've heard that," says Pinkie. She offers me a grape and a crust of bread as I go on with my story.

"That first La Rocha believed that the rodents who dwelled here needed a guide, a benevolent voice to help them through the trials and tribulations that came of living in this dark underworld. And so he began to scatter his wisdom around the tunnels . . . messages of hope he'd inscribe on found bits of paper. He knew these scraps were just human refuse—coupons, grocery lists, sports programs, movie tickets—but to the rodents who deciphered them, they were mysterious and wonderful. He would add his own good advice or inspiration and leave them as gifts for his followers to find. Soon the Mūs compiled them into a sacred book. That pleased the insect greatly. But eventually even a being as nearly immortal as a cockroach grows weary."

"So he quit?" Pinkie guesses.

"No, he didn't quit. He decided the position of La Rocha should be a titular one."

"A what?"

"An office that gets handed down, passed on to begin anew. In that way he knew his spiritual leadership could be everlasting, it would go on eternally, as long as there was always a creature worthy to take up the mantle."

"In this case a three-legged rat."

"Precisely."

"So how did you become part of the legacy?"

"I had not been back in the tunnels long. I was still in hiding, eagerly awaiting the day my family would join me. But when it became clear that this reunion was not to be, I was devastated. I had lost your mother and would never know my litter. The ache in my soul nearly destroyed me, so I decided I would seek out the mystical being in the hope of finding solace. Imagine my surprise when I discovered that he was not some all-seeing cockroach sent down from on high in a platinum chariot pulled by phosphorescent dragonflies. . . ."

At this exaggeration my daughter laughs, and the sound fills the locomotive, as well as my heart.

"The chipmunk La Rocha was growing old. He'd held the title for longer than most. When I told him about Firren and the Rangers and our goals to bring down Titus, he said that if I would be willing to step in and take over for him, I could use La Rocha's authority not only to bring comfort and direction to the believers, but also to put an end to the evil peace accord and the hunting ground. How could I refuse?"

"I still don't understand why you didn't tell Zucker or Firren that you were alive and fulfilling the duties of the buggy prophet," says Pinkie.

"Because there were rules. I could not be seen. I could never speak to another living rodent. And I could not disclose the secret, for if the truth was ever revealed, the tunnel rodents would forever more be deprived of their La Rocha, and for most of them that faith was all they had to cling to. And by the way, now that you know this, you are a part of the secret. So you must tell no one, ever. Not Hopper, not Pup. No one."

Pinkie is quiet for a long time. "I'm still confused about why Mother told Hopper to find the Mūs, and why you put forth the prophecy of the Chosen One. You knew if we came here, we'd be entering a world at war. We'd be exposed to grave danger."

I nod slowly. "There would be risk, to be sure, but no more than the risk you lived with in the pet shop. Your future there had but one possible outcome."

"Snake food," Pinkie grumbles.

"Right. And while I dreaded the thought of harm coming to you and your brothers here in the tunnels, I welcomed the possibility of you knowing what it meant to be truly heroic. What a rare opportunity that is! You see, Pinkie, it is not often that a mouse gets the chance to accomplish something. I wanted you and Hopper and Pup to know the satisfaction of making your mark, of doing something that would be remembered long after you were gone from the world. I wanted you to understand there are things worth fighting for, and those are the things you must protect with your whole heart. Just because the heart of a mouse is small, that doesn't mean it can't be brave."

"I have one question."

"Please . . . ask."

"I understand that the first mystic really was a cockroach. But why have all who have followed him allowed that part of the legend to stand? Of all the forms you might have adopted, of all things you could have pretended to be . . . why that?"

"Because, Pinkie, there are so few things in this world that are indestructible. One of those things is the humble cockroach. And the other is—or at least should be—faith."

Now my daughter, with her white circle and wounded ear, approaches me.

And she unlocks my chains.

They would march under the patchwork banner.

Hopper asked Firren to carry it, because he loved and respected the warrior rat and because he knew Zucker would approve.

The rodents had begun to gather at the iron gate, assembling one by one or in small groups. Hopper saw many familiar faces and a few new Atlantians whom he'd never met. He wasn't surprised to see that Marcy wasn't among the group; he knew that if she was choosing not to fight, she had a very good reason.

He was also gravely disappointed that Ace had still not shown up. He tried not to imagine the worst, chalking the cat's absence up to something as harmlessly simple as being snowed in at the deli or having forgotten the location of the portal on the subway platform that would have deposited him into the tunnels.

Ace is probably fine, Hopper told himself. Still, he worried.

He stood now at the head of his army, their

undisputed leader, although in his heart he believed that all who would go into battle this day were equally worthy.

The soldiers were busy dividing the troops into three separate battalions. Each of these would consist of a roughly equal number of mice, rats, squirrels, and chipmunks possessing varying degrees of battle skills and military expertise. These three divisions would be headed up by Bartel, Pritchard, and Fulton. Ketch, much to his disappointment, would not fight due to his injury.

The fourth battalion was Hopper's corps of specially selected rodents. Garfield stood to his right, and Polhemus to his left; falling in behind them were the basketball rats, Valky, Driggs, and Firren and her Rangers. They would follow the map provided in the note he'd received last night, and to his mind, theirs was the most dangerous path because it was the one most likely to deliver them to Felina's lair (not to mention Pup's hiding place). He felt confident that the warriors marching with him were the ones best suited to a battle against the ferals, and he took some comfort in knowing that the well-meaning novices who made up the other three battalions were almost guaranteed not to see so much as a skirmish.

Almost guaranteed.

It was a calculated risk. If he could, he wanted to spare them the horrors of battle, and if the mysterious note was to be believed, that's exactly what he was doing.

If the note was a fraud, however, these hastily trained rodents with only a handful of actual soldiers among them could turn out to be the ones facing the enemy.

Hopper didn't *think* his hunch was wrong, but if it were . . .

He felt sick just thinking about it.

He knew that once they reached the Great Beyond, they would have to disperse, each section heading off into a different area of the tunnels. For the moment, though, they were a single, brave, united force. And the sight of that made Hopper's chest puff out with pride. He lifted his paws for their attention; the rodents fell silent.

"Thank you all," said Hopper, "for joining with me today. This fight has been long in coming, and although the thought of it appalls me, I know that we have no choice but to confront the fiend Felina."

A murmur of agreement rippled through the ranks.

"As you know, our search for the feral queen will require us to separate the moment we get beyond these walls . . . these walls, which all of you have worked so diligently to rebuild. Please know that although we will march separately to points east, west, north, and south, we are all united in the name of Atlantia."

"Atlantia!" Garfield cried out, lifting his sword.

"Atlantia!" the rodents chimed.

"Because we march willingly into danger," Hopper continued, "I wish to share with you something I learned from a very dear friend in a place called Brooklyn. It is a means of calling for help in dire circumstances." He took a deep breath and executed the SOS whistle he'd used to summon Pilot.

The rodents echoed him, and the distinctive whistle exploded through the tunnels.

"If any of you run into trouble, just use that call, and your brothers- and sisters-in-arms will come swiftly to your aid." He paused to look around at the city in its hopeful state of change and renewal. Stalls were popping up in the market square, and buildings that had been half burned and crumbling once again stood tall and sturdy.

"Before we set out," said Hopper, "let us take a moment to remember all those who so recently suffered and died here in the name of justice and freedom. Remember their courage, remember their friendship, and know that when you march today, you do so in their worthy footsteps. The fight that they began is now ours to finish. Let us finish it today!"

A cheer rose up from the army. Newly forged weapons—some made of keys—clattered proudly and menacingly. Hopper could not help but smile.

Felina wouldn't know what hit her.

"Chosen One?" Firren prompted, raising the banner.

Hopper gave a nod, but before he could open his mouth to command the army to march, the tunnels began to shake with a familiar, distant rumble. Then a light bloomed in the darkness and the noise followed. A subway train appeared from the shadows, rocketing past like something alive, screeching and throwing off sparks.

To Hopper, the majesty and power of the speeding vehicle boded well for their mission.

They were ready.

"We march!"

CHAPTER TWENTY-THREE

HOPPER'S ELITE CORPS MARCHED through the gloom and the dust and the muck. They marched for what felt like miles, but not a single rodent grumbled or complained or quit. Hopper was grateful for their loyalty. He knew that the uplanders were fighting to express their gratitude for his acts of bravery on their behalf. As for Driggs and the soldiers and Firren and her rebel Rangers, he suspected these brave warriors were fighting for more personal reasons: a lost loved one, a home destroyed, a profound belief that evil should never be allowed to prevail.

Hopper was fighting for many things. He was fighting to honor the memory of Zucker, and Beverley, and his fallen cagemates who'd died beneath an angry broom. He was fighting because he'd been inspired by a selfless, wounded pigeon who'd put aside his own pain to save a friend, and he was fighting to save Pup and to show him that goodness would always be more important than power. He was fighting for the mother he barely knew and for the father he'd never meet, and for Firren's parents, who had perished in a hunting ground long ago. He was fighting because Felina was cruel and self-serving and unbelievably arrogant to think she had the right to defy nature for her own entertainment.

Today Hopper, son of Dodger, Chosen One of the great Mūs tribe, pet-shop mouse who'd found his way to the subway tunnels quite by accident, would stand up and do battle for every last rodent who'd ever suffered at the paws of Titus and the wicked feral queen.

Now they had come to an area of the tunnels where Hopper had never been before. The air around Atlantia was fusty, but the atmosphere here was wet and clinging and dank in the extreme.

"We're getting close," he said, squinting at the map.

"This is certainly Felina's kind of real estate," muttered Firren. "If her lair isn't here, she might want to think about relocating."

Relocation. Rescued rodents. *Ace.*

Hopper's heart began to hurt.

But the battalion trudged on, dirt caking onto their paws, mildew seeping into their fur. Firren's blazing-white garment faded to gray before Hopper's eyes as the dust and grime that permeated the air settled into the tunic's fibers. Twice the Chosen One twitched mold spores off his whiskers.

"Look over there," said Julius, pointing. "Is that a shoe?"

Hopper whirled, honing his vision through the gloomy shadows until he spied what indeed appeared to be a lost and rotting piece of footwear—an old wing-tip loafer, creased and stained. It looked as though it had once been adorned with a tassel, but that decorative touch was long gone. Whatever became of the foot that had worn it would forever remain a mystery; the old shoe was now a bunker. A hideout.

And Hopper was certain that Pup was hunkered down inside it. He threw back his shoulders and started toward the shoe.

"Wait," said Firren. "Maybe we should call out to him. We have no idea who or what he's got in there with him. Weapons, other rodents . . ."

"No." Hopper shook his head. "I'm going in." Again he strode toward the shoe; there was a rustle behind him as every paw settled on a sword handle. Hopper tried to ignore the implications of that.

As he drew closer, he saw that the seam of the old loafer's backstay had been split open to create a V-shaped entrance. Hopper crept toward it, peering inside.

"Pup?" he whispered, stepping inside. "Pup, it's me."

There was a shuffling sound from deep inside the toe of the shoe—a scuffing that sounded like a lot more paws than Hopper had been expecting.

"Pup . . . are you alone? Pup, please—"

Swiitttzzzzzzzzssssshhhh.

Hopper's face was suddenly entangled in clinging strands of silk, a gossamer mask that stuck to his fur and sealed his mouth and eyes shut. Sputtering, he clawed at the mess; it came away sticky and weightless in his paws.

"Looks like we have company, Hack." A cruel chuckle rumbled from the depths of the shoe. "Hopper, meet Hacklemesh. Hack, this is my brother, Hopper. Mr. Chosen One himself."

Again Hopper heard the scuttling sound. He fought against the gooey film that held his eyes closed. Then he felt something spiky and hairy reach for his face.

Spider legs!

He leaped backward, colliding with shoe leather.

"Oh, relax," Pup sneered. "He's not going to hurt you."

Hopper held his breath as the spider—Hacklemesh, it would seem—began peeling away the silken strands and knots that covered the Chosen One's face. It was an unpleasant pinching sensation that left him shuddering.

Finally the bulk of the web came away, and Hopper opened his eyes.

He immediately wished he hadn't.

What he saw was his tiny brother dressed in rags. The black circle he'd drawn around his eye back in the Mūs village had been darkened; the eerie marking seemed to have bled into his fur to leave a permanent, bruiselike mark. The sweet smile Hopper remembered was now a steely smirk, showing Pup's pointy little fangs.

"What have you done to yourself?" Hopper breathed. "Oh, Pup, what's happened to you?"

"I'm making a name for myself," the little mouse bragged. "I want to be taken seriously. If clobbering Felina is the only way for me to achieve that, then so be it. I'm tired of being everyone's responsibility."

Hopper let out a heavy sigh. "It wasn't like that, Pup."

"Wasn't it?" Pup's eyes flashed. "Do you know what Pinkie said when I told her I wanted to join her personal guard?"

Hopper didn't, but he guessed it was probably something terribly insulting.

"She said they'd never be able to make a uniform *tiny* enough," Pup informed him, snarling. But beneath the snarl Hopper heard the humiliation, the hurt.

"That was very unkind of her," Hopper agreed. "But, Pup, do you honestly think you can take on Felina by yourself?"

"Hacklemesh is with me. And as you've just seen, he can be very useful."

"I suppose he could," Hopper allowed. "In fact, shooting webs might be a very effective way to subdue a charging feral . . . assuming the ferals attack *one at a time*. The problem is, one good stomp of a feline paw would be equally effective in crushing your spider friend into the dirt."

Pup seethed. "Why do you have to belittle me that way?"

"Technically, I was belittling Hacklemesh."

This earned Hopper another squirt of spider silk, this time to the back of the head. "Well, I'm sorry," he said. "But it's true. You're small, Pup. And Hacklemesh is small. *I'm* small. But I have an army behind me, standing shoulder to shoulder . . . and that's something big." He pawed at the gossamer glop sticking behind his ears, losing patience. "Being stubborn and reckless is not the same as being brave, it's just . . . well, it's just stubborn and reckless, that's all!"

Pup folded his arms across his petite chest. "Then let me be a part of your army!" he demanded. "Let me march alongside you, with a weapon."

Hopper glanced away. "No."

"Why not?"

Because you're the size of a pistachio nut! Because Felina could devour you in a single gulp. Because you're my little brother, and if anything ever happened to you, it would destroy me.

"Because I love you," Hopper answered truthfully. "Because protecting you matters to me more than anything. It's why I came back. To rescue you."

"But I don't want to be rescued!" Pup fumed. "I don't want to be protected. I want to fight. I want to be like you and like Pinkie! And if I'm part of an army, it won't matter how puny I am."

"How puny you are on the *outside*," Hopper amended. "But, Pup, there's such a thing as being small on the inside. In your heart. This mission you're about is selfish and singular. You're angry, and the bigger the anger, the smaller the mouse."

Pup lunged forward, his paws grasping the handle of Hopper's newly forged sword. For one mad second Hopper feared Pup would impale him . . . but what he actually did was almost worse.

The tiny mouse used Hopper's sword to stab himself in his own ear, cutting a jagged slice into it!

"Pup!" Hopper cried. "Have you lost your mind?"

Pup's eyes were wild. Blood poured from the delicate flesh of his maimed ear, but he tried to mask the pain by laughing. "I take after my big brother and sister now," he cackled. "See? I've got the circle and I've got the scar. Am I Chosen enough for you now, Hopper? Am I?"

Hopper flew at his brother, grabbing the sword before Pup could damage himself further. Then he turned frantically to the spider. "Stop the bleeding!" he commanded.

Hacklemesh obeyed; Hopper watched as glistening filaments of spider silk shot through the air to coat and cling to Pup's injured flesh. The sticky-strong web instantly acted as a natural bandage to stem the flow of blood. And not a moment too soon.

Pup's eyes rolled back in his head, and his face went deathly pale. Heart racing, tears flowing, Hopper reached for his brother, who was swaying on his feet.

Gently he guided Pup downward until he was lying on the supple leather of the shoe's lining.

"Take me with you," Pup begged, his words as wispy as spider thread. "Please, let me fight." The icy fury was gone from his voice; only his innocence remained. It nearly broke Hopper's heart to hear it.

As he leaned over his little sibling, a tear spilled from Hopper's eye, falling onto Pup's face and blurring the dark circle, but not washing it away. "You wait here, brother," Hopper whispered. "I will come for you. I promise."

With that he pressed a kiss to Pup's forehead and climbed out of the shoe.

"There, up ahead," said Ranger Leetch. "That's Felina's lair."

The company halted in a scuffling of paws and clanking of weapons. Hopper squinted through the dusty dimness but saw nothing resembling the feline metropolis he'd been expecting. No bustling township, no comfortable cat community alive with commerce. Perhaps he was missing something.

"Where?" he asked. "Where is the city? I don't see a palace or a market square or anything."

Firren consulted the map. Then she examined the ground and lifted her dainty snout into the air and sniffed. "This has to be it," she said. "Not only is this the spot indicated on La Rocha's map, but the paw prints and fur traces in the dirt confirm it." She wrinkled her nose. "Not to mention the feline scent is unmistakable."

This was true; Hopper's nose convulsed at the powerful smell of cat permeating the dusty air. But he was still having a hard time believing that the feral queen lived *here*. He'd been expecting Felina's sovereign territory to be sprawling and upscale, like a larger, more opulent, feline-friendly version of Atlantia. He'd imagined a grand, glitzy castle rising up in a cluster of turrets and towers. But what he saw was a decrepit collection of old cardboard boxes turned on their sides.

Could these tattered boxes actually be the feral cats' living quarters? Hopper had had a bit of experience on the inside of a cardboard box, and to his mind there was nothing cozy or welcoming about it. And these boxes were far worse than the one he and Pinkie had broken out of. Some were bent or crushed at their corners, others were warped and water stained. Every one of them bore the swipelike gashes of cat claws marring their outer walls, and from what Hopper could see, the boxes boasted no interior furnishings beyond the occasional moldering blanket or torn, rotting pillow. More depressing accommodations he'd never seen.

And where in this nasty mess did Felina sleep? She called herself a queen, but her lair was dirty and dank, stinking of cat waste and crawling with fleas. There was nothing posh or pretty or prosperous about this village.

Felina's lair was nothing like Atlantia. Felina's lair was a dump.

"I guess this just goes to show you," mused Firren, "you can take the cat out of the alley, but you can't take the alley out of the cat."

Hopper's first thought was that he was glad it was his expert corps, and not one of the less experienced battalions, that had marched directly into this dangerous locale.

His second thought struck harder, bringing a tight, cold knot to his stomach.

"Does anyone else find it odd that there aren't any cats about?" he whispered. "Where *is* everybody?"

Garfield stepped forward, peering ahead at the empty boxes, the deserted grounds. Not a single feral cat prowled the encampment. It was eerily silent. "That's an excellent question, Chosen One."

"Maybe they're out scavenging," guessed Polhemus.

"Perhaps they've moved on in search of more prey," Driggs suggested.

"Or maybe," croaked Hopper, his fur suddenly bristling, his whiskers quivering madly, "they smelled us coming and they're at this very moment . . . surrounding us!"

He drew his sword just as several pairs of gleaming yellow eyes appeared in the darkness, blinking and glaring from the shadows, pressing toward them from all sides. The air was suddenly alive with the sound of hissing and spitting.

"Prepare to fight!" Hopper commanded.

The battalion drew their weapons as the ferals revealed themselves, slinking like smoke from the dark edges of the tunnel. Hopper could see the hunger on their faces, the hatred in their eyes. There was no grace in their movement, no shine to their coats.

Hopper's key-turned-sword, sharp and gleaming, sliced the air in threatening arcs. Firren's blade was, as ever, circling above her shoulder as her glittering eyes darted from one stalker to the next.

The cats pressed themselves toward the rodents, slowly, slowly. . . . Their paws slapped into the dry dirt, creating small, dusty explosions.

The enemy circle was closing in.

Hopper readied himself to strike.

"Charge!" shouted Polhemus.

The rodents sprang into action, and the tunnels erupted with the sound of their voices ringing out— war whoops, howls, primitive growls that resonated with the righteousness of their purpose. This was the brave, emboldened battle cry of a small species at last standing up to challenge their tormentors, to fight for justice, determined to take back the tunnels.

The ferals swatted and bit and stomped, but the rodent warriors were strong. Blistering screams of pain and surrender sizzled through the air as blades and rapiers found their targets again and again. Injured cats whimpered and meowed in defeat as they limped or hobbled or scurried away in retreat.

Hopper punched and kicked, and dodged bladelike claws and fangs. He took a swipe to his snout and tasted his own blood but kept fighting. Firren was all but a blur, her sword a silver flash as it whistled through the air, slicing off whiskers and shortening tails. The basketball rats moved as one, shooting rocks and throwing craggy-sharp stones with deadly accuracy.

Before long only two cats remained; they were the newest of the glaring—Hopper recognized them as the two that had skulked into the ruins of Atlantia and threatened the small mouse who'd judged Hopper so harshly and reminded him of his failure.

Hopper realized now as he backed away, panting and wheezing, from the bigger of the two cats that the small mouse had not shown up to fight today. Whether he'd met some tragic fate in the tunnels or was simply a coward, Hopper could not guess. But right now he did not care. He had more than enough loyal rodents beside him for this battle. And he was happy and relieved to note that while some bled and others clutched at broken bones and injured limbs, none lay lifeless on the dirt.

Even this small battalion had managed to hold its own against the vicious cats.

In fact, it seemed as if they had *won*.

Because the new cats who remained, despite their size, were outnumbered.

Hopper raised his blade. Firren coiled herself, ready to pounce. The soldiers and the basketball rats did not hesitate; they were already steaming forth in pursuit of these last two opponents like a speeding subway train.

Then Hopper caught sight of something that froze his blood. A cloud . . . a billowing puff of pure, snowy white emerging from the darkness. For one crazed second he thought the upland blizzard had found its way into the tunnels.

But the white shape was no icy storm cloud, and when Hopper realized what he was seeing, a single word tore from his throat—a desperate command, a panicked plea:

"NOOOOOOOOOOO!"

The racing army halted itself in a confusion of stumbling paws and weapons stalled in flight. Every eye—even the four poisonous-yellow eyes of the remaining two ferals—gaped at Hopper, who stood with his own eyes locked on the elegant white creature drifting cloudlike out of the shadows.

Felina.

Because she was not alone.

Dangling from her daggerlike fangs was the prince.

And he was alive.

Chapter Twenty-Four

Zucker.

Alive.

Barely.

The two ferals saw their chance for escape and bolted, kicking up grimy swirls of dust as they ran.

Felina's searing, mismatched eyes remained on the Chosen One as she skulked forward, holding the prince in her mouth like some ill-gotten prize. Clasped in her jaws, Zucker dangled like a wet rag. Hopper could see that he was cut and scratched and bitten in more places than he wasn't. His ears and tail were crusted over with scabs and welted with fresh scars. His eyes were closed and his head lolled as he hung there from Felina's mouth.

The purr of her smug contentment rolled from her throat like thunder, and her eyes snapped with triumph as they bored into Hopper. She could not speak, of course, occupied as she was with clamping the royal heir between her teeth. But her expression, icy and ferocious, spoke volumes.

"Zucker!" Hopper cried.

The prince flinched in his toothy prison. When his eyes opened, Hopper saw they were glazed and vacant.

Hopper knew that a single movement from him or

any of his troops would result in Zucker being eaten. The sense of helplessness shot through him like an electric shock.

Felina was once again calling the shots, making the rules.

Hopper's only hope would be to surprise her somehow. But with her devilish eyes glaring at them so unwaveringly, there was little chance of that.

"Zucker . . . ," Hopper whispered, tears springing to his own eyes.

"Hey, kid. How ya been?" Zucker's voice was a hollow croak, trembling with pain, but somehow his grin did not falter. "Heard you went upland."

Hopper nodded. "I did." His mind flashed on all the things he'd seen and done in the daylight world, things he would so love to share with Zucker. He thought of whom he'd met and what he'd learned. . . .

And slowly an idea came to him.

"I made a wonderful friend up there," Hopper went on, keeping his voice light, the conversation casual. "He's a cat, if you can believe it."

"I can believe it, kid. You're a likable mouse."

Hopper could see that Felina's brow was knit low. She was smart enough to know he was up to something; he was smart enough to know that the trick would be not letting her know what it was.

"This friend taught me how to do a really amazing thing. Would you like to hear it?"

Zucker winced. "Well, this ain't exactly the time for a floor show, kid, but if you really want to—"

"Oh, I want to," Hopper assured him. "I really want to!"

Then he lifted his head and began to whistle. The shrill sound carried itself away, far into the tunnels.

Felina's eyes flashed as she slid her glance left and right, wondering what Hopper had intended with all that noise. When nothing happened, she seemed to relax, although she did not release her hold on the prince.

Hopper turned to Firren, who was staring at Felina with fiery eyes. Garfield and Polhemus and Driggs all held their swords aloft, and Hopper knew even the slightest nod from him would send them tearing at the cat with a single, bloody intention.

But he also knew that such a charge would result in instant death for Zucker.

"What is it you want, Felina?" Hopper asked. "You've lost the fight. Your ferals have deserted you. Even if you . . ." He paused, searching for a word he could say without being sick. "Even if you . . . *consume* . . . our prince, you will win nothing."

Felina clearly did not like having her failure pointed out to her. She narrowed her flashing eyes and ever so slightly tightened her jaws.

"Aaaahhhhggghhh!" Zucker screamed as Felina's teeth bit into his flesh.

"Stop!" cried Hopper, raising his sword toward the queen cat's chest. "Stop or I'll—"

Again the cat bit down on the prince. Zucker winced. This time the noise that escaped him was an agonized growl.

"Release him!"

The voice came out of the darkness, blazing with authority, echoing with might.

Even Felina started at the sound of it, nearly dropping Zucker from her clenched jaws.

"Release him," the voice commanded again. "Release my son."

"Titus!" gasped Hopper. He could barely believe what he was seeing. The exiled emperor of Atlantia—his robe tattered, his face drawn—was standing before him.

And then he wasn't . . . because he was moving.

Forward and with great force, heading straight for Felina. A rasping scream tore from Titus's throat as he flung himself at her front leg and sank his teeth into the fur.

Felina opened her mouth, letting out a blood-chilling shriek and releasing Zucker from the grip of her jaws.

Firren sprang forward, as did Driggs, placing themselves between the prince and the ground. It was a clumsy catch, but their quick action spared him from a bone-breaking landing.

Felina ignored her lost prize; baring her teeth, she began to stalk the emperor.

"You disgusting beast," Felina hissed, circling the rat. "You think I won't devour you simply because we once enjoyed a mutually profitable business arrangement?"

"Devour me," Titus said, lifting his chin in a defiant pose. "Go ahead. I deserve to meet such a violent and undignified end. Just spare my son. I will gladly sacrifice myself so that he may live."

Felina laughed, then reached out her front paw and gave the frail emperor a firm swat. The force of the blow knocked him to his knees.

"Oh, Titus. How familiar this all is," Felina sneered. "Do you remember how you fell to your knees and begged me for mercy before?"

"What are you talking about?" Zucker asked, gritting his teeth against his pain. "What is she saying, Father?"

Titus expelled a ragged breath. "It's a long story, my son. And it doesn't matter now."

"It matters to me," said Zucker. "When did you ever beg Felina for mercy?"

"Tell him, Titus," Felina drawled. "You know how I love reminiscing."

Titus clenched his jaws. "It was long ago," he began, his voice hollow and distant. "Your mother had just given me the news that she was expecting. I was thrilled and terrified, and I went to Felina to ask her what it would take for her to leave my family alone."

The emperor's craggy paw went to the scar that snaked so hideously across his snout.

"She told me that she would spare my litter, and any other rodent to whom I chose to grant my protection, if I agreed to bring her as many rodents as I could lay my filthy paws upon. As I could see no other way to save the pups I had already begun to love, I offered my paw and my word to this evil queen. I thought just one such offense could not be too difficult to endure, so I did as Felina asked. But after the first . . . sacrifice . . . she was so pleased with the arrangement, she decreed that our foul covenant would not be put asunder until she declared it so."

"I was brilliant," Felina purred.

Zucker's face was an unreadable mask. "There was a litter? Where are they?"

"Died," said Titus with a sob. "All of them. At birth, and of natural causes." His weary eyes flickered toward Felina, and the hatred in his gaze was unmistakable.

"Time went by," Felina continued, glowering at Zucker. "You grew up without a clue as to how the peace accord worked. But one day your royal mother came to me, all dressed up in that dangly blue-and-gold necklace of hers, to appeal to my good graces. Unfortunately for her, I've never had any of those." The cat laughed; it was a mirthless cackle. "She had finally learned the truth about the camps and wanted me to do away with the atrocity of the hunting ground. I told her that was fine with me, I would gladly put an end to all of it if she would just give me one teeny-tiny little thing."

"And that was . . . ?" snarled Zucker.

"What else?" Felina's eyes narrowed to slits and her fangs glistened. "Her *life*."

Firren gasped; Hopper let out a yelp of revulsion.

"And she *agreed* to that?" asked Zucker, appalled.

"Well, now, I'm not really sure," said Felina with a flick of her fluffy tail. "She never did get around to answering the question, you see, because . . . I had already devoured her in one tasty bite."

Zucker roared with anguish; Titus merely closed his eyes.

"But you never did put an end to the camps . . . ," shouted Hopper. "Or the hunting ground! You told her you would stop the sacrifices, but you didn't."

"I happen to be a wonderful liar," Felina crooned. "In fact, it was a lie that got me this beautiful little bauble." She craned her white neck to show off her famous red collar. "It belonged to a trusting mother cat I met when I was on death row in an upland animal shelter. She had a litter, three male kittens, all named for playing cards, if I recall. I knew the humans would never take the life of a mama, so I conned her into letting me try on the collar, knowing they would think *she* was *me* . . . and guess who got the needle! I got to live, *and* I walked away with her pretty red collar."

"You're diabolical," said Hopper.

"Yes. And I also happen to be hungry." Felina glared at Titus, who was still huddled on his knees in the dirt. "I'm in the mood for rat, Your Majesty. Shall I feast on fresh young rebel flesh?" She tossed her head in Zucker's direction, then leaned down so that her nose was touching Titus's. "Or should I just settle for rancid old emperor meat?"

Hopper felt his stomach clench as Titus turned his desperate, grieving eyes to Zucker.

"For all that I have done wrong," he whispered, "I apologize."

That was his answer.

In one lightning-fast motion Felina dipped her head and clamped her teeth around Titus. A second later he was gone.

Zucker let out a howl of fury just as a streak of black-and-white fur rocketed out of the darkness and slammed into Felina.

"Ace!" cried Hopper.

The cats fought wildly, a tangle of striking claws and gnashing teeth, until the upland cat had pinned the feral queen in the dirt. Dust rose in a choking cloud, and Ace's green eyes glowed in the midst of it as he bared his fangs and went for her throat.

"Mrrrrowwww!"

When Ace jerked his head up again, Hopper's
stomach turned over at the sight of something red
that appeared to drip from his mouth.

"Is that blood?" Firren whispered.

"I hope so," seethed Zucker.

But as Hopper squinted through the dirt cloud, he
saw that it was not a bloody piece of Felina's flesh
that hung from Ace's jaws . . . it was her collar.

"Get out of here, Felina . . . ," Ace snarled, gripping
his jeweled prize in his teeth. "And don't ever come
back."

He released Felina, who bounded off, hissing and snarling, into the tunnel.

Hopper watched until her white tail disappeared around a sharp bend. And at that very moment he heard the familiar rumbling from the depths of the gloom. Shadows flickered as a blinding stream of light ignited the tiled walls. Metal wheels screamed along their rails, spitting sparks . . . and the cat queen was running straight for them.

The last sound she made was a shriek of horror that was instantly swallowed by the roar of the train.

Felina's reign had ended.

The Queen of the Ferals was pronounced dead by Polhemus. The train had done what the rodents had thought to do themselves. And as much as Hopper believed that taking their revenge against Felina would have been justified, he was just as happy not to have her blood on his paws. He may have become a seasoned warrior, but he still did not relish the idea of killing another living creature.

"What shall we do about the lair?" Driggs asked.

"Torch it," said Garfield. "Burn it to a crisp. Let the memory of Felina and her wicked ferals vanish with the smoke."

Everyone looked to the Chosen One, who nodded. It was decided that the basketball rats would carry the severely wounded prince the long distance back to Atlantia. Hopper covered him with the patchwork banner for warmth, and Firren would walk with her paw wrapped around Zucker's limp and trembling one.

Valky, Driggs, and the soldiers, their weapons at the ready, fell into formation, flanking Zucker.

Hopper and Ace would meet up with them in Atlantia later; they had a stop to make.

Then Hopper pointed a steady claw into the tunnels.

"To Atlantia," he said.

"And mind those train tracks," whispered Ace.

The triumphant rodent army headed home.

They approached the shoe warily. From a distance Ace examined it with the discerning eye of a typically fashion-conscious Brooklynite.

"Your brother's got good taste," he declared, pointing out the quality leather and hand tooling. "Where I come from, humans pay a fortune for shoes like these."

"I don't think Pup chose it for its stylishness," said Hopper. He moved closer to the shoe and cupped a paw around his mouth. "Pup . . . Hacklemesh. It's me, Hopper. I'm coming in to get you. I just want to bring you back to Atlantia, so please don't shoot any of that spidery gunk at me this time."

Hopper waited for a reply.

None came.

His heart thudded.

"Maybe he's just being stubborn," Ace suggested.

"Or maybe he's not. Maybe he's . . ."

Hopper bolted for the shoe, leaping through the V-shaped opening in the torn seam. "Pup!" he cried, searching the shoe with frantic eyes.

The soft leather insole was stained with blood.

And Pup was gone.

All that remained was a message (written by the spider, Hopper assumed, but dictated by Pup), scrawled in dark stone dust on the interior sides of the shoe. It was a rather long statement; fortunately for Pup, the original owner of the pricey wing tip had had very big feet.

I DIDN'T DIE, the message said.

This declaration came as a great relief to Hopper. He took a moment to still his racing heart before reading on:

> I EXPECT YOU HAVE ALREADY FOUGHT
> FELINA AND PROBABLY WON. BUT I DID
> NOT ASK YOU TO FIGHT MY BATTLES
> FOR ME. I CAN TAKE CARE OF MYSELF.
> I DO NOT WANT, NOR DO I NEED, YOUR
> PROTECTION.

The next line made Hopper's blood turn frigid.

> FROM NOW ON, BROTHER, IT WILL
> BE YOU AND OUR SISTER WHO WILL
> REQUIRE PROTECTION.

If this prediction weren't bad enough, it was the final three words that actually made Hopper dizzy. Because Pup had concluded his message with this fur-bristling phrase:

PROTECTION . . . FROM *ME*!

When at last Hopper had recovered from his shock, he and Ace set out again.

"I think maybe he's bluffing," said Ace.

"Maybe." Hopper sighed. "I suppose there's nothing I can do about it right now."

"Exactly," said Ace. "I say forget about Pup for the moment. You should be celebrating. You just defeated the wicked Queen of the Ferals. I think that entitles you to be in a very good mood."

"Yes," Hopper agreed. And despite the memory of Pup's haunting proclamation, he smiled. "We really did it, didn't we?"

"Nice going with that SOS," said Ace.

"I'm just glad you made it," said Hopper.

About halfway back to the city the two ferals who had survived the battle appeared in their path.

"Want me to handle this?" Ace whispered.

"Thanks, but I've got it." Hopper stepped forward toward the spitting cats, his tiny shoulders squared, his paw on the hilt of his weapon.

"Are you hungry?" he demanded to know.

The ferals exchanged glances as Hopper took a step toward them, gripping his sword. "Where did you go when you left Felina's lair?"

"To the upland platform where the humans wander," said one.

"Did you find food there?" Hopper asked.

"Some," said the other. "Bits and scraps. Enough."

Hopper nodded. "Then I will ask you again and you will answer with honesty. . . . Are . . . you . . . *hungry?*"

"No," said the first cat.

"Then leave us be."

Again the cats looked at each other, confused.

"This is how it is to be in these tunnels from now on," declared Hopper. "Hunger is the only purpose to hunt . . . not vengeance, not sport, not power. Nature will see to the balance; nature deals the cards."

Cards. Ace. Hopper suddenly remembered what Felina had said about the litter in the upland shelter—*kittens named for playing cards.*

As the ferals prowled off toward their smoldering lair, Hopper turned to Ace, who had slung the red jeweled collar loosely around his neck.

"You had a family once, didn't you, Ace?" Hopper ventured softly. "Brothers named King and Jack?"

Ace confirmed this with a nod.

"And that's why you wanted to be the one to relieve Felina of her collar?"

"That's exactly why." The brave tuxedo cat gave his friend a sad smile. "Because it was my mother's."

Chapter Twenty-Five

HOPPER STRODE THROUGH THE gates of Atlantia feeling bigger and braver than he ever had in his life. He knew that the tunnels would never be completely without their dangers, or entirely free of challenge . . . but then, neither would life. And that was the adventure of it. From this day forward nature's justice—not Felina's fury—would prevail, and that was all any mouse could ask for.

The rodent warriors who'd made up the other three battalions had returned from the march and exchanged their weapons for tools. They were already back at work, repairing the city. Hopper was glad to see it; there was still much to do (as La Rocha had once told Hopper in a note), and although Pup's threat still lingered in the back of his mind, the Chosen One found himself looking forward to all that lay ahead.

The elders were waiting to welcome Hopper, the conquering hero, on the steps of the palace. They congratulated him and explained that the basketball rats had brought Zucker to his bedchamber, where his wounds had been cleansed and treated.

Hopper was eager to check on the prince. He was about to head into the palace when Valky appeared and laid his key sword on the top step. He turned to Ace.

"The Nets are playing the Knicks tonight," the chipmunk said. "Think we can manage to avoid that traitor with the broom and grab ourselves a couple of seats?"

Ace laughed. "Sure. I'm counting on Brooklyn to beat the spread. Capone's a New York fan, so there's a sausage-and-pepper grinder riding on this game."

"Wait," said Hopper, his head swiveling from Ace to Valky, then back to Ace. "You're going back?" He felt tears stinging his eyes. "You're not staying?"

"We can't stay, Hopper," said Ace, swishing his tail to pull Hopper in for a friendly squeeze. "I've got a job to do, remember? There are lots of rodents who still need to be relocated, and Valky has to be there to show them how to survive in the grasslands. Especially now, with all that snow on the ground."

Hopper knew Ace was right, but he hated the thought of saying good-bye.

"Julius, Kidd, and Dawkins are going to stick around for a while," Valky told Hopper, "long enough to build a basketball court in the playground for the little ones."

"That'll be nice," croaked Hopper, biting back tears.

"Hey," said Ace. "You know you can come up and visit us anytime."

"I know," said Hopper, dabbing his eyes. "And I will.

I promise." He took a deep breath. "Good-bye, Ace. And thanks. For everything."

"I knew you were something special the minute I saw you dangling from that bridge," whispered Ace, leaning down to brush his silky face against Hopper's back.

"You're special too," Hopper said. "Say hi to Capone for me. And send Carroll my . . ." He almost said "love," but since the thought of that made him blush, he said "my best" instead.

Valky snapped Hopper a little salute, then turned and trotted down the steps. Ace followed. When they reached the bottom, Ace looked back and gave Hopper a wink. "You're going to accomplish great things down here, Hopper," he called. "I can feel it."

Then he was gone.

With a stab in his heart Hopper entered the palace.

Hopper was touched to see that the flag he had sewn with his own two paws, the banner that had acted as a blanket for the prince on his journey home, now lay folded neatly at the foot of the bed.

Zucker had been fed a hearty meal. His wounds were cleansed and bandaged. He told Hopper and Firren all about his captivity under Felina's watchful glare, about how she'd deprived him of sleep and nourishment, tossing and bouncing him around the lair whenever the mood had struck her. The only thing that had kept her from eating him alive, he told them, was that she thought he would make a better hostage than a meal.

Hopper decided to give the prince and the rebel warrior their privacy. He knew Firren had a great many things to say to Zucker, and he suspected, from the way that Zucker smiled a big, dopey smile every time his eyes met Firren's, that he had a few things to say to her, too. When he took his leave, Firren was sitting vigil beside the prince's bed, not because she worried his condition might take a negative turn, but because every few minutes the prince attempted to throw off the covers and get out of bed, announcing that he wanted to oversee the activity in and around the palace.

"Must I remind you," Firren was saying as Hopper tiptoed through the door, "that I'm holding a very big sword?"

In the entry hall Hopper was met by a servant, who handed him a note addressed to the Chosen One. According to the servant, it had arrived just after they'd set out for battle, hand delivered by a mouse bedecked in full military regalia.

"What color was it?"

"The mouse?"

"The uniform."

The servant frowned. "Oddly enough, it was pink."

Hopper laughed and tore open the note:

Dear Hopper,

I am sure you know by now that Pup has gone off on his own in a misguided attempt to prove that he is a capable warrior. I am guessing you received this information from that sneaky rat-rebel friend of yours, Firren, who managed to escape me.

Although I am not ordinarily the sort to extend an olive branch, I have decided that for Pup's sake you and I must now consider forming an alliance. If we don't, the little fool will most likely get himself killed.

My grand plan, if you're interested, is to continue my efforts to lead the Mūs. They are our family, and they are good and wise. They can be fierce, too, and you know how much I like that. But I've recently had it pointed out to me, by someone for whom I have a reluctant respect, that as a leader I have certain, shall we say, faults. And so, based on the advice of this respectable

SOMEONE, I HAVE VOWED TO TRY
LEADING WITH FAIRNESS AND JUSTICE,
JUST AS OUR FATHER, DODGER, WOULD
HAVE DONE. I DOUBT IT WILL BE AS
MUCH FUN, BUT I WILL DO MY BEST.

   TO REITERATE, I INTEND TO MAKE
MYSELF AVAILABLE TO JOIN FORCES
WITH YOU ON A MISSION TO SAVE
PUP. IF YOU WANT TO GET TOGETHER
TO DISCUSS THIS, AND TO DETERMINE
WHETHER TOGETHER WE MIGHT
SOMEHOW POUND SOME SENSE BACK
INTO OUR CRAZY LITTLE BROTHER,
PLEASE LET ME KNOW.
SINCERELY,
YOUR SISTER, PINKIE

P.S. HEY, HOPPER, REMEMBER THAT
MORNING IN THE PET SHOP WHEN THE
BOY CAME IN WITH THE SNAKE? EVEN
THOUGH I TRIED NOT TO ACT LIKE IT,
I WAS PRETTY SCARED. JUST THOUGHT
YOU SHOULD KNOW.

P.P.S. I'M SORRY I BIT YOUR EAR.

P.P.P.S. YOU'D BETTER BE SORRY YOU
BIT MINE!

Hopper folded up the note and slipped it into his pocket. He would reply with a similar missive, telling her all that had transpired in that old wing-tip loafer. He would explain that although Pup had not gone to his death in a one-on-one battle with Felina, he was still MIA and in need of their prompt intervention. To that end Hopper would graciously accept her offer of an alliance.

He would also extend to her an invitation.

An invitation to a wedding.

The whole of Atlantia, as well as the entire Mūs tribe, turned out for the celebration of Zucker's royal wedding to the rebel leader, Firren.

The ceremony was to be held on the steps of the palace. A very enthusiastic crowd had gathered at the base of the sweeping staircase, spilling into the streets of Atlantia as far as the town square. The young, newly crowned emperor wore his customary purple tunic, adorned with the gold-and-blue jeweled chain that had once belonged to his mother. Hopper, of course, was Zucker's best mouse, and Ranger Leetch had been awarded the honor of walking Firren down the aisle. Lilting strains of beautiful music came from an orchestra of crickets.

As Hopper took his place on the top step beside a very nervous Zucker, a blue-robed figure emerged from the palace.

"I wish to preside over the ceremony," came the stranger's voice from deep inside the cover of his hood.

"Sure, fine . . . works for me." Zucker barely glanced at the stranger; he was too busy watching Firren make her way gracefully up the stairs.

"Who is that?" Hopper whispered to the prince-turned-emperor.

"No idea, kid. As long as he's official, I don't care who it is."

Hopper frowned and eyed the robed figure with interest. There was something strangely familiar about the blue fabric of his cloak.

When Firren reached the pinnacle of the staircase, Leetch placed the bride's dainty paw in Zucker's. Hopper tore his eyes away from the stranger in the blue robe to survey the happy crowd. When he spotted Pinkie in her golden robe, he noticed she had an odd little smile on her face, as if she were in possession of some terrific secret—as if she knew something Hopper didn't.

Now Leetch stepped away, and Zucker and Firren were looking into each other's eyes while the stranger in the blue robe raised his arms in a mystical blessing.

"Dearly beloved . . . ," he began.

The cloaked stranger was an eloquent speaker. He spoke of love and loyalty, of partnership and promise, and when he invoked La Rocha's name, Zucker didn't even roll his eyes.

Hopper thought Firren was positively glowing. He was especially relieved that the groom managed to remain standing through the entire service, despite the fact that his royal knees never stopped shaking.

When the ritual was complete, the stranger nodded inside his hood. "And so it shall be," he proclaimed. "The rebel Firren and the newly named emperor Zucker are united in an endless bond. Together they will guide and protect the good citizens of Atlantia with patience and wisdom, integrity and kindness."

When Zucker leaned forward to place a shy kiss on his bride's cheek, Hopper led the crowd in a round of rousing applause.

As the guests headed into the palace for the reception, Hopper caught a glimpse of Bartel and Pritchard, and it dawned on him that he hadn't seen their sister, Marcy, since the night before the battle with Felina. Odd that she hadn't attended Zucker's wedding. He was sure she had her reasons, although he couldn't imagine what they might be.

"Thank you for that beautiful ceremony," Firren was telling the robed stranger.

"Yeah," said Zucker. "That was some top-notch officiating you did there." He reached out his paw to shake the stranger's hand. "Thanks."

The stranger removed his hood and smiled broadly

at the groom. "You are most humbly welcome . . . Zuck-meister," he said.

Firren gasped.

Zucker stared.

And Hopper—the Chosen One, the son of Dodger—blinked once . . . twice . . . then collapsed in a faint, right there on the steps of the palace.

Hopper heard voices.

He was aware of Zucker saying, "We've missed you like crazy, pal," and Firren saying, "Thank goodness you're all right," and then Zucker saying, "Where in the heck have you been hiding all this time?"

But as Hopper awoke, what he reveled in more than the sound of these familiar voices was the feeling of warmth that surrounded him, the strong, steady heartbeat thrumming against his fur. Slowly he opened his eyes to look up at a white circle of fur, into the eyes of his father.

His *father*.

As the daze lifted, Hopper realized that he was in Zucker's bed with the banner of scraps tucked around him. Dodger . . . his father . . . was perched on the edge of the bed, close beside him. Just like he'd been so long ago in the nest of aspen curls. His heartbeat lulled Hopper now as it had then. But this time, Hopper knew, it wasn't going to disappear.

Hopper sat up and looked around at his friends and family. "Sorry I fainted."

"Can't say I blame you, kid." Zucker chuckled. "Nearly passed out myself when I saw the late, great Dodger standing there . . . alive . . . on the steps of my palace."

"We were so worried about you," said Firren, gently stroking the fur on Hopper's forehead.

"Personally, I thought you were never going to wake up," came Pinkie's voice from across the room. She was seated at Zucker's desk with her arms folded and her eyes narrowed. "You are such an attention hog, Hopper."

Hopper decided to ignore the barb; after all, she was there, waiting to see that he awoke safely. That had to count for something.

Now Hopper turned to Dodger with an expression of disbelief. "I don't understand, Father. We all thought you were—"

"It was all just a ruse," Dodger explained. "So I could continue to work in secret toward our goal of liberating the camps."

"Wish you would have let us in on it," joked Zucker. "Spent an awful lot of time mourning your loss."

Dodger looked sheepish. "I'm sorry about that, my friend. I thought it was for the best to let everyone believe that Cassius had done what he set out to do."

"So Firren's theory was right all along," Hopper

said. "Cassius only injured you and you went upland, and now you're back."

"Wanna hear something nuts?" said Zucker. "There were a few moments there right after you disappeared when I thought . . . well, when I found myself wondering if maybe . . ."

"Maybe what?" asked Dodger.

Zucker shrugged. "Well, I had this gut feeling, this strong hunch, that maybe . . . possibly . . ." He scratched the fur on the back of his neck and sighed.

"Just say it," urged Hopper. "You thought . . . what?"

"That Dodger had become La Rocha," the emperor blurted out.

For a moment no one said a word, their eyes moving curiously to Dodger, who sat beside Hopper with a blank expression on his face.

Then Pinkie let out a loud snort, and everyone started laughing at once.

"See?" Zucker frowned. "I told you it was crazy."

"Not as crazy as you might think," said Dodger, giving the Zuck-meister a chummy clap on the back. "But I assure you, old friend, as certain as I'm standing here before you *right now* . . . I am *not* La Rocha."

Here Dodger paused to slide a quick glance at Pinkie, and Hopper could have sworn he saw his father wink.

"I'm just Dodger," he continued, "an ordinary Mūs, a mortal being. But La Rocha will live forever in these tunnels."

Hopper smiled. He liked that La Rocha brought faith to the underdwellers, because he knew that everything that really mattered began with hope.

"In fact," said Dodger, "I can guarantee that La Rocha is somewhere out there right this very minute, spreading his . . . or her . . . goodness and wisdom, and giving all of us something to believe in."

The gathering took a moment to let this sink in. Even Zucker looked convinced.

Then the emperor and empress took their leave, so the newly reunited family could have some time alone in one another's company. Hopper's heart ached for the absence of Pup. How his brother would have loved knowing that their father was alive. At least, the old, innocent Pup would have loved it. This new, frightening Pup was an entirely different story.

Hopper took a minute to fill Dodger in on the episode in the wing-tip loafer and Pup's second disappearance.

"Your brother, it seems, is experiencing some growing pains."

"Yeah," grumbled Pinkie. "He's growing, and we're the ones feeling the pain."

Dodger smiled at her ready wit, but his face soon turned serious again. "We will do everything we can to find him," he promised. "We'll work together and we'll bring Pup back."

"My Mūs army is at your disposal," Pinkie offered magnanimously.

"And I'm sure Zucker and Atlantia will do whatever is necessary to locate Pup," added Hopper.

Dodger nodded. "It is nice to see you two agreeing on something," he said with a grin. "I know we are all afraid for Pup, but at least he's in far less danger now that Felina is gone."

"Heard she made quite a nasty splat," said Pinkie, her lip curling up in a wicked smile.

"That's disgusting," said Hopper.

Pinkie rolled her eyes, and Hopper quickly changed the subject.

"Father," he began, suddenly nervous. "I was just wondering . . . where are you planning to live now? I'd love it if you decided to stay here in the palace."

"Hey!" Pinkie scowled. "I'm sure he'd rather come back to the Mūs village with me. After all, that was his home."

Dodger stroked the white fur around his eye thoughtfully. "I was hoping there might be room for me in both places. Zucker has already asked me to sign on as one of his advisors, so naturally, I'll spend a significant amount of time here in Atlantia. But I would also like to see about expanding the Mūs Tribunal into a quartet. I have great respect for Sage and Temperance and Christoph, and I would like to be a part of our ancestral community." He smiled at his two Chosen children. "What do you think about that arrangement?"

Pinkie let out a huff. "I suppose I can live with that," she said.

Hopper was slightly less enthusiastic. Now that his father was back in his life, he hated the idea of losing him . . . even if only on a part-time basis. For a moment he considered swallowing his pride and asking Pinkie if he could join them both behind the gray wall.

But then his mind spiraled back to the day on the palace steps when they'd led Titus out in chains, and he heard the echo of Zucker's words:

Becoming a guiding force in the future of Atlantia is pretty much your destiny.

Hopper knew in the marrow of his bones that this was the truth. As much as he loved and respected his Mūs brethren, Atlantia was his home. Even during his time in the daylight world with Ace he'd yearned for it. He'd worried for it. He'd tried to push it from his mind and his heart, but he couldn't do it. When he first arrived in the tunnels, he'd been frightened and without hope, but with Zucker's help he'd looked deep into his mouse soul and discovered courage there, courage he'd used to help the city rise above its own evil past to begin a new and magical journey.

Atlantia needed Hopper because Hopper was Atlantia's destiny . . . and now more than ever Atlantia was his.

Feeling safe and content, he settled back into his

pillows. Dodger motioned to Pinkie to join them on the bed, and to Hopper's surprise, she did, tucking herself in at his feet. They sat together quietly for some time. When at last Pinkie spoke, her voice was so gentle Hopper almost couldn't believe it was hers.

"Father," she whispered. "Will you tell us about our mother?"

"Yes," said Hopper, pleased that she'd thought to ask. "Tell us."

"All right," said Dodger, reaching out to take first Hopper's paw, then Pinkie's. His eyes sparkled as he let himself remember. "Your mother was lovely. Smart like you, Hopper, but also fierce and determined, just like our Pinkie. Like many of the rodents who are born to Brooklyn, above or below it, your mother was given a name to honor the city. I was named for a proud band of warriors who once battled in a grand stadium for which my own father was named. Your mother, like your friends Garfield and Polhemus and Ketchum, was named for one of the city's fine streets. In my opinion, she was given the loveliest name of all, after the most pleasant and beautiful street in all the borough."

"What street was it?" asked Hopper, his voice reverent. "What was Mama's name?"

"It was more than just a name, really. It was a promise, a prophecy, a reminder of the greatest gift

that any of us can ever give to one another." The great Dodger's eyes shone with pride as he looked from his feisty Chosen daughter to his courageous Chosen son. "Your mother's name," he told them, "was Hope."

La Rocha's journal—from the Sacred Book of the *Mūs:*

> *I, the mystical and revered La Rocha, begin my life anew as the eternal voice of these tunnels.*
>
> *My predecessor is at this very moment enjoying the company of his beloved children for the first time since they were newborn pups. He has served us well for some time now, and he has earned his retirement. For the last several weeks he has been preparing me to take up his mantle and carry on this important work.*
>
> *Much will be expected of me in my new role. This is an enormous responsibility I have accepted, but I believe in my heart that I am equal to the task.*
>
> *What I want for all who dwell here is to live in peace, governed by justice. But before that can happen, I fear that we must first endure the challenge of a new and powerful enemy.*

He is out there now, in these subway tunnels, seething and simmering, nursing his wounds—both real and imagined—fanning the flames of his anger and awaiting the moment to release his wrath.

He is small, but his plans are big, and his pain is deep.

There is no opponent so dangerous as he who acts in desperation. For in his mind he has nothing to lose. I must find a way to impart this to those who believe in me. Perhaps I will look to my former existence to see what wisdom I can borrow from the life I used to live.

A life in which I nursed a prince and protected a Chosen One.

And watched a revolution grow from its infancy to a promising but tremulous conclusion.

I have seen great suffering, and immeasurable courage. I have witnessed what amazing success can come from the simple act of rodents believing in themselves; they will need to hold fast to that faith when this lurking threat unveils itself.

And it will be up to me to guide them . . . to comfort and advise, to teach and inspire. To watch and listen, and share the secrets of these tunnels with all those who strive to make them safe.

I will begin now by going to the Runes to inscribe this message:

BEWARE THE TINY VILLAIN

RINGED IN A CIRCLE OF GLOOM.

FOR HE IS THE THIEF WHO STEALS HOPE.

AND THE LOSS OF HOPE IS DOOM.

EPILOGUE

FOR DAYS PUP'S MIND had raced, shifting back
and forth between the moment's reality and the
blistering images of the past; these were mingled
with vague, bewildering possibilities for the future.

As he stumbled and staggered away from his shoe
shelter, he flashed back to his arrival in the tunnels.
His terrifying drop out of the subway car, his crash
landing into the hard-packed dirt.

And Cassius.

Cassius, the general who, with a small legion of
Atlantian scouts serving at the pleasure of the emperor
Titus of the House of Romanus, had found the little
mouse crying and cowering beside the rusted metal
rail of the subway track. With a smile that reminded
Pup of the snake he'd just so narrowly escaped,
Cassius had told the wanderer that there was nothing
to fear. Atlantia would provide; Atlantia would offer
care and shelter and the promise of a whole new life.

Pup had followed willingly. He'd thought he'd been
saved.

Now in his mind's eye he pictured himself enjoying

the comforts of the refugee camp and rejoicing when his brother arrived.

Then things became complicated. War whoops and battle cries and a bone horn sounding its warning. Smoke and chaos.

A battle witnessed from deep within a metal cup.

Pinkie's reign, his own escape . . . and Hacklemesh, the hideous-looking but surprisingly friendly creature who possessed the most remarkable ability . . . that of spinning webs.

It was thanks to Hack that Pup had survived as he combed the tunnels in search of Felina's lair. The spider had trapped flies and shared them with the near-starving mouse.

And then Hopper had shown up and ruined everything.

Hopper always ruined everything.

ACKNOWLEDGMENTS

I WISH TO THANK the following people who have added so much to my Mouseheart experience, and more important, to my life:

My deepest affection and gratitude to Shannon and Ricky, who remain my most loyal and trusted companions on every adventure. You guys give me courage when I need it (which is most of the time).

Thanks and respect to the extremely cool people at Simon & Schuster, Ruta, Katy, and Paul, who've helped make being an author more exciting than I ever knew it could be.

Adoration and appreciation to my "Ode Friends," who love writing (and dessert) as much as I do.

High-fives to my cousins—all of them! The ones I have looked up to and the ones for whom (I hope) I've set a good example. For this only child, you have always been a comfort and a gift.

Love to Dolores, Erik, and Jimmy . . . not the family I was born into, but the one I was lucky enough to marry into.

And finally, I offer something bigger and more profound than even I have words to describe to my mom and dad, who never laughed at the little girl who said she wanted to be a writer. . . . They just bought more paper.

Take a sneak peek
at the epic conclusion
to the Mouseheart trilogy,

RETURN OF THE FORGOTTEN

THEY STOOD ON A LEDGE far above the city with Atlantia sparkling below.

Sparkling and growing still, thought Hopper; the metropolis was improving and expanding, it seemed, every minute of every day.

"Tell me again how Atlantia came to be," came a sweet voice from beside him.

Hopper smiled and looked down into the snapping black eyes of his goddaughter, the princess Hope.

"Well," he began, delighted by the tiny rat's interest in learning her own history, "Atlantia was the dream of your grandfather, the late emperor Titus. He was an ambitious upland rat from Brooklyn, New York."

Hope shuddered. "But he was nasty!"

"He was misguided," Hopper corrected, but this was being generous. The truth was that as emperor, Titus had made a host of extremely poor choices, and countless innocent rodents had suffered because of his politics. It was also true that Titus had taken a forgotten subway platform deep beneath the borough of Brooklyn and transformed it into the spectacular city that lay before them now. But to maintain this prosperity, he had been forced to spend most of his reign sacrificing unsuspecting tunnel wanderers to the evil cat Queen Felina. Titus justified his own evil as being necessary to buy peace for Atlantia.

In the end, he paid a much greater price.

But Hopper did not like to discuss such gruesome details with his little friend. Instead he told her a far more palatable version of the story.

"Long ago, Titus happened upon this abandoned platform and chose it as the site on which to build his dazzling city. Under Titus's leadership, Atlantia bloomed into a great civilization."

"But my grandfather was hiding a dark secret," Hope cried, knowing the story by heart.

"Yes he was." Hopper gave her a solemn nod. "A secret that brought a great deal of pain to many . . . including himself. But thanks to your mother and father . . ."

"And you! The Chosen One!"

Hopper blushed slightly. "Right . . . thanks to all of us, and the rebels and the refugees, Titus was overthrown, and then, not long after, Felina, too, was defeated, putting an end to the brutality and the tyranny."

"But in the aftermath of battle Atlantia fell to ruins," Hope gushed, her eyes brimming with intelligence and excitement. "Now you and the emperor and empress—"

Hopper grinned. "Otherwise known as your mommy and daddy. You know they do not wish to be called by such titles anymore, now that Atlantia's government is shifting away from a monarchy to something more democratic and fair."

Hope rolled her eyes and pouted. "I know. I also know that *that* means they don't want me to wear beautiful crowns and gowns and jewels, like my grandmamma, the empress Conselyea, did."

"In the scheme of things, crowns and gowns don't count for much," Hopper reminded her.

"But *I like being a princess.*"

"I know, little one, but your parents would much rather you liked being a good and wise leader instead." Hopper patted her between the ears. "They are determined to see Atlantia rise again, so it can welcome all rodents and offer them protection within its walls. And without any dark secrets this time. Come along, now."

As they started toward the palace, Hopper turned his attention back to the bustle of the city below. There he saw progress. Mice working beside rats working beside squirrels working beside chipmunks. Atlantia was on its way to once again becoming the magnificent place it had been the first time he'd seen it. After many long months of thrilling innovation and intensive labor, the underground urban masterpiece was nearly complete; the city was thriving again.

But it was more than just structural and commercial changes that Emperor Zucker and Empress Firren were striving for. They had an entirely new vision of the way Atlantia should be governed, and to this end, their empire was in the midst of great political improvements as well.

Citizens could now vote on civic decisions, and express their ideas at public hearings. Zucker had gotten the idea from a book in Titus's library. He called it a "republic," and together he and Firren were determined to make it a reality for Atlantia.

But they understood that even positive change took time, and they respected the fact that their subjects needed to get used to the idea.

So they stopped wearing their opulent jewels and elegant clothing. Zucker wore the same workaday attire his subjects did (which he found far more comfortable than his royal garb), and Firren always donned her beloved Rangers tunic. They requested that the Atlantians call them by name, not title.

Even still, the rodents insisted on bowing and curtsying to them and calling them His and Her Highness. The habit, it seemed, was difficult to break.

It seemed strange to Hopper that the rodents needed to be convinced of something that was in their own best interests, but there it was. He wondered: Did they believe that outward finery and glitz represented ability and competence? That was *exactly* the kind of superficiality Titus had relied upon to justify his authority. And look how *that* turned out!

In truth, when it came to governing, Hopper knew

that it was what was *inside* a rodent that counted. The character, not the crown, was what defined a ruler.

Sadly, little Hope did not yet understand this particular truth, but Hopper wasn't worried. She was still very young and she had many things to learn. At the moment, his darling godchild might be easily dazzled by her empress grandmamma's old tiaras and dresses (which she'd determinedly dug out of the palace basement and claimed for her own), but he truly believed she'd come to understand the value of invisible things like honesty, loyalty, and integrity. He was confident that she and her four littermates would one day step up to take part in the wonderful new government their parents were working so hard to set in motion.

This gave Hopper great joy indeed.

But mingled with his joy was the faintest prickle of sadness. It brought to mind his own littermates . . . his brother and sister. The last time he'd stood upon this ledge, he'd had no idea what his own future held and he'd been desperate to know what had become of Pinkie and Pup.

He knew well enough where Pinkie was *now*—safe behind the gray wall of their ancestral village, ruling the Mūs citizens with her newfound wisdom and benevolence. To Hopper's great relief, Pinkie had undergone a change of heart after discovering that their father, the legendary rebel Dodger, was still alive. She was still given to grumbling and bossiness, but she was no longer angry or unkind. Dodger split his time between assisting Pinkie in ruling the Mūs, and advising Zucker here in Atlantia. Hopper was thrilled about Pinkie's new outlook.

But Pup. Pup was another story entirely.

Where in these vast tunnels their diminutive sibling had taken himself off to still remained a mystery. And what Pup might be up to was anybody's guess.

"Uncle Hopper! Look!"

"What is it, Hope?" Hopper asked, shaking off his dark thoughts. "What do you see?"

"Over there!" Hope leaned so far toward the rim of the ledge that Hopper had to lunge forward to grasp the hood of her tiny pink cloak (a gift from Pinkie, of course). "In the market square! That chipmunk is selling whirligigs! Can I please have a whirligig? I can, can't I? I can have anything I want—after all, I am a crown princess of Atlantia!"

"Hope," said Hopper, gently but firmly, "it's wrong to demand things just because you happened to be born to Zucker and Firren. You should focus on *earning* the things you want."

Hope gave him a pout. "But I *didn't* demand. I asked politely." She gave a heavy sigh. "So . . . no whirligig, then?"

Hopper chuckled. "I didn't say *that*. I only meant that if you *do* get one, it won't be because you are entitled to it as a princess. It will be because your parents and I like to see you happy and because you've earned it. But for now the whirligig will have to wait. You know you're expected in the schoolroom."

Hope let out a little snort. "Do I have to go? The tutor smells funny and my brothers and sisters pick on me. And there's no one else to play with."

Hopper smiled. "Well, I'm sorry to hear that, but you can take comfort in the fact that soon you'll all be enrolled in the public school," he promised. "Your mama is determined to see that happen sooner than later. It's just a matter of getting it built."

"Well, it can't happen soon enough for me!" she huffed. "My siblings all think they're so smart!"

"You're just as smart as they are."

She smiled at the compliment, then frowned again. "Not as smart as Brighton is. She's a genius. They call *her* Bright-one. Of course, *she* never has any fun."

Hopper laughed. "She is the serious one of the litter, isn't she?"

"Yes," Hope agreed. "And Verrazano is the great leader and talented swordsman. Fiske is the clown but also a philosopher, and Go-go is the one who all the little boy rats of the city fawn over and make goofy eyes at." She frowned. "Princess Gowanus, the royal heartbreaker."

"Go-go has her good points," Hopper said, biting back another chuckle. "You all do. Which is why

Zucker and Firren and all the rest of us are so proud of each and every one of you. You're a wonderful little bunch of future upstanding politicians."

"I prefer princes and princesses," Hope teased.

"Royal heirs," said Hopper, compromising by using the commonly accepted term for referring to Firren and Zucker's offspring. "Will you settle for that?"

"I guess," said Hope, placing her paw in Hopper's.

Hopper recalled the night he'd sat down with Firren and Zucker to discuss recasting the public's impression of their babies by coming up with a better, more down-to-earth term than the "royal heirs."

"You can call them the Patriot Pups," he'd suggested. "That has a nice ring to it."

"It's not bad," Zucker had allowed. "But how about the Children of Democracy?"

"That's still a bit lofty," Firren had observed with a grin. She'd thought for a moment, then clapped her hands. "We can continue to refer to them as royal heirs, as long as we're very clear about the fact that what they are heir *to* is responsibility and purpose, and *not* riches and unqualified adoration."

Zucker had smiled, his eyes twinkling. "I like it," he'd pronounced. "They'll be the heirs to our best intentions and our most worthy efforts."

Hopper had thought that was the perfect way to look at it, but in truth he would have loved the little rats no matter what anyone called them.

Now Hope was tugging at the sleeve of his tunic, giving him her most glowing smile. "Of all us royal heirs, *I'm* your *favorite*, aren't I, Uncle Hopper?"

Hopper beamed at her. It was true that Hope held a special place in her godfather's heart. And with very good reason:

When the royal litter had arrived, Hopper and Pinkie had both been there to provide Zucker, the nervous first-time father, some much-needed support and distraction. Marcy, back in the palace on one of her rare visits, had skillfully assisted the midwife, Maimonides, who'd come all the way from the Mūs village to lend her experience and expertise. When Mamie, as the midwife was called, handed Zucker his firstborn—a daughter—he'd kissed the squirming infant on her forehead and promptly named her Gowanus.

Marcy gave the second pup, a boy, to Pinkie to hold.

"We'll call him Verrazano," Zucker decreed. "Raz for short."

Little Raz's first royal act was to spit up all over Pinkie's golden cape. Hopper took some brotherly pleasure in seeing that.

Two more pups arrived, mewling and cooing— twins, one male, one female. They were christened Fiske and Brighton, and handed to Dodger to snuggle. At last the fifth and final royal rat-ling entered the world. Yet another precious baby girl.

"Hope," Firren whispered, exhausted but happy. "Her name is Hope. After your mother, Hopper."

Hopper had been too choked up to speak at first, so touched was he by such a tribute. "It's a lovely name," he whispered at last, when Marcy placed the babe in his arms. The rush of love he'd felt was nearly indescribable. *Such innocence,* he thought, gazing down at her scrunched-up little face. *Such possibility and promise.*

READ STORIES, PLAY GAMES,
AND LEARN MORE ABOUT
THE WORLD OF MOUSEHEART AT

MOUSEHEART.COM!